THE MOST IMPORTANT THING HAPPENING

A NOVEL IN STORIES

MARK STEELE

David C Cook
transforming lives together

THE MOST IMPORTANT THING HAPPENING
Published by David C Cook
4050 Lee Vance View
Colorado Springs, CO 80918 U.S.A.

David C Cook Distribution Canada
55 Woodslee Avenue, Paris, Ontario, Canada N3L 3E5

David C Cook U.K., Kingsway Communications
Eastbourne, East Sussex BN23 6NT, England

The graphic circle C logo is a registered trademark of David C Cook.

LCCN 2012954695
ISBN 978-1-4347-6690-8
eISBN 978-0-7814-0884-4

© 2013 Mark Steele

The Team: John Blase, Andrew Meisenheimer, Amy
Konyndyk, Nick Lee, Renada Arens, Karen Athen
Cover Design: FaceOut Studios, Jeff Miller
Illustrations: Connie Gabbert

Printed in the United States of America
First Edition 2013

1 2 3 4 5 6 7 8 9 10

122012

CONTENTS

Nick —
You're joining a great family!
Enjoy the read.

OZ. OF GOD

He stood at the peak of the dune, the thing she had surrendered to him clenched in his blood-soaked hand. He was panicking now. There was no undoing what he had done. Until he skidded into the fresh sand to gain his balance, he had not realized the ferocity of his sprint. Sweat suddenly burst in a torrent from his hairline, his temples feverish. He had expected to wash in the waves, but of course there were night swimmers. His knee-jerk reaction was to thrust his palms deep into the meshy granules, allowing them to scrub the evidence raw like steel wool. He buried the item deep down where the sand was saturated. Calling it a mere item seemed disrespectful; he was still in shock to have it in his possession. When his hands emerged, the bloodstains had dried and darkened, the look of soil.

He remained on all fours, scoping the horizon, a deep bestial cough bullying its way out his burning throat. The sunset peeked through the rainclouds like the iris of an old man fighting off sleep. He had minutes—mere minutes—before he would be found out. Before they would give chase. After the discovery, the roadways would be blocked for miles. He would not get far unless he traveled by sea. He began to make his way toward the boardwalk.

The stretch of the dock, normally abandoned, was awake with a small crowd of revelers due to the carnival. There should have been more, but the majority of regulars were gawking at the building collapse downtown. It gave him slight hope that the authorities would be short on men, distracted from this additional manhunt.

He staggered his way down the planks, between the booths and tents, rides and freaks, simulating drunkenness so no one would approach. Each excited scream startled him, reminding him of the earlier part of the evening.

And then, at the end of the pier, he discovered that the schooners and yachts normally residing here were gone, having abandoned this bacchanalia of merriment. He turned aghast, trapped amid the crowd, having lost precious minutes of escape. His eyes darted, conniving. A rope was coiled on the edge of the dock. He could fool them, he thought. He could gather food from these merchants, enough sustenance for days. He would lower himself down the rope into the maze of wooden support beams underneath. He could camp there for a week perhaps, though eventually, they would come. There wasn't a place to hide that would go unsearched. But among the chum and flotsam, the dogs would lose his scent, and those officials who would eventually venture underneath would be sloppy, deeming the location a last resort, nothing more than a no-stone-unturned. They would not see him, for they would not truly be looking. And then. Then. When the sailors returned, he would seize a vessel. The authorities would send very few men after it because they would deem the pursuit a distraction from the real crime, the one, ironically, of his own making at the church.

He had his plan. He glanced at his hands under the pale glow of the gaslight. Blood still under the fingernails. He must be swift. The crowd lurched twenty yards up the boardwalk. It made him uneasy;

perhaps a fight was breaking out. Perhaps not. The ruckus was tumbling toward him like a reckoning. It could be the police.

Instinctively, he slipped under the cuff at the rear of the nearest tent, the only one from which he heard no voices. It had a rural scent about it: horse urine upon hay bales, the fermentation of rotten vegetables. He eased inside silently. There was very little light, save one lantern on the far end. It swung upon a limb growing awkwardly over a tree stump serving as a table. On either side of the stump set a rock large enough for sitting. On the stump itself, a very small bottle, the sort belonging to an alchemist, filled with a dark liquid.

His instinct told him to remain in the murkiest portion of the shadows, unmoving. But something intangible tugged at him, a distraction from his urgency. The tent was small. He could not approach the lantern too closely without concern of casting a shadow. And yet, there was something about that bottle. Something to that liquid. It was more than a simple yearning to inspect the bottle. There was a *necessity*.

It was only after he made up his mind to begin stealthily making his way toward the stump that he realized he was already halfway there, his arm outstretched, his fingers involuntarily forming the grab. Within six feet, he was stopped cold by a voice.

—You hesitate.

The words startled his heart into a new section of his chest where it did not normally reside. He gasped louder than he intended. He dared to speak, though hushed still.

—Who's there?

—You want what you see and yet you hesitate. I am surprised.

—Who is there? I'm not trespassing.

—Surprised and impressed, said the voice from the darkness.

—Show yourself.

—I should say the same to you. After all, you are the trespasser.

—This is a public place.

—This is a ticketed attraction. Until I see your ticket, it is not for you to decide what is or is not public.

—I don't have a ticket.

—Then, how do you ride the rides, play the games, et cetera?

—Et cetera? I don't believe I've ever heard anyone say that out loud.

—It's pleasing to the tongue. One of many things people think but do not say. For instance, you. You do not say anything that you actually think.

—I don't have a ticket.

—Ah. Then, you have a need.

—I don't understand.

—Mine is neither the most intriguing attraction at this carnival nor the most publicized. There are only two reasons someone enters my tent: happenstance or desperation.

—Then, it is happenstance.

—We both know that isn't true.

The source of the voice emerged, quickly and silently straddling the farthest rock. A thin man, his left eye taped shut with gauze, a fresh scar originating from under the bandage streaking up his face. His hands were also wrapped like a burn victim's.

—You, my friend, are not attending this carnival, he said. —You have entered my tent ticketless from the rear in silence. You are not here at random. You have been drawn here.

—I don't believe in that sort of thing.

—I wouldn't expect you to. If you believed in that sort of thing, you would not be here. You would, instead, decide for yourself where you have been drawn. It ruins the whole process, really. Shame. I would now like one of your cookies.

—Pardon?

—That I smell. Give me one of your cookies that I smell. It is a small request, I think, in light of the fact that you are trespassing with no ticket.

—I don't have a cookie.

—Are you certain?

—Very.

—Unfortunate. Then, it must be the scourge settling into my brain. Upsetting. I would have never thought it would smell like cookies. All the more timely that you have arrived.

—What happened to your face?

—What happens to any of our faces? Time takes a boot to it. But I would imagine you mean the scar.

—It is a very unpleasant scar.

—I could say the same for you.

—Mine wasn't all that unpleasant. I didn't even feel it until well after it happened.

—I didn't mean unpleasant for you. I meant for me. To look at.

—As is yours.

—Yes—well—mine is new, the scarred man said.—So tell me. Euphoria or rage?

—Pardon?

—You didn't feel the scar when it was made. That can only be because of euphoria or rage. Or numbness. Were you at the dentist?

—Rage.

—Of course rage. If it were euphoria, you would not be here.

—And why is that?

—Because you are here to escape, and if you had ever known euphoria, you would have escaped there.

—Unless it didn't work.

—Touché. What is your name?

—I would rather not …

—If my assumptions are right, then I am probably going to save a life here. I suggest we become acquainted.

—How could you save my life? I am in no danger.

—A criminal and a liar. This is unlikely to end well.

—You accuse me …

—Let's review: ticketless, silent, rear entrance, evasive, impersonal, no cookie, rage scar, and standing in the shadows when the police march by my tent. If you are not a criminal, you certainly wear the burden of one.

He stood in silence. Something inside urged him to flee, but he found that he couldn't. He literally *could not.*

—What exactly do you believe is the significance of me being drawn here? he asked.

—You have not answered the first question.

—du Guere. My name is du Guere.

—Is that a name? That's not a real name. Or a fake name. Isn't that a French breakfast cereal?

—My mother was French.

—But now, she is suddenly not French?

—Dead. She's dead.

—Suddenly?

—If giving birth is sudden, said du Guere.

—Sometimes.

—I couldn't tell you. I was preoccupied with being born.

—Now, we're getting honest. Why do you believe you have come here?

—I have no idea. Why do you believe I have come here?

—For redemption.

—I'm sorry?

—No, you aren't. That is precisely the predicament.

—Redemption?

—You are scourged. At the moment, you are at the most dangerous stage.

—What stage is that?

—When the scourge begins to eat you, but you cannot yet feel it.

—You are mad, du Guere retorted.

—Probably. But I know scourges. And you are curious.

—What if I don't want to be fixed?

—I said nothing about being fixed.

—You said redemption.

—Clearly you have not experienced the word.

—Redemption how?

—I believe you know how.

du Guere allowed his eyes to drift downward to the small glass container, its contents shimmering.—That.

—You disrespect with your impersonal pronouns.

—I don't know what that is.

—So you spit out something meaningless? "That?" It's profane.

—What is that?

—An ounce of God.

The next words forming on du Guere's tongue were choked out of existence. Certainly, he had heard incorrectly.—An ounce ... I beg your pardon?

—Save the begging, said the man with the scars.—You'll need it later. One ounce. One concentrated, unadulterated ounce.

—Of God?

—Of God.

—*The* God?

—I wouldn't say "God" if there were several.

—I don't understand.

—Yes. That is expected.

—You're saying that in that bottle ...

—... is an ounce of God. My goodness, is there an echo in here? One sixteenth of a pound. Are we clear?

—How can that liquid be God?

—This liquid is not God. This liquid is one ounce of God.

—You're a liar, du Guere said.

—I don't have to explain myself to you—because you know it is true. You feel it. That rising in your rib cage. It is reverence and fear.

You are hungry for and afraid of this. You are certain, think what you will of me. And you will think many things of me before sunrise.

—How did you get it?

—I will give you one more free answer. The rest will cost.

—How did you get—

—One free answer. Consider it carefully.

—What … What does an ounce of God do?

—Given the proper circumstances, it could bring you redemption.

—Redemption from what?

—You tell me, Sebastian.

—I didn't tell you my name was Sebastian.

—No, you said your name was du Guere.

—It is.

—I know.

—You said the proper circumstances …

—This is a rare item, interrupted the scarred man.—There must be a price.

—But, I have told you; I do not have a ticket.

—No worry. I need something much more important, of far more value than a ticket.

—And that would be?

—The thing you buried.

Sebastian du Guere was not known for being rattled. He had spent twenty-eight months building toward the thing he buried. Slightly over two years of his life devoted to deception, manipulation, the gaining of trust. It required commitment and absolute confidence that in the end, she would willfully give him what he was after. But, the thing he buried, he did not want that at all. No one had seen the exchange—and no one could have foretold of its role in the con. Nonetheless, he had held it, warm and dying in his hands. As this stranger made mention of it, something acidic lodged near Sebastian's esophagus.

—I buried no thing.

—The item? I believe you called it an item? Though *item* is a touch disrespectful?

—Who are you? Who exactly are you?

—I smell the sand, the blood, the salt in your fingernails, the scarred man continued.—There is no use in debate, and there are no more free questions.

—I … I never called it an item. I thought it. I only thought it.

—I suggest you bring me what I have requested. Or run away. That would also be nice. But, do so without an ounce of God.

—I have no idea what you …

—You hesitate.

Sebastian did. He stopped midsentence, his mouth hangdog. Something shifted inside of him. He found himself pivoting about-face, slipping out the tent the way he had entered, this time scraping his knee on a spike. He faced the ocean and then walked toward the dunes.

The authorities were there, faster than he had calculated. Perhaps a quarter mile from the spot in question. Sebastian debated whether their location was downwind as he dragged earth slowly away in palmfuls. The wet sand gathered in the creases of his clothing, a small well of seawater being created between his knees. And then, the water began to bubble. Sebastian knew he was close to the thing, for it was still hot. So hot it was heating the water around it. Peculiar—and yet as Sebastian grasped it and it oozed amid his fingers, it did not scald him. It merely pulsed dark and struggling just as it had when it first emerged from her mouth.

It had been his third substantial con.

Sebastian had never stood for anything. Never believed in anything cerebral or spiritual. His uncle had repeatedly illustrated to him that the only authentic force is manipulation and that truth is whatever the most powerful people decide is truth. When his uncle disappeared, eleven-year-old Sebastian ran away from the foster home and made his way from fishing town to fishing town on the currency of his imagination. Little fibs fed him. Larger deceptions landed him floors to sleep on. In the late teen years, full-on scams acquired him the cash to move onto larger cities, though he never strayed far from the coast. The ocean sang an unending lament of escape. Inland meant commitment, and a grifter can't have that.

Upon adulthood, Sebastian decided to make a habit of the con, and eventually not a career. He had stowed away enough to disappear for a decade but found life morose and degrading if he wasn't focused on the next mark.

His first gave him the scar on his cheek. Ironic, because the scar on his cheek had been used on every mark since as proof that he

---

was sincere. It was the classic misdirect: the scar gave a frightening first impression, an impression that Sebastian had to remedy over time with unexpected kindness. The common man believes that first impressions are next-to-impossible to change. Sebastian knew this was hogwash. It is the second impression that sticks because marks never make room for a third. To be proven wrong once is perceived as enlightenment; to be proven wrong twice is foolery—and no one thinks himself capable of that. The marks never detected the manipulation again after accepting the scar.

In that first con, he befriended a blind codger worth a fortune, serving as his guide and confidant, skimming off of every payment he made on the old man's behalf. The man told Sebastian he loved deep-sea fishing, and Sebastian had obliged him. Once they were twenty miles off shore, the old man chided Sebastian, saying he knew of the scam. He himself was once in the con game and had made a small killing grifting the women in his retirement condo—nothing, he said, like he would have made had he ever been able to pinch the Cymbeline, but, living near it these three decades, he had convinced himself that it was an impossible mark. When Sebastian told the old man he didn't know what the Cymbeline was, the old man laughed an ugly laugh, revealing the scum affixed to his dentures. He was, he continued, fully aware of all the finances Sebastian had taken from him over the past month, and a few young goons were back at the dock, waiting for them to return and to take recompense from Sebastian's hide.

Then, he laughed more. He laughed and laughed just the way Sebastian's uncle used to laugh at him. The old man made a quick off-handed comment about Sebastian's failure in life—his inability to pull off a single illegitimate caper on a feeble mark. It was the exact sort of thing Sebastian's uncle would say, and without thinking he beat the man with a decorative oar that adorned the inside of the ship. When Sebastian swung it in rage, he did not even feel the fishhook fly off and embed itself in Sebastian's own cheek. Sebastian had never spoken of the incident again, but recollected it foggy as if from something he had read, hardly feeling as if he were the character in the story. His fury detached him.

He fled into the water, leaving the battered body on board to be discovered a day later.

This was how Sebastian created his false name. It was painted on the old man's decorative oar: Sebastian. He was uncertain where du Guere came from—it surfaced from a craw in the back of his brain. Probably one of the spy novels his uncle made him read aloud after dark. He was able to state the name with certain conviction because he could hardly recall his true moniker. Paul probably. Or perhaps Dan or Alan. It had been so long, and as a rule he did not consider the earliest portion of his life to hold truth.

The second con was more fortuitous. Having soured on the elderly, Sebastian did research in the library of a nearby prep school and found fast profit playing on the boredom of wealthy adolescents. Boarding school kids with flexible trust funds. Sebastian became the fellow around town who could provide them with contraband either forbidden by the school, the parents, or the law. He would begin small with cash exchanges for items in paper sacks. But, once the young were hooked, it was only a matter of time before they craved quantities beyond the realms of cash on hand. Sebastian timed it well and, having gained their trust, obtained eleven credit card numbers—all extremely lucrative. He found it difficult to muster any regret, considering the boys conscienceless scavengers upon humanity. They deserved far more than the hand slap that would define their comeuppance. It cemented his decision to never breed.

But the third.

The third con changed things.

He had seen her from the stern of the sailboat he had bought with the Rorster kid's money. They had glided by one another subtly. He was stunned at himself for the double take. Sebastian had found that he thought in cycles, that nothing distracted him or caught him off guard because he was always weighing the next scenario, the closest means of escape. But, she had caused him to glance a second time. That surprised him.

He liked it.

He followed her boat back to the marina where her Daddy was having a Board Retreat for the Whathaveyou Trust of Something Unimportant. Sebastian imagined her a cotillion sort of daddy's girl and slipped into a nearby vacation condo to nab a tux. He slipped in through the rear French doors that stood ajar behind the children watching television and stole the clothes while steam emanated from the bathroom. Sebastian found this to be the best sort of thievery. Fleece a household while the victims are absent and they assume they have indeed been robbed. Rob a household with them present in the next room and they absolutely know they must have misplaced the item themselves.

No one considers themselves the fool.

The woman's name was Robin.

Robin Chivenchy.

And her father owned the Cymbeline.

The Cymbeline: a unique and famed opal containing an abnormal percentage of sandstone for a gem with such dark colorization. It is remarkably translucent and its monetary value has been estimated to exceed the rare Aurora Astralis. The Cymbeline, passed down through the Chivenchy family for centuries, has only been viewed publicly on the rare occasion of a Chivenchy daughter's nuptials.

Sebastian met her through a friend of a friend (neither of whom actually existed) at a rather intimate dinner party. He wore the tux unkempt and barefoot in his role as the exhausted reveler after a day of celebration, making it look as if he were passing Robin happenstance upon his own exit. She thought she noticed him first and invited him to her table for one last (first) drink.

The easiest of marks.

He decided upon the swindle that would burn the slowest. He became the casual cad about town, allowing her to stumble upon him repeatedly. He waited patiently for her to initiate the chase. Three weeks. Seven run-ins. That was when she first mentioned the scar.—Now, why would someone with your money not have that fixed? It taints an otherwise perfect face.

He was flattered, turning an involuntary shade of red, and it troubled him. He was aware that she could see him. More than a stare, a knowing. A con man lies all the time, but a con *artist* knows when anything but truth will out him. This was a moment made for fact.—I don't want it fixed. It reminds me of someone I don't want to be any more.

She bandied an olive about in her closed mouth, pensive but playful.—I have one of those, too. She said it like it was the end of the conversation, but Sebastian persisted.

—Let's see it.

—It's not that sort of scar, she replied.

That was two years ago. Twenty-eight months, actually.

He courted her for eighteen months before taking the necessary steps to secure her father's blessing. Her mother had died at childbirth: an odd coincidence, but strangely comforting to Sebastian. To think that even the haves lack something of pivotal importance is a thought that goes down hot and electrifying like scotch.

He had studied the best of proposals and thought her a traditional sort. Down on one knee, ring in hand. But, at the last moment, he reconsidered. That would be treating her like a mark. She deserved more. No, he did not love her; he loved the con and, yes, she was integral to it, but that did not make his feelings for her the sort called affection. To give her the proposal she would expect, it simply seemed careless. He took her to the shore at midnight; this shore, where even now, Sebastian held the hot dark part of her in his hands. He took her to this shore and stood next to her, both of them transfixed on the lights of the vessels floating upon the night sea. He reached out for her hand, her warm hand, and felt a catch in his heart, a desire to make sense of this moment.

—What word is in your head right now? She often asked personal, startling things.

—Why would that matter?

—You're stalling, she coaxed.—The one word you don't want to tell me.

—Away.

—Away is a sad word.

—Depends upon what is here, I suppose.

—Is it a sad word to you?

—Not today.

—Your turn. Ask a question.

—I hate this game, he lied.

—Ask.

—What do you love least about me? The words startled him as they came out of his own mouth. Her answer was without pause.

—The distance, she said.

—I'm by your side most every day.

—Some days, yes. Right now, for instance. But the evenings, not so much. You've never told me of your time at sea.

—They were painful days, he replied. The lie was immediate, automatic as if it had been stowed on the inside of his cheek for such an occasion.

—Yet you want them back, she persisted.

—I—what? No.

—Don't lie. Our love may be new, but there are evenings when I can tell I am not enough. Your thoughts drift. You gaze into nothing in ways I've never seen you gaze at me.

—Then you don't pay attention. My glances of you, I steal. When I get lost in the distance—

—You are dreaming of escape.

—No. Of the future. Only the future.

—Don't do this.

—Robin.

—I'm not the sort who fancies. I have not allowed my heart the freedom of most girls. I haven't loved much.

—You've loved me much.

—I haven't loved beyond you. There was a suitor three years ago. But he was not really pursuing me.

—He wanted your father's fortune?

—What would make you say such a thing?

—It is an obvious truth, he said.—Many say it of me. I know you think it.

—I have never thought it. And he was not you. He was a man of folly. His words were playthings. We would go to the show and he would only be interested in the car chases. Nothing true interested him. He only wanted to watch very expensive things move quickly toward an impending destructive end. And that was all he and I were. So, I need to know for certain whether or not anything true interests you, Sebastian.

—I assume you mean something specific.

—When you stare into the sea, your eyes come alive. Is the longing really for the future? For the future alone?

—I—I don't know that I understand the question.

—Do you ever consider God?

—God? *That* is your question?

—To me, it is an important question.

—You mean do I consider whether or not God exists?

—Really. You don't seem the sort to question the "if."

—I would think everyone is the sort to question the "if."

—Not everyone.

—I see.

—I think God has to be there, Robin said.

—Why so?

—Because occasionally, I find the good.

—The good?

—I understand that *people* aren't good. They just aren't. They are self-serving and cruel and short-sighted. They want things.

—Ironic coming from a woman of means.

—It doesn't matter that I have things. I still want things. Because I am still stumbling for the good. Aren't you?

—Is that all you think of me?

—It's all I think of anyone. It's all I think of myself. I think it because I know it is true. Even of you.

—How can you believe that I am only interested in things? he asked.

—Aren't I a thing?

She caressed the sand with her bare foot, her train of thought sidetracked by something she didn't want to say. There was a moment of silence as she stood transfixed upon a distant foghorn. She met his eyes. She went on.

—Aren't we a thing? Isn't love? Aren't we all just things someone else wants to have because it might lead to good?

—To call it a thing seems disrespectful.

—Yet a thing is still what it is.

—And that is why you believe in God?

—I must. I have felt the good. The legitimate, genuine good. And I have felt it amid being attracted to illegitimate things. Illegitimate people. The good was real. The people, it turns out, were not. I know what you have in your pocket and I know what you are going to ask me tonight and inside me, a yes is bursting. I want to say it out loud. I really do, Sebastian. But I've been here before. I considered a yes before and when it fell apart, I was shaken. When you look for God in the good and the good goes bad, it is brutal. It hurts in a way that doesn't seem temporary, but as if my soul itself were so torn and damaged that it could crawl out of my mouth and shrink away to nothing. If God is real, God must sometime speak and act and convince and console—and the only way I can figure to do that is through *people*. But how can we see God if we don't first give ourselves to people? Trust people? And people are not good. So, God must not be inside the goodness of people. I suppose people must instead stumble toward the goodness of God. I've been searching for someone who will do that with me. Together. Or there will be no good left to be found.

He couldn't help himself; something was forming in the cold corners of his heart. The ring emerged from his pocket in the palm of his hand. His knee hit the cold wet sand and he stared her dead in the eyes.—Will you be my wife?

She responded, not with an answer, but with a question of her own.—Do you think it's possible? Could we stumble—together?

—We will, he said.

—Then yes.

He wished to be married that very evening, but her father believed in extended engagements. Ten months, and with each passing week, each passing scheduled commitment, each announcement and proclamation of familial duty, those recesses inside Sebastian began to turn away from the sun. Yet he loved Robin more. He found himself coveting the soft quiet fleeting moments, the few they would have outside the scheduled constraints of the privileged. He would trace the veins on the back of her hand with his finger delicately, memorizing them. Afraid to let go of her hand, lest it grow cold, her affection the assumed con.

With every fête, his contempt for her father grew. He paraded his daughter like a *thing*, always flaunting the display of the Cymbeline at the nuptials, as if their wedding were a museum opening. Each time he mentioned it, she would wince almost imperceptibly. Her left eyebrow would shake and her smile would grow briefly close-lipped. He knew this was what she did when her father proved his frailty.

He imagined the wedding day, whisking her away with the Cymbeline around her neck. A new life funded without her family. Yes, she would grieve who he really is, but she would also be drawn to the change. For what he had become was greater than what he had been before her.

The evening before the wedding (last night, actually), he lay with her in a hammock behind the guesthouse, staring into the cloudless night sky. He should have seen stars, but they were nowhere to be found. Robin fell asleep aside him and he was at peace, for the first time, debating a permanent change. What if he didn't do it? What if he did not seize the jewel? No more living the lie, but instead drifting seamlessly into this new man he was successfully pretending to be. It couldn't be difficult. He had been a different Sebastian for so long, it began to feel natural. He did not wake up each morning rehearsing lies any longer. He went to bed believing them. He had allowed himself to breathe easy, let his guard down, for months now. He sat up and stared at her. He had promised her he would chase the good. Was she worth that?

He decided unequivocally that she was.

He would change. And it wouldn't take much, for he had feigned change for a very long time indeed.

Minutes before the wedding, he had stared alone in the mirror. The groom's chamber just inside the vestibule leading to the sanctuary was cold and echoing. Sebastian struggled to tie the cravat around his neck. Really. A cravat. He felt a knee-jerk loathing of the haves and quickly choked it down. He thought to himself that the knot was near perfect when he was startled by the rattling of ice behind him.

It was her father on his third bourbon.

—You watching the news?

—What? Of course not. I'm—I'm about to be married.

—Building just collapsed downtown, he spat out. Morbid small talk.

—What?!

—Just came down in a cloud of smoke. Nobody knows why. Pretty bad omen for a wedding day, wouldn't you say?

—I don't believe in omens. He returned to the cravat, though it needed no modification.

—I have seen that you love her.

—Of course I do. I am marrying her.

—It's unfortunate, really. We were all certain you would have run by now, given us an opportunity to seize you in secret. The one thing I didn't count on was you actually loving her.

Sebastian's heart sank.—What are you talking about?

—There are at least three attempts to seize the Cymbeline every year. Did you know that? Three.

—How would I know that?

—Always clumsy, amateur attempts. So foolish. As if the Chivenchys are not men of means—men of plans.

How could he know? Sebastian's mind was racing. He could still talk his way around.

—One fellow. Arturo Lomini. He has attempted the robbery three times. Including six months ago. Finally caught up with him. He was released from prison last month.

—Why would he be released?

—In exchange for information, Chivenchy stated.—Quite useful. He slid a photo across the small settee footstool. Sebastian measured the emotion that could be read on his face as he glanced at the crumpled and aged snapshot. In it, the blind old man. And there, standing behind him like a good son, Sebastian saw himself.

—I helped him—assisted him. I didn't know he was a thief.

—Then why the name change? Chivenchy persisted.—A bit convenient, don't you think?

Sebastian sat, dissolving.

—You hid it well, but there is something with all of them. Always something.

—All of them?

—Her suitors. So many. I would imagine she didn't tell you much. They each represented a different level of embarrassment for her. You do realize that you have wasted months, years. It was an

27

impossible heist. How did you imagine snatching it, transporting it? The Cymbeline is secured with a lockable clasp. Only the security guards who will retrieve it immediately after the ceremony have the key and it requires the fingerprints of both to unlock even that. You never had a chance because you never had a plan.

—You have to believe me. I have no intention of stealing the Cymbeline.

—No. I would imagine that you do not have that intention any more. Here is how this will play out. My daughter is a fool and she has fallen for fools four times now. What happens next must hurt her. This must hurt so much that she will never attempt marriage again. You will take the ceremony as far as possible. You will make the declaration of your vows and she will respond "I do." Then, it will be your turn. And when it is your turn, you will confess. There will be no apologies. No declarations of being transformed by love, because I will be standing close behind. And anything that reduces her pain will play into how long you remain incarcerated. When your ruse is proclaimed, I will call the guards to seize you. I will be very dramatic. Very publicized. Mortifying. And she will never—

Sebastian had not recognized the fire doubling over within him as rage, but in one fell swoop, he knocked the bourbon glass from the man's hand, sending it crashing to the floor. He tackled the gentleman and began pouncing upon him, blow after blow. Whether it was the bourbon or not, Sebastian did not know—but her father did not fight back. Instead, he laughed.

He laughed and laughed. A cruel sort of laugh. Like the old thief. Like Sebastian's uncle.

Sebastian du Guere took a large shard of bourbon glass off the floor and shoved it into the side of the man's neck to make the laughing stop.

It did.

A rap on the door. It was time.

Sebastian would have to fix his cravat again.

The wedding was rushed. She was perplexed that he never looked her in the eye. Not once. Yet the crowd fawned. All they could see was the Cymbeline.

They were pronounced man and wife and he kissed the bride. He seized her hand, the veins hard and prominent like the black keys on a piano. He ushered her swiftly out to the private vestibule where a guard awaited to escort her to those who would retrieve the stone. He looked at her in the eye for the first time.

She knew. The one look was enough.

—Oh, Sebastian.

—That isn't my real name.

She turned away as Sebastian reached around and throttled the guard, squeezing the ball of his fist deep into the man's Adam's apple. The guard slid to the ground, groaning and kicking every which way, smearing the wet soil from beneath his shoes on the hem of her wedding gown. She did not flinch. She did not turn back around. The guard collapsed and Sebastian seized his gun.

He stood, her back to him, the subtle movements of her shoulders syncopated in rhythm to a cry she did not allow him to hear.

He would not think of her. Months from now, years from now, she would survive this. She would not forgive, but he would not need her to. She would move on. Eventually. This was only right.

That she knew the scam completely. That she was, in the end, aware. He owed her that much.

He called urgently for the other two guards. They entered as Sebastian pulled the trigger over and over spastically, barely aiming, hitting one guard in the shoulder, then in the small of his back as he turned and fell. He was normally not this reckless, having never felt emotion seep so deeply into the equation. A bullet hit the other guard directly in the face. She stood, blood splattered upon the white, Sebastian slipping to a fall amid his deliriousness and the carnage. The guard who had been shot in the back wrestled Sebastian to the ground, Sebastian smashing his nose into the floor. The guard's last breath was a brutal, gargled one. Sebastian slid both men's forefingers onto the appropriate place on the small case one had handcuffed to his wrist. It opened. Inside was the key. He approached her gently, face-to-face for the first time as the true grifter.

—You had to know. You had to sense this.

She stood silent.

—This is who I am. You don't need to understand.

—You changed.

—I didn't.

—I felt it, she insisted—I saw it. He changed you.

—Who?

—God.

Rage boiled. And sadness. It was over.—This was a con. It was all a con! Sebastian was shouting now.

—Don't resist what has happened in your heart.

—Nothing real! Nothing real has happened in my heart.

—Don't say it as if it's final, she pleaded tenderly.—You don't know, you don't really know. This is just weakness. In a moment of anxiety, you fell into old habits.

—Give me the stone.

She appeared to be holding back a reflex. As if she wanted to wretch.

—Sebastian. I am yours now. I am your wife. I am Robin du Guere. This doesn't have to be you any more. Please, Sebastian.

—My name is not Sebastian. It never was.

She fell to the floor, a crumpled heap of white and red.

—The stone, Robin. Now.

—Give me your hand.

He did. His hand shook. He did not know why. Adrenaline.

She took his hands in hers, warm and soft.

She stared into his eyes. Another convulsion. Was she about to be sick? He hated the thought of her anxiety, but it was a necessary evil, so they say. So they say.

—We are strangers. But, you loved me. You did. We were good.

—I don't have the capacity for good.

—You did. You do.

—Give me the stone.

She stared at him, her eyes moist and bloodshot.—Goodbye, Sebastian.

An enormous convulsion, like birth pangs. He held onto her hands tightly. She convulsed again. Did she need a doctor? He found himself concerned and repulsed. One last convulsion and something …

Something.

Oh, God.

Something was exiting her mouth.

A billowing form, a cloud but solid, a dark, dark thing, seemingly liquid but with a shape of its own came out of her mouth—not down, but upward like crows from a belltower.

Sebastian gasped aloud, a primal child's yawp that surprised him. He attempted to let go of her, to push her back, but her hands held his all the more tightly—imprisoning him to observe the moment.

The thing rushed out of her, painfully, like the expulsion of life itself, formulating and hovering. Sebastian sat upon his own knees in abject terror. This thing, this horrible beautiful thing that seemed to stare at him. It knew him. It owned him. It filled him with remorse and foreboding.

He knew exactly what it was—and he knew exactly who had summoned it out of her. He had. It was Sebastian who had polluted and ruined the most beautiful parts of her. His final betrayal. It had proven there was no good, no God, and it cemented her end. The thing—no, not merely a *thing*—lessened in size as it hovered, becoming small and organ-like. No more the size of a kidney or a human heart. It completed its expulsion from her mouth, and she collapsed. It floated lightly down into Sebastian's hand, and he held it, wet and hot.

Her soul.

Her dark, scarred, polluted soul.

It was only now that he realized it was not black at all, but blue.

It was only now that he realized Robin lay dead before him.

He ran—abandoning the Cymbeline, leaving it dangling around her lifeless neck.

He ran and ran—for the beach. For the ocean.

Standing outside the tent, Sebastian had not noticed his own tears. He did not recall how long he had stood here, staring at her soul. It was shrinking smaller, pulsing blue in his palm like a dying baby bird. He stood in the shadows. There was chaos about him, chatter within overheard conversations of a police presence. Rumors of a murder in the air. A new bride found amid three others. All dead. Her father dead as well. The husband nowhere to be found.

Sebastian swallowed a breath too hard and his chest hurt. The husband. He felt captured already, not by the law but by something far more formidable. All that mattered now was the possibility that something—anything could assuage the terror inside of him, the dark matter that would make even a free life a hell of his own making.

His only hope was this ounce of God.

Robin had believed—she had believed until he had driven that faith to ruin. It was his only option left.

He slipped quietly back into the tent the same way he had entered the first time.

—You have brought the scourge with you this time, the stranger observed.

—I do not believe this was a scourge to her.

33

—Not the thing in your hand. You have brought the scourge deep within yourself. More pungent, more scathing than before. You have done a lot of thinking while you were away. You must understand now where it came from.

—I have not felt it before today.

—Of course not. You breathed it in.

—What?

—When it emerged from her mouth. The cloud. The realization of what you had done, what you had stolen from her.

—I did not take the jewel, Sebastian said.

—You took much more.

—I took her life.

—Oh, much more than even that.

And Sebastian knew it was true. For Robin's soul was worth much more than her life. The guilt—the scourge, whatever this scarred man chose to call it—was eating him alive, a weight too crushing.

—Give it to me, Sebastian insisted as he motioned toward the small bottle.

—Manners.

—I can't survive this. Give me the ounce of God.

—But, you cannot be certain what the ounce will do.

—You said it would probably save my life.

—I remember what I said better than you. An ounce of God is volatile, Sebastian. I am very willing to make this trade. Trust me—very willing. But, it is not entirely in my control.

—How can you say that after I brought you her soul?

—Bringing me her soul is a good start. A necessary step, but now comes the real conundrum. You must initiate the trade.

—The trade?

—The words must come from your mouth. I have led you as far as I can on my own. Now, you must actively pursue the answer.

—A trade? Sebastian stood, thinking through his crisis. He needed the ounce, but could think of nothing he owned that would be considered valuable.

—You have to believe that I do not have the stone. I did not take it.

—What use would I have for the stone? The stranger was smiling now.

—What else do I have but her soul?

—There you go.

—Robin's soul? You want Robin's soul—for yourself?

—Are you initiating the trade?

—What does that mean?

—This has to come from you.

—You want me to …

—Stop! Not what I want.

—What?

—Ask me.

Sebastian could not believe the words coming out of his own mouth. What could this man possibly desire of this lump in his hand? Would it be a final betrayal to barter it away? Or is this awful thing something Robin would want discarded for eternity? Sebastian certainly wanted to be rid of it.

—I am asking you. Could I—trade this—exchange this—could I exchange Robin's soul for the …

—Stop. The stranger held up a bandaged palm. The man gave him an intentionally knowing glance.—Do not get ahead of yourself. Know all of the facts first.

—Know all of the—what?

—Ask. The stranger mouthed it as if he wanted the words hidden. *Ask the question.*

Sebastian thought long and hard about what he truly needed to know.—Before I make the exchange, I need to know. What will the ounce of God do to me?

The man smiled, took a deep breath, and answered.—An ounce. It doesn't appear to be much, but beware. An ounce of God is more fury than this planet can contain. It is immense power or poison, depending upon the state of your soul. It has been known to dissolve a man into nothingness, to burn like fire down to the fingernails, to turn a man inside out. It is a raging, wild thing—an ounce of God. Not face-to-face or ear-to-voice, it is a portion—a portion within you. It searches for permission to do its business—and let me make it clear, the business of God is not for the faint of heart. Are you certain, Sebastian du Guere? Based on the current state of your soul, are you certain that you desire this ounce of God?

Sebastian stood, his brain boiling. He did not believe he could withstand what the man described—and yet he needed change, immediate change. The pain raging, he struggled to complete his sentence.—Perhaps only a drop, he said.

—Make your request.

—Yes. That is the exchange. Robin's soul for one drop of God.

—Louder, the stranger said, salivating.

—Robin's soul for one drop of God!

—How much? You must be certain.

—One drop! ONE DROP of what is in that container! Please. Please give it to me! Please give it to me now!

—Not until you surrender that which is in your hand.

Sebastian gave the man the blue beating thing. It was unacceptable that it had come to this. He felt his fingers release the warm soul, and he felt it cling to his palm ever so slightly as if it did not wish to be transferred.—Your hand, the stranger pleaded, your hand now. We must exchange at precisely the same moment.

Sebastian extended his left index finger. The man carefully allowed a lone drop to settle on his fingertip as Robin's soul released itself from Sebastian's possession.

—It is warm.

—Hurry.

Sebastian paused, his insides tumultuous. He touched the finger to his tongue and waited.

Waited.

Waited.

The man grinned.

Suddenly, the space around him expanded and contracted like birth. Sebastian's entire existence. His lies and crimes became a pair of brick walls, Sebastian writhing in between them. The weight of his choices, of all he had destroyed in the wake of his own damaged life, he saw it all there before him. And he felt remorse—remorse like he had never known. He had always been able to stave guilt away, considering it for the weak, but this lone drop of liquid laid an exclamation point on his life's actions, and he found himself crumpling to the ground, kneeling before his crimes—his chest bursting, his eyes madness.

—What have you done to me?

—You have done it to yourself, the stranger stated.—You made the request. You made the choice.

—It is too much! Too much! When will this guilt be lifted?

—I'm afraid it will not.

—What?!

—As I recall, you were quite unwilling to take it that far. You only wanted a drop. A taste. As you see, a taste of God shines the light on much pain. But, forgiveness from that pain? That requires willingness to accept all that comes with it. And you did not want it all. You only wanted one drop.

—You *lied!*

—I did nothing of the sort. Everything I said the ounce would do, the way it would feel—it is all accurate. But, that pain was the road to what you truly wanted.

—You didn't tell me that.

—I also didn't tell you the opposite. I simply trusted that you would be unwilling to suffer the consequences.

—What kind of a cruel God would trick me like that?

—God didn't trick you. I did. The man with the scar rippling down his cheek laughed. He laughed like the men in Sebastian's life who had brought him such pain. A laugh like every failed father figure he had known.—Just because I hold the ounce of God—just because I know what it does—doesn't mean that I work for Him.

—But—you said I would be healed.

—You selfish man. You simply don't listen. I said *someone* would be healed. That someone is *me*.

As Sebastian lay contracting on the dirt floor of the tent, the man took the bandage off his eye. The socket was a cavity, the eye itself absent. He took Robin's soul in the palm of his hand and slid it into his mouth, it turning into steam and then gas and then dissipating as the man's eye returned and his scar disappeared.

—What are you? Sebastian asked.

—This world was almost rid of me. But, thanks to you, my scourge is gone—and yours is just beginning.

—Give me the ounce! Sebastian was writhing now.

—You have nothing left to trade.

—Anything.

—You have nothing that I want.

—My soul. *My* soul!

—Well, now. Why would I need to trade? I'm going to have that soon enough.

They stared eye-to-eye.

—My hands—they are beyond repair, the stranger stated as fact.—I will give you the ounce—if it is what you really want, but not until you bring me one more soul.

—*Another soul?!*

—Before sunrise. A fresh one, unpolluted. That last one tasted gamey. That is my trade. The ounce of God for one more soul.

Sebastian lay there, the truth of his scourge a blanket atop him. He was here by devices of his own making. Any other option—any—would seem a miracle. But, as his guilt reached its tentacles throughout the folds of his brain, he knew that no miracle would come his way tonight.

—How am I supposed to accomplish that?

—You're a con man, Sebastian. Do what you do best. Think like me.

—But, in the middle of the night—how will I find a damaged soul?

—Such a sad little man—only consumed with your own crises.

Sebastian stared, the fly deeply entrenched in the web. Against all better judgment, he must do as this man says. His life depended upon it.

—There was a tragedy in town today, Sebastian. A tragedy much further reaching than yours. A building collapsed. So many despair tonight. All I ask is that you find one. Preferably a girl.

The new eye twitched and settled, glowing blue.

—Find her. And bring me her soul.

THE MOST IMPORTANT THING HAPPENING

I am above the chaos. Always above it. Observing without the ability to help. Though sometimes I prefer to be across the street from the chaos in an eatery of some sort. They have large windows and pie, and I can observe with a mustard pastrami on sourdough. At this moment, however, I am above the chaos. Prostrate on a fire escape with my nose smashed to the grate, peering seven floors below into the alleyway where the stranger I am observing cannot imagine life continuing as she has previously recognized it. But, she is incorrect. I know. I've witnessed this sort of incident every day of my adult life. Ever since the age of twenty-one—the birthday itself, actually. Without so much as a whisper of warning, my surroundings disappeared. I found myself whisked away, and I've kept whisking away ever since. It isn't time travel, because my watch has never been inaccurate, save the time zone in question. Funny. But it isn't all bad.

I mean, yes. Much of what I witness is bad. Ugly. That's the nature of this modern age. At any given moment, the Most Important Thing Happening is more than likely destructive. That seems to be the way we like it. And by "we," I don't mean Magnets. I mean people. I don't think there are any other Magnets. At least, I haven't met any. Perhaps there has never been another. Perhaps there is only one of us at a time.

So, yes, I suppose some would call me special. I do. I call me special. I've seen the Gaza Strip and inaugurations and death-row executions and Ground Zero. I observe and I take notes. I've attempted to do more, but—well, I'll explain later. I've seen lives begin and end, sometimes simultaneously. I've observed treaties signed and contracts betrayed and, last Tuesday, I watched a three-year-old girl almost drown, except an eleven-year-old boy jumped in and saved her. I don't know if I'll ever unearth the long-term significance of that. My best guess is that she will grow up to either save the world or destroy it—or, perhaps the boy will. He was the one who did the saving, but maybe doing the saving turned *him* into someone significant. Despite the patterns, it's actually quite challenging to tell what makes any moment the Most Important Thing Happening. My hand gets tired writing that out so many times, so I have shortened it to MITH. Get it? It's an acronym—or maybe an acrostic.

Yesterday, I was in Tel Aviv for seven minutes. Seven minutes. I found myself outside a telephone booth as a young man spoke quite passionately inside. I couldn't even hear him. His eyes gushed tears. But, not the tears of melancholy. Anger intermingled. Rage boiled. It was true grief. And then, I was gone. What is the value in overhearing that? Especially when it was so muddled? I am frustrated and do not know.

Normally, I'm here and there for hours, or potentially a day. I like it when it's a birth because I can count on being around for a few hours, possibly sneak in a nap. Deaths are rough. People everywhere. You sort of have to squeeze up against a wall. There's always a lot of food, though. Food is good. And no one seems to notice an extra person at a funeral.

Not that I am *ever* noticed. I know I'm not invisible. The mirror proves it. It's one of those little pocket mirrors that ladies use to touch up their makeup in public. I snagged it a few years back at one of those cheap cosmetic jewelry stores during a mall shooting—it reminds me that I'm real. That I am present. It's pretty easy to debate your own existence when you spend your life fading into the background. So, I pull the mirror out every few days—or hours—I suppose I've gotten a little more insecure about it lately. Besides, it's someone to talk to, right? It also comes in handy sometimes to see around corners when there are attacking cougars or a jihad or whatnot.

There is a reasonable reason I disappear, actually. As long as you behave like you fit somewhere, no one seems to notice as you come and go, especially in tragedy. Human beings simply do not know what to do with themselves in moments of crises. I, however, have become quite at peace about it. I am a comfortable transient. An observer of historic moments in the making. That is far less interesting than it sounds.

So, after Tel Aviv, I thought I would give Marci a call from wherever I ended up after the headache dissipated. Every time I

Transition, the head pounds. My guess is that it has something to do with air pressure or altitude—though it feels a bit more like a hangover. The way your eye rolls into the back of your head when you hear a high-pitched whistle. That sort of thing. Anywho, it has its upside. When the pain begins, I know I'm just about to Transition to somewhere else. And if I'm with Marci that means one last kiss.

After Tel Aviv, I ended up in Omaha in a business complex. It would have been 6:13 where Marci lives. She would just be getting home from work. I had to be quiet because I found myself standing beside a round table of gentlemen who were debating whether or not to include a warning label on the box of their fashion doll accessories since the smaller pieces were known to come off quite easily. They voted against the label. It would hurt sales of the doll, the business-man said. The one with the hair implants—the businessman, not the doll. It's that sort of moment where you think at least one person would stare at me (the bearded fellow in the blue jean jacket) and ask, "Who let him in here?" Instead, they each gave me their sand-wich order and kept on conversing.

I only heard small portions, however. I was ringing up Marci.

Answering machine again.

Marci and I met near the beginning. She was working as a stockbroker's assistant in the city, and I was there moments before a significant disaster hit. It was an awful time, just awful. And yet, it was the Most Important Thing Happening for at least three solid weeks, so it gave me something I craved—time in one place. Time to develop a relationship. Actual love. I was in a library reading up on quantum mechanics, and she walks in to hang up pictures of her missing cat. Turned out she lived three blocks from the tragedy and he hopped out her apartment window the night before. We forged a real bond marching up and down that ghost town of a city searching for Mr. Pepper. (That was the cat's name.) I asked why Mr. and she said she had never been able to decide between calling him Doctor or Sergeant, so she settled for something in between. She was very concerned for him, wondering if he was alive or dead. I told her that Schrodinger would say that he was both. She smiled because it was a joke—not because she understood it.

Slowly, the rest of the city scrambled for peace while we fell in love. My awkwardness turned slowly into stories about the ills of the world outside her city. This seemed to bring Marci great solace. The fact that she was present for the lengthiest MITH in recent history— and survived, that was something.

It was a wonderful time. I don't think I ever pulled out that mirror.

And then, after three weeks, another MITH happened and I was away. From that point, Marci and I have been a relationship of cell phones and postcards. Postcards bought in Lagos, written in Miami, and mailed from Pakistan. We rarely meet, though I landed a block from her apartment almost ten months ago for a drive-by shooting and we eloped. Best three hours of my life.

Wait. She's calling back.

—Hey, Sweetie.

—Where are you? She was being short again.

—Over an alleyway—on the fire escape. It's cold, so I want to say maybe one of the Dakotas.

—They don't have alleyways in the Dakotas.

—Maybe Vancouver. Are you in pain?

—Always. And I bought that calico table skirt I liked so much.

—What's calico again?

—I showed it to you last month.

—Did you budget first? I need to get some toothpaste.

—How can I budget when I don't know how much you're spending? Have you been able to earn anything?

—No. There's not been any time.

A distinct sigh on the other end of the phone. Marci does a lot of sighing these days. You'd think someone who has the power to Transition unpredictably through wormholes would get fewer sighs from his wife.

—When do you think you might be back in New York? She said it as if any answer to the question would be ill-received.

—You know I don't know that, I said.

—It would be easier to have these detailed conversations in person.

—You knew what being married to me would look like.

—But, that doesn't mean … Another sigh.

—It's not my schedule. It's—it's the will of history. It's the MITH.

—You're not actually still calling them that. I thought that was just a phase.

—It's easier.

—So, if I were a little more important …

—You're important to me.

—Ohhh. I can hardly breathe any more. She stated it with a dull pain.

—Have you tried walking around?

—When I walk around, my feet swell up. I need this baby to get out already!

—Three more weeks.

—I don't know if I can last … Ohhhhh!

—What?! What!

—Just another Braxton-Hicks. Distract me. What's going on in the alleyway?

—A few floors down, there's a woman who was scraping the ice off her windshield—and a couple of guys came and knocked her on the back of her head with a tire iron. They took her purse, car—everything.

—That's terrible. What did you do?

—I wrote it down.

—You think there's a chance you'll jump to New York in the next few hours?

—How would I know that?

—Because I'm out of mayonnaise.

—You're craving mayonnaise?

—Yes. With celery. And I hate going out looking like this.

—I have no idea whether or not I'll be in New York.

—We should develop a system that gets you here at least every other week.

—That's not going to happen unless you start orchestrating international incidents or kill someone important.

—Don't tempt me. I'm hormonal. Wait! Here's another jar in the pantry.

—Crisis averted.

—What's she doing now?

—Who?

—The woman in the alley.

—She hasn't moved. It always amazes me how so many hurtful things go unnoticed. She's been lying there for ten minutes and not one person has even glanced her direction.

—Except for you.

—Well, sure.

There is a lengthy pause on the other end of the cell phone. I listen as Marci chews up the celery. It makes its own special crunching sound. A wet crunch. Strangely identifiable as celery—just by the sound. And another headache sets in.

—Hoo boy. I'm about to Transition again.

—I *hate* it when you call it that. It's like you're comparing it to childbirth. If you're comparing your hobby to childbirth, so *help* me …

—I don't think you can call it a hobby.

More wet crunching. More headache. She continues.

—I wasn't going to tell you this.

—Tell me what?

—I was at that Thai Food place you love.

—Oh—in Khon Kaen?

—No. By my apartment here in New York. Not in Thailand. How would I get to Thailand?

—Sorry.

—I'm not you.

—I get it.

—I was at that Thai Food place and there was an awful taxicab accident right outside the front window.

—Sorry to hear that.

—Turns out the Mayor was in the other car and he was drunk. Saw it with my own eyes.

—That, hmm—when did you say this happened?

—Three days ago. About seven fifteen in the evening.

This time, the silence was on my end of the phone.—That seems like it would be considered a Most Important Thing.

—I know. It did to me, too. So much that I hurried out of the restaurant to find you. And, it wasn't easy to hurry, mind you. My feet are swelling.

—But, I wasn't there.

—I know. You weren't. But someone was.

—What sort of someone?

—Another fellow with a journal. Just like yours.

—Another—a what?

—Another fellow. There was another man. In a blue jean jacket like yours. Standing on the side of the road all creepy, like the way you do it—and nobody even looked at him. He took notes. But peculiar. He was just like you except for one very unusual thing—or at least I thought it was unusual—

And I suddenly move through dimension and space. Hurtling across the globe—or perhaps through it. Or across the galaxy and back like satellite signals. I clutch the cell phone to my face as I feel that familiar rush, like I'm standing under the hand dryer in the mall bathroom. The new mall bathroom hand dryer. The one that blows the skin down so that you see the outline of your finger bones. I land—although I never have determined if "landing" is what I am actually doing. I panic, anxious to finish the conversation with Marci. But, I have no cell phone service here. I look around. I'm in a rainforest of some sort and I smell smoke. I wander over a hill where a nearby village is ablaze. There are people running, terrified. I watch as they file a line from the river in order to douse the flames, but instead of putting out their homes, they first focus on an altar they have built in the center of the village.

They go at this for several hours. There are children there. Screaming children. This is where it always gets to me—but I have to steel myself. Because there is nothing I can do but record these details in my journal.

It begins to rain, a cold mist, enough to soak my clothes, but not enough to put out the fire. Of course, I am prepared. I've been through this sort of thing before. I unfold my thin metallic-looking thermal suit and strip down, placing what I had been wearing into a Ziploc freezer bag. Best to tuck myself next to a tree base underneath the forest cover. I could even sleep a bit, if hard-pressed.

A second Magnet.

Not possible.

Well, I suppose possible, but not explicable. How could two people observe the Most Important Thing Happening at the exact same time in two different places? Is it feasible to think that there is some sort of ranking? A number-two Magnet who observes the Second Most Important Thing Happening? And, if so, is he the Second? Or am I? Is there a Magnet Control Room somewhere with yet another fellow pulling the lever on who goes where and when? Is it a room full of guys? And why would you need a room full of guys unless there was a world full of Magnets? Are there female Magnets? Do they have to wear the blue jean jacket, too? Because it isn't slimming.

I take out the mirror and stare at my own brown eyes. Focus. Get my bearings.

I came up with the label Magnet myself. It seemed to make the most sense. I'm constantly attracted by an invisible force to the most significant of happenings. The moment something once significant becomes unimportant, something more significant pulls me away. At the same time, I am never allowed to experience the mundane or insignificant. Those moments turn and repel me like—well, no need to belabor the analogy. Magnet isn't the only name I've come up with. I've got a page in the back of my journal where I've brainstormed names for lots of things. Chocochunk. That's a kind of candy bar. Magnazoom. It's a toy. I don't know what it does, but I've got the name handy. Fozeneeper. I'm saving that one. It makes me laugh even though it's nothing but a word. Crazy.

Why was I chosen to be a Magnet? That's the conundrum of the decade, isn't it? I spend a lot of time thinking about this. Of course, it's plausible that I wasn't chosen at all—that some random act propelled me into this role. The best I can figure is that history needed an observer to chronicle these pivotal moments. I'm like a walking textbook, but with a first-person perspective. I'm good at that. I can do that really well. I am fascinated by the human condition, and I've really grown at not getting so emotionally attached. I think this is an important detail of the Magnet's job description—if I get too attached to the crisis or people in question, I might not want to leave, and then it would be a real challenge to pay attention to the next place I'm supposed to go. And, as I learned the hard way, when a Magnet gets attached, a Magnet wants to "do something." This is clearly a no-no. Let me explain.

August 6. Three weeks after I turned twenty-one and all this chaos first began. It took me three weeks just to grab hold of the idea. Up until then, I spent a great deal of time gripping my skull from the pain or weeping in a corner or cowering from Bengalese tigers and Malawian thugs or parasites in the Amazon. The change was sort of thrust upon me, like Shakespeare says of greatness, and it kept shoving me headfirst into walls. But, after three weeks, I accepted my lot, and that is when my homegrown empathy set in.

His name was Alexei and he was eleven. His father, upon swilling significant amounts of vodka, would utilize the boy as his punching bag. I stood in a shadow in the corner and I just couldn't take it. The father reached his hand upward to strike the child. So I reached out for the father and suddenly thought I was about to die. The electric shock that ran through my body rattled every fiber of my being. Like a round fence encircling me, keeping me at bay, maintaining my status as the disengaged third party in the room. The father beat down on Alexei again and again—and I reached out to help over and over, but it was like my bones were on fire. I ended up on the floor, helpless to assist.

Alexei died.

I wept.

And then I pulled out what was in my coat pocket. A journal. It had been the last gift I opened on my birthday, right before I transitioned the very first time. It was in my hand at the exact moment. That's how I learned I could take things with me. I cracked it open and I chronicled Alexei's travails so that they would not be in vain.

Although I believe that they were. I've attempted a little effort from time-to-time to assist what I'm clearly meant to observe—but there is always the electricity. I am always shocked and stunned because the boundary remains, circling me like my own little atmosphere.

So, now I write it all down.

Because that is something.

The rain is very cold. You would think that a rainforest would be warm. I don't know why you would think that—but there it is. I'll write that down. I put away my mirror and bring out the journal, shielding it from the drizzle.

You don't think it's a competition, do you? A contest between two Magnets to ascertain which one is doing the better job? Couldn't be. There is no job; at least, not one that has ever been thoroughly defined. I don't have business cards. No one has ever pulled me aside or left me a pamphlet clarifying the daily to-do list. I don't like pamphlets. I like magazines.

Those villagers are still at it. From my angle on the hill, it appears to be a pretty pointless exercise: the village is burning down. It simply *is*. Let it go and expend your energies building another. Then maybe I can move on to a locale with a few bars of wireless service.

I open my journal—not to write—to read. It is a rare luxury for me. These sorts of moments are traditionally very panicky. The only real exception was last week, I want to say Tuesday. I leaped into the most beautiful green lea I had ever seen. Must have been some untouched part of Ireland—but sunny. Perfect. And there was no one around. So I lay there waiting—and surprising no one more than myself, I fell asleep. I must have slept for hours—the only thing eventually waking me was the headache signifying I would leap again. How was that the Most Important Thing Happening? I have no clue. But, it's possible that the Universe considered it of vital importance that I had a good nap.

Way to go, Universe. You rock.

But, back to the present. Me under a tree reading. I've had worse days.

I find an entry that seems rushed, which is odd. My handwriting normally slants upward to the right, but here it slants up to the left. I never do that. I must have been writing in an awful … Oh! Never mind. That was last Monday in Afghanistan. There was crossfire. That makes more sense.

I tend to like my prose. Especially when I'm describing moments that are practically a scene from an action movie. Like this one:

> A tumult of bullets rains down from every side, like I'm one of the three little pods of dirt at the bottom of the screen in Missile Command. Everyone else is wearing Kevlar and helmets and whatnot and I'm lying down in a foxhole wearing Adidas jogging sweats. Weird. I don't know who's winning. I don't even know who's shooting. But, I'm going to wait this sucker out. COME GET ME.

I stop reading.

COME GET ME.

Those words are not in my handwriting.
And they are written in red ink.

I don't understand. What? How? This journal never leaves my possession. Never. I curl it up like a magazine and stick it in my back pocket. I feel it there, all day. Every day, comforting my right buttock like a full wallet. How could anyone write in my journal? I turn the page again. A blank page between journal entries. Only the page is not blank. There are more words. More words in red.

NEVER MIND HOW. COME GET ME.

The greater realization comes upon me. Not of how he did it—but of whom it must have been.

The second Magnet. This someone Marci observed.

The entire idea is absurd. A second Magnet? What? What? What?

Who? How is this—let me gather my thoughts for a moment. The headache is back. *Finally.* Jump me to civilization so that I can call my wife. I strum through my journal to search for more red ink. I now notice it is here and there. It is everywhere. A red X here. Another disapproving comment a few dozen pages later. Here I have written the phrase *must be important* and mister red ink has followed it with **WHY?** What is that? What is that? What? I have read a dozen words in this man's handwriting and I already loathe him. The rain intensifies and so does the pain underneath the base of my skull just above the neck. I am—

And I Transition.

You know, it is rather like falling after all. Only falling upward if that is possible. Like I might die when I slam into the ceiling.

I will call her the moment I land. I will call Marci.

Darkness.

I stand and immediately ram my head onto something solid. This does not help the headache. Not at all. I am in a prison cell of some sort. Perhaps solitary confinement. That certainly doesn't make any sense. I can't observe anything significant if I am alone. I slowly acclimate to my surroundings. There is paper of some sort strewn about the floor. Dozens of napkins. I slip on them. And these are shelves on which I hit my head. Staplers everywhere. Stacks and stacks of packaged paper reams.

This is a closet. And it is filled with office supplies.

And *napkins*. Why on earth are there so many napkins?

There is a small square window in the door. I turn the doorknob slowly and quietly. Locked from the inside. Good. I can hide. I peer out. An office space—and it is in shambles. There are pools of water about, as if the internal sprinkler system was triggered. Must be the aftermath of an earthquake. Strange, though. I'm usually brought in during the big moment itself rather than afterward.

Unless I've been demoted.

Oh no.

That is exactly what must be happening. I have been relegated to documenting the aftermath. The cleanup. They are making me the janitor after the Most Important Things have Happened. That is bogus. I won't stand for it.

I fumble for my phone. I should have bars now.

Out of battery?! When? What? I shouldn't have checked it so many times in the rainforest. I rustle through the detritus in my pockets. I try to open my fanny pack, but the zipper is wet and stuck—probably some rainforest fungi. I use my mirror to see out the closet window without being seen. There are seven people in the business office, all with their backs to me. A woman, who appears to be the youngest of the seven, is speaking into a video camera on a tripod while the others observe her. What is happening here? No time to think about that. Ah! The zipper. I extricate my power charger. An outlet. An outlet? An outlet! Why is there not an outlet in an office supply closet?! I search behind bottles of copier toner. I slip against the supplies and they tumble to the floor.

KEE-RASH!

I stand absolutely still. Not good. What if I am discovered in the closet? Right now. Being mistaken for the sandwich boy is one thing, but how on earth could I explain being in here? I scramble to pick up the paper and accidentally pick up one of the napkins. It has writing on it. Looks like it was written in lipstick. A love letter of some sort. As a rule, I really do loathe the average workplace.

I sit quietly for some time, listening.

Now, there is suddenly chaos on the other side of this door. I take a quick glimpse to see that the girl and the five others are hovering over the remaining man, who is now on the floor, bleeding profusely. Oh. Unusual. I didn't hear a gunshot. I use the melee to my advantage by scrambling to find an electrical outlet, but there is nothing. Nothing. And the headache is back.

Great—I never wrote any of this down. I am certain this is going to be used against me, so I grab the journal. But, where is my pen? I reach around in the darkness. I feel a set of keys, no. Ah! A pen! I scribble down details as my head pounds.

*Girl talks to camera. Man on the floor bleeds out.
He is now dead. The girl clutches a napkin. Identical
to the napkins here in the closet. Second woman waves
a gun. Second man picks up the camera and aims it
at the proceeding. This will not end well.*

I am immensely grateful I am not expected to make sense of
any of this. I lose my place in the journal and flip back and forth
frantically among its pages.

Wait. In the bleeding light of the lone small window.

More unexpected words.

I WILL END THIS.

This is not good. I must get to a phone.

I unlock the closet from the inside and ever-so-quietly turn the
knob.

Electricity!

A thousand volts shoot underneath my skin. No. Oh no. I have
done something I was not supposed to do. I have changed something.
Assisted in a revision of the circumstances. But what? Opening the
door?

I hold in the pain and peer through the crack. The door is ajar
no more than a half-inch.

And I Transition once again.

My skull is on fire. It is the most painful yet by a long shot.

And I arrive.

An SUV screeches to a halt inches from my squatting form. It takes me a moment to realize I am in the middle of an intersection. None of the cars stop to ask why I am here. They speed on and around, hurling profanities in other languages.

I must be in New York City.

I WILL END THIS.

Is that some sort of veiled threat?! Actually, not veiled at all. Yes, that is exactly what it is. I am at the Five Points Intersection in Lower Manhattan. Manhattan! And yet, at least a dozen long blocks from our apartment.

So close and yet so distant. I might as well be in Albuquerque.

But I can call.

I discover that I never stopped clutching my phone, even through the leap. But my charger is gone. I must have left it in the office supply closet. I am such a yutz. I spot a Convenience Store on the corner. Don't they make those paper phones now? I mean, not really paper, but what am I trying to say? Disposable. Yes. Disposable phones. That's a convenient thing, isn't it? They will have them at the Convenience Store.

I rip open the packaging.

Twenty-three dollars. Marci will have a field day. I bought a seven-dollar Tom Waits bootleg once when I leaped to Kuala Lumpur and she about had an aneurysm.

I dial. It rings.

She'll ask why I haven't called in nine hours and then I will explain, which will lead to the detail about purchasing the disposable phone and then she will just go ballistic. Absolutely ballistic.

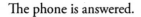

The phone is answered.

—Hello, Gary.

Uh oh. It's not Marci.

She doesn't know my real name is Gary.

—Who exactly is this?

—I think you know who this is.

—I have a suspicion, yes, based on your ominous tone and a car accident my wife described to me. But, that doesn't explain away the details.

—You certainly do have an affinity for the details, Gary.

—How do you know my name is Gary?

—I was at your twenty-first birthday party.

—You wrote in my journal! How did you do that?!

—You were sound asleep. Ireland is lovely for napping, don't you think?

—HOW—how did you leap to—to ME?

—I suppose me getting to you was of the utmost importance.

—I don't understand. I don't understand at all.

—Oh, I believe you will if you think hard enough.

—Where is my wife?

—She's in the next room.

—That's a lie. She would never let you into the apartment.

—We're not at your apartment.

I stand.

I am more than a bit stunned. There is silence on the other end of the phone. My eyes are stuck, staring at a yellow fire hydrant across the street. All is peaceful with the exception of the tuned-out din of New York City.

Moderately quiet.

Mundane.

And, it suddenly dawns on me.

—Why am I here?

—Why do you think you're here?

—Why am I right here? There is nothing happening where I am standing.

—Nothing?

—Nothing that could be considered the Most Important Thing Happening.

—Perhaps there are no MITHs left.

—That's MY acronym. Stop reading my journal!

—It's my journal, too, Gary.

—What do you mean it's your journal too?

—I mean it was my journal before I gave it to you. But, I can hear Marci screaming, so I'd better go.

—Don't you dare! What?! Where?! What?!

—I can't answer your questions, Gary.

—*Why do you have Marci's phone?*

—They put it in a plastic bag with her other things at the hospital front desk.

Not possible. Not now. Not with this man.

—You.

—Me.

—You've been sent for the birth of my child.

—I have?

—Why is the birth of my child the Most Important Thing Happening?

—Well—you've been at this long enough, Gary. You can probably guess.

And the headache begins.

It is somehow more intense than any that have come before. I go light-headed and the wrist holding my phone drifts down the side of my face.

Oh no. I cannot; I cannot leap. I cannot leave. Not at this moment.

—If you touch either of them …

—What will happen, Gary? What will you do?

And the line goes dead.

Marci. My baby. My baby. They are there and so is he and I am on the verge of going far away. I feel myself drifting. That chain yank at my navel signifies I'm about to be hurtled across the planet.

No. I will not let it happen. I cannot.

But how to stop?

I have never stopped a leap before. Never brought a transition to a halt. I have never even tried. I have always been rather relieved to be departing. I reach out as far as I can. Shock. Agonizing pain. It throws me to the curb. Physically to the curb. I smell burnt hair. My own. I reach again, more tentatively this time. Again. Agony. Now, I smell burnt flesh. Acrid filthy skin.

I stare into the distance, defeated. Head pounding. I want to die. I want to just die.

My breathing slows to the rhythm of my own heartbeat. My pulse. I gaze down the road. The long, unwinding path of New York City in between these monstrosities. The distance. I haven't fixed my eyes much on the distance in the past fifteen years. Only what was right in front of me. That which I could not fix—that which I could not even nudge.

I realize I am still clenching my mirror in my left hand.

I stare at myself.

My breath slows.

I do not like what I see.

I break into a run.

I burn. Volts course through me like lightning to a kite.

Curse it all. Curse these rules and these leaps. Curse we Magnets. Curse the pain I am in—my boiling blood. Curse every Most Important Thing Happening.

And as I tear the air apart with the sheer force of my will, something happens.

The electricity that had kept me fenced now propels me forward. Like a Taser to my heels, excruciating pain forces me forward at a gallop—and just in time as I feel the sudden pull of fate attempting to scurry me away.

I run. Perhaps I could out-effort this rope around my life. Can one out-jump gravity? I don't know, but I run.

I know where she must be. She has spoken of it often and never thought I cared to remember. It is partially true, but only partially because I intended to forget so that the pain of being absent would lessen.

My body is thrown into a hardware store window. Those around me gasp. It breaks into shards that cut me. I bleed and have no time to feel it. I hurl my physical form forward again. I will not be yanked away without a fight.

A significant burst backward. This time, I am thrust upward into the top of the streetlamp. I grab hold of the pole as my feet flail above me. The pole is hot. Is it hot here today? I had not noticed.

I shimmy my way downward, clawing at the grooves in the sidewalk like an anchor. Dragging my form along as a dog licks at my ear.

I always knew I would miss his birth. It was an assumption. What a fool. A fool.

I grasp. I struggle.

I clutch. I crawl.

Then—electricity.

A burst.

I run. Like a feather in a wind tunnel, I run.

I know she needs me and I would have once again been absent.

Still I run. Propelled not from hate for the other Magnet, but from love for the child unborn. I know that this is how it will happen. This is the breaking of the unspoken rules. This futile attempt at escape. This hurried and vain passion I suddenly have. This is how he—he who observed the car accident—this is how he will end this. This is how he will end me. Because I have broken the rules.

I am getting involved.

It is the first urge I have acted upon in so many years. And it will certainly be my undoing. No matter. I run and run and run. My tendons untangle. Am I faster now? Atrophied muscles begin to remember this feeling: urgency. I feel the pull from moment to moment behind me, but it changes from the resistance of a bungee cord to the tug of an ear. The pull has become an irritant. A buzzing mosquito. As my legs throb from years of disuse, I feel things. Concern. Desperation. Pain. So much pain. Where have these feelings been?

I scream as I hurtle past pedestrians. The fire in my legs, tremendous. Like a terror there. A fever. Such pain I have never—well, the headaches were pain, but dull, like when a nap lingers too long.

The headache. It is gone. Burned out by the distraction of other More Important Things Happening. My legs loosen. They begin to feel unshackled. I fly. The wind tunnel reversed, I am now the breeze, obsessed with nothing more nor less than my wife and boy. My wife and boy.

My son.

I stop. I vomit into the sewer. I have not run full out in a while.

I run again. I have clarity now.

I am moving forward. Not away. Toward home. I am not about to leap. I am here. Present. The pull gone. The pain gone. The electricity gone.

I burst into the hospital entrance, and he is there. There, sipping on a cup of complimentary coffee. I did not know they would have complimentary coffee, but I swiftly knock it out of his hand and tackle him to the ground. I begin to pelt away at his face, not causing much damage—I am, after all, new to this sort of thing. I grab his jean jacket lapels and pull his head off the linoleum flooring until we are practically nose-to-nose.

—What did you do to them?!

He smiles. An odd choice.—I didn't do anything, Gary. She's fine.

—And the baby?

—The baby's not quite born yet.

—You said you would end this!

He stands. He brushes himself off and limps to the entrance. He picks a book up off the floor. Oh. It is my journal. I must have dropped it in the melee. He hands it back to me. He is calm. At peace. I am perplexed. My mouth hangs open for a good eleven seconds. I do not notice until some saliva slips out onto my shoe. It is then that I speak.

—Yes, Gary. This. He motions back and forth between us.—I will end *this*. Not *them*.

And this brings to mind what I consider the more important question.—Why are you here?

—Is that what you really want to ask, Gary? Really?

—No. What I want to ask—what I mean to ask—is why are *we* here?

—I couldn't tell you for certain.

—You—you don't know?

—I don't know any more than you know. There's a job and it requires someone jumping from one important moment to the next.

—I have an acronym for that.

—I know and I don't care.

We stare awkwardly for a moment. I really wanted to tell him about the acronym. Marci's contractions must be building. I should go.—One more question.

—Yes?

—Why do you think there needed to be two of us?

—Two of us?

—At a time?

—Gary—There is only supposed to be one of us at a time.

—No. There were two. You and me.

—There was one. Until today it was only *me*, said the other Magnet.—I've been trying to pass the job to you and leave it behind since your twenty-first birthday. And today, I can. Because, at long last, you are truly taking my place. The man wrapped his blue jean jacket more tightly around his torso and slipped out the door. I was desperate for more answers, but could only muster one last thought.

—The electricity. Will it always hurt?

—Only if you're doing it right.

The elevator arrived at the ground floor full twice before I decided to scamper up the fire escape to room 1623. Marci was astounded to see me. She wondered the obvious: is there something about this moment that is the Most Important Thing Happening?

I say—It is to me.

She asks if she is going to die. Is the baby going to be great? And will the great be a good or bad sort of great?

I tell her I do not have this information, but I do not believe I leaped here for her or the baby.

She says this makes no sense.

And the conversation ends abruptly with the onslaught of another contraction. Between contractions I explain the running. I explain the red words. Meeting him in the lobby. I explain that the complimentary coffee is bad. Another contraction. I find myself explaining everything to her. Everything. My feelings for her and this child. I explain the reasons I have chosen emotional distance. I explain everything. Everything except for any of the Most Important Things I have witnessed.

Right now, none of them seem to matter all that much.

He is born. And as I stare into his eyes, I feel more in this moment than any moment that has preceded it. Marci chooses to name him Gary. And I don't have the heart to explain why this is a terrible idea.

It's been hours now. Hours of peace. A few terrible hospital meals. And I have not felt the slightest twinge to leap. Have I done this to myself? It seems ironic. The moment I understand what a Magnet is truly designed to do—the second I get what a MITH really is—it seems the need for them has slowed to a crawl. All this time, I assumed the pain was there to keep me from taking action. It never dawned on me that the pain was mine to push through.

Marci sleeps peacefully with little Gary curled up by her side.

My hands ease into my pocket and I cut myself.

It seems my fight with gravity this afternoon caused the mirror to break in my pocket. I pull out the largest piece and stare into it.

I know my reflection too well.

And then—the tug at the navel.

The slight nausea as if a roller coaster is lurching. I am filled with hope and dread wondering how this time will be different from all the others. Will I regret getting involved—or will it change me? How badly will it hurt and why does the thought of that make me finally feel alive?

I grip the mirror and smile. I am nervous, but I am prepared. And as I feel my body shove away into the dark unknown, all I can think about is what Marci will have to say when she realizes I am not there in the morning to bring her a decent breakfast.

BLAH BLAH BLAH

—And that, my followers, is a pound of fact, a pinch of opinion, and you can keep-a-change!

The crowd went wild, but the crowd always went wild when J. Aaron Epsom signed off from rehearsal. They were mostly paid crew and interns, but either way, J. Aaron was used to applause. His trademarked brand of faux hubris caused *Now* magazine to declare him "the Rock Star Pundit on a Muzak Broadcast landscape." The saucy news he served up on a nightly basis was at first off-putting to the network's programming chief, Howard Howard, but Howard warmed to J. Aaron when he saw the overnight ratings spike seven months ago when he first went on the air. Now a pending book deal was merely the appetizer toward world domination.

J. Aaron gave a few last-minute notes to prep for the 8:00 p.m. live broadcast and retreated to the greenroom where his hot chai awaited. He did not particularly care for the taste of hot chai, but drank a mug nightly out of superstition. The evening of his very first show had gone so well, he had felt electric, and as he stepped backstage, one of the interns, a cute thing named Tamala, handed him a sample of the beverage. He had shouted out *HOTCHAI!* while improvising a pose that some would call a samurai/ninja hybrid and others would call desperate. Tamala laughed and then slept with him. He hadn't refused a cup since. Though the night of the fourth show, he fired Tamala. Her laugh ended with a snort that was grating.

He passed the writers' room. Barry remained. Barry Gooz always remained.

—Look who's making me shine, J. Aaron said.

—Yay. It's you.

—Pretty great monologue. Pretty fair. Especially the third joke. Why is it always the third joke that kills? I love third things. Someone should write a doctoral theorem on that.

—Thesis.

—Even if the second joke bombs. Crazy. You didn't write that one, did you? It felt more like I wrote it.

—But you didn't.

—Well—some might say that in delivering the joke so well, I crafted it anew in the moment.

—You didn't craft it anew, insisted Barry—because you didn't write it.

—Who did? Lorenzo?

—No.

—Shmoopy?

—Again, no.

—Z-Dog? Puppy Pound? Shahanga? Felt Tip? Klargle? Moonwash?

—No. And why hasn't Howard given me a nickname yet? I've been here longer than everyone you just mentioned. I've even been here longer than Schnauzerhaus.

—You go home to your kids right after the show every night. Howard doesn't give nicknames until he's stone-faced drunk. That's why Steve's nickname is Stonefaced. Wait! Was it written by Stonefaced?

—No, said Barry.—It was gpownin74_yapwow.

—I don't know that nickname.

—That'd be a complicated nickname. It's a username. We've been encouraging viewers to blah in their own jokes.

—Blah in?

—You know. Blahblah. The newest social media craze. If you don't update your "whatchadoin" every 20 minutes, it makes up something for you.

—That sounds really productive.

—It is a wellspring of humor.

—Just like you—sometimes. Speaking of, where's the rest of the writing staff? Got hot dates before the show? I do. That goes without saying.

—Yet you said it.

—With Rojeta. That new intern. Where did we find her?

—She's Tamala's sister.

—Whoosh. Their parents have got to stop naming people.

—You said "whoosh."

—I did.

—Out loud.

—I'm trying it on for the show. New shtick. I'm gonna say words that are actually just sound effects.

—Onomatopoeia?

—No thanks, I just went. Here's another word I'm trying on. Poom.

—Poom isn't a word.

—Are you sure? I think it's the sound a bag of flour makes when it hits a swimming pool.

—How would you know that?

—Check your swimming pool.

Barry forced his own glasses askew as he rubbed his closed eyelid with his thumb. It gave the impression he was exasperated, but with what J. Aaron hadn't a clue. He sighed all the way down to the fluid building up in his lungs and attempted to end the conversation.

—Well—have fun dating the second crazy-named sister.

—Hey! I wonder if there's a third? I love third things! What do you think her name would be?

—Shahanga. She's on our writing staff.

J. Aaron yanked his smoking jacket off of the only chair in the room with wheels and hurried to the elevator, tapping the v̂ button nine times before—

—ROMCOM!

—Mr. Howard!

—Please. Call me Howard. Mr. Howard's my father, may he rest in peace someday soon.

Howard caught J. Aaron before the elevator doors could close, but Howard Howard always caught J. Aaron. If there was anything that irritated him more than the nickname ROMCOM (the etymology would make very little sense even with a backstory), it was the giver of that nickname: Howard Howard. Howard gave nicknames but did not have one himself even though he desperately needed one.

—Smoking jacket's a beauty, Howard Howard insisted.

—Actually, the smoking jacket is to impress a beauty.

—How kind. My niece will be flattered.

Poom. J. Aaron had completely forgotten that he had agreed to take Howard's visiting niece Saphsa to—where was it?

—Not everyday she gets to eat at a restaurant that looks like a mini Big Ben.

That's right. Howard Howard had specifically asked J. Aaron to escort Saphsa to "Whales," the all-you-can-eat British-themed eatery in City Square.

—You should definitely try the Haggis Loaf appetizer.

—I thought haggis was Scottish.

—Hey, if Americans can serve French Fries …

—I'm thinking maybe a change of plans.

—Oh, stated Howard with more than a hint of disapproval— she really has her heart set on Whales.

—Great. You can take her there yourself. My change of plans involves a different individual of the feminine variety.

—You don't have to talk like that. There isn't a camera on you.

—I'm taking Rojeta to doughnuts, then steak. These European models need a pillow of carbs to line the intestine before the beef scoots in.

—The model will understand when you cancel. I am, after all, your boss. Saphsa will meet you at six.

—That's cutting it awfully close to the 8:00 p.m. show.

—You've shown up five minutes before and been fine.

—I've shown up five minutes before and been great—but I never had a stomach full of haggis. You know I can't eat that sort of thing or …

—Or you'll balloon to your old weight?

—I was going to say, "Or I'll lack energy for the show."

—Then have the lamb fries.

—I would if I were going.

—You will and you are.

He stated the last five words with a face that reminded J. Aaron of his father. His father wasn't much of a father. Probably why J. Aaron didn't particularly care for fathers. Either way, the face had its intended effect. J. Aaron found himself walking the sidewalk toward Whales, trying to get all the laughs out of his system he might subconsciously associate with the name Saphsa over dinner.

Man, that third joke killed. What is it with the third joke? The truth of it stuck in J. Aaron's craw. Blahblah, huh? He wondered what it might take to join in on the socialness. He typed the URL into his MiniPowerPad 3.0 and assessed the instructions:

```
Email:
Username:
Password:
Confirm Password:
```

It seemed miraculously simple. Though others tended to tend to J. Aaron's details, J. Aaron knew all four of these details by heart. In fact, three of them were identical. This social media thing really was easy. He took ten minutes to type in the information (his clumsy thumb continually replacing the j with a k), and felt nervousness in his stomach as the first prompt appeared:

```
Compose your first blah: 110
characters or less.
```

Characters? What's a character? J. Aaron didn't realize he would need to write some sort of story. Unless character referred to the amount of letters, which made no sense as just saying "letters" took less time than saying "characters." After assessing other sample blahs, J. Aaron assessed that characters indeed meant letters and considered the process of blahing futile. He was just about to delete the account when another prompt appeared:

```
You have 133 followers.
```

Glory be to the Creator. J. Aaron knew he was successful—popular even, but he had no idea that 133 people per minute were ogling him (the fashionable term for using the Ogle.com search engine). They had social networked their way into being his loyal subjects in less than sixty seconds. And he hadn't even blahed anything yet. This was remarkable.

He was late for dinner.

Just one, he thought. He stood in the center of Center Square and pored over the line. He gazed into the distance and allowed his eyes to glaze while staring at the twinkling lights atop the Hardaway Building. This was important. His first missive to his followers. It could be philosophical. No. That would go against his newsman-next-door persona. An ironic perception about this trash bin of a city? No. He was supposed to love this city. It was in the bio that his writing team had crafted.

Hmm. He knew just the thing.

```
In City Square. Preparing my
bowels for both the haggis and
the blind date awaiting me.
Whoosh.
```

He made himself laugh so he knew it was awesome and started walking.

He approached the tourist portion of City Square. Every eatery had a theme and every store had a ten-foot-tall icon in front: a toy sculpture or soap carving or brownie tower. All the while, flashbulbs popped as sightseers recognized their witty nightly news anchor. J. Aaron feigned a wave as he tripped over an animatronic jaguarundi outside the Endangered-Species-Themed Casino.

```
You have 478 followers.
```

Wow. He had been advised to mind his ego, but this sort of reinforced it as fact.

He entered the restaurant through the mouth of a humpback whale wearing the bearskin cap of a British Royal Guard. Just inside, a hostess stood at a kiosk on the part of the tongue that would otherwise taste bitterness.

—I believe I have a reservation.
—If you have any hesitancies, you should eat elsewhere.
—No. A reservation. An appointment to eat.

—Oh. Sorry. I'm a literalist. And we don't take reservations.

—Not even for J. Aaron Epsom?

—I don't know what that is.

—It's not a what. It's a who. It's a guy with almost 500 followers. Me.

—Your first name's Jay?

—No. It's the letter. The letter J.

—And you say it out loud?

—Am I on your list or not?

—Did your Union Jack vibrate?

—I beg your pardon?

—If I didn't give you a wireless flag buzzer and if it didn't vibrate, then your name hasn't been called. Kapish?

—Poom.

—What? the hostess asked.

—Sorry. I thought we were making up sound effects.

—Unless, that is, you're meeting a lady friend, the hostess stated as if she had only just remembered it.

—Lady friend?

—Someone said to call her if a handsome famous fellow shows up. Could that mean you? Had she ever seen you before?

—You see this face? You're welcome.

—Her Union Jack vibrated twenty minutes ago. She's over there eating a second helping of Buckingham & Cheese Salad.

J. Aaron tiptoed past the Renowned Nannies Pictorial History and peeked around the corner. A fluorescent velvet Stonehenge framed her head like a halo, which was unfortunate because black-light was not at all flattering to Saphsa's girthy silhouette.

He sauntered over, making certain to brush past a table where he heard his name whispered—you know, give them a thrill. And then, the inevitable: he squeezed snug into the booth, the table pressing into his belt line.

—Tiny booth.

—I had to scootch the table your way, she said with a mouthful of green and brown.

—Scootch. That's a neat word.

—I didn't invent the word. I just did it to the table.

—Wow. Salad. Why do I smell onion rings?

—It's the deep-fried cubed ham.

—There are fried cubes in the salad?

—Of ham.

—Clever. Almost like a meal.

—You don't remember me, do you?

J. Aaron Epsom knows there are four stages in a successful performer's life. The first is called the urge. It is the moment when the epiphany hits a certain someone (who has no other skill set than performing) that performing is what he/she was born to do. The urge convinces the performer that singing/comedy/jazz-hands were inbred from the fetus stage and that they will die—oh just *die*—without making a life of art or at least consistent applause.

The second stage is called the bottom. This is when the performer becomes convinced that he/she is no better than the eleven thousand others auditioning for the same jobs. That he/she should have seized the opportunity earlier to learn a functioning motor skill. That unpaid repertory is a reward, not a due. This is also the stage when the performer makes his/her first actual friend in show business. The actual friend is special. The actual friend understands the performer's lowest moments and needs. The actual friend becomes empathy rather than competition. The actual friend truly gets you. For some, this is the final stage. Performing life remains at this level while plasma donations and barista gigs pay the utilities.

Only a handful reach the third stage.

The third stage is called the ceiling. Brazen, overflowing success. This is the stage where the performer eventually forgets the actual friend ever existed. As J. Aaron glanced up from the Andrew Lloyd Webber crossword on his menu into the eyes of Saphsa, he was instantly cognizant that stage three was peaking and that he was about to be thrust down the mountain into stage four.

Oh, Howard Howard—what have you done?

—I beg your pardon?

—We were in the Hordelings together.

—What? Were we? In that building with the tree in the lobby?

—Yes. We improvised together.

—There were, like, a hundred of us in that troupe.

—There were seven. She said it after a prolonged moment of silence.

—I mean, including the audience. Did you say your name is Saphsa?

—Yes. Saphsa Eloquin.

—That is one bizarre stage name.

—That's my real name. I was using a stage name back in the Hordelings.

—Of course! You were—Pam.

—I was Rhonda.

—Yep! Rhonda something with an M.

—No.

—With a consonant.

—Rhonda Oerboerseau.

—I meant in there somewhere. A few consonants. In the middle. Sandwiched among a lot of vowels. Wow.

—You don't remember me at all.

—I have no recollection of a Rhonda Oerboerseau. Is that Dutch?

—How should I know? I made it up.

—You were really good. Really good at making up a name. Did we do any sketches together?

—Yes. We were in a seven-member comedy troupe for three years. We did many many sketches together, Orvin.

—Shhh. Hey now. I know I've upset you, but there's no need to call me Orvin.

—How is Aaron any better?

—It isn't. That's why I made up "J. Aaron."

—That's ridiculous.

—No. It's famous. I'm famous. I have nearly 500 followers.

—Yes. I know.

—You what now?

Turned out Saphsa Eloquin *née* Rhonda Oerboerseau had an ongoing Ogle alert that notified her when any online action occurred for "J. Aaron Epsom." She had been among his first 133 followers. She had read of J. Aaron's bowel preparation for the date and how she had been compared to haggis.

He took a quick gulp of his water to cool the steam. He was not going to let this girl grab his goat in public. Grab his goat? Is that the saying? It should be. He pondered the nuances of the euphemism while a lone ice cube lodged itself between his cheek and uvula.

—This is all really bothering you, she stated with both pity and disappointment.

—Why would it bother me to forget you? I'm supposed to just take your word that we did all these things together? Ha. Ha ha. Do you know how many people wish they were seated in your chair at this table at this moment?

—I know one who wishes she wasn't.

—So, you invited me here to humiliate me.

—I'm not the one who winced at the fried salad cubes.

—That salad has chocolate-covered hardboiled eggs in it. It's begging for ridicule. You can't penalize me for that! And Howard should have told me that you were a previous acquaintance.

—Howard doesn't know.

—What do you mean Howard doesn't know?

—I've never told my uncle that I perform. I don't want any favors in the business. I'd rather make it on my own.

—Lady, the business *is* favors!

—"Saphsa"—you don't get to call me Lady.

—You expect me to believe that you arranged to have dinner with me—ME—and that you are NOT looking for a job.

—I don't need a job from you, Orvin.

—Stop. Calling. Me. That.

—I came to have dinner with you because you hurt me.

—Here we go.

—Stop it. I don't expect you to understand. You weren't the same person. We all make mistakes, but you hurt me and it has been hard for me to let go of that hurt.

—What's the angle here, Orca? What do you think I'm going to give you?

—No fat jokes. Please.

—You've got to be kidding me.

—I'm not interested in anything you can give me. I've allowed the way you hurt me to rule me for a very long time. It's turned me into what you see before you.

—I can hardly see you behind that menu.

—Stop it. You becoming famous—on every billboard and magazine—it just made things worse, so I thought if I reconnected and reminded myself of the friend you once were—

—This is a hidden camera show.

—A what?

—This is that show. What is it called—*Doinked*! Where they mess with celebrities' heads. Am I getting *Doinked*?!

—Please lower your voice.

His eyes met hers. His smile dissolved.—You're serious.

—This is important to me. Necessary, she muttered as her eyes fell to the salad.

—You thought we were friends? I don't even remember you.

—Clearly. I am not here to gain anything from you. But, for my own well-being, I needed closure and it appears I have seen the extent of how much of that is possible with someone like you.

—Someone like me?

—Forget it. I will now close this chapter. Tomorrow, I begin an opportunity that will change my life.

—Right. Reverse psychology. Make me think you have a better opportunity so I offer you an internship because you read somewhere that I date interns.

—For your information, I have a book deal with Shrub & Sons Publishing.

There it is. J. Aaron could feel the rage broiling behind his right eye. Why the right eye before the left? J. Aaron didn't know. Perhaps rage moved like it was reading a manga comic in Japan.—So, we cut to the chase. An exposé. You're here to extort money out of me to stop you from tearing me apart in some exposé.

—It's not an exposé. It has nothing to do with you.

—Of course it doesn't. I just happen to be the only famous person who has hurt you. I suppose it isn't about me at all. It's probably a photo book of baby seals dressed like people.

—It's a book of paper dolls.

—What?

She pulled out a sample.—Only for adults. With real fashion. I always found great escape in paper dolls as a girl, but every adult escape I've found is destructive. I've decided to create an innocent one. But, instead of paper clothing, it's actual clothing.

—Are those tiny pajamas?

—Mmhm. And they're made of the finest materials: silk, cashmere, leather. It's a high-end coffee table book for the child in all of us.

—Children shouldn't be drinking coffee.

—You're missing the point.

—This is real? This is really the book deal? Not some factual trash about me?

—I'm here to forgive, Orvin. Forgive and move on. I really need to. For my own well-being.

J. Aaron peered through narrowed eyes for the slightest of moments before bursting into laughter.

—You're laughing. Saphsa quivered. Don't laugh.

—You really—you just don't—don't get it.

—Don't mock me.

—You aren't giving me much of a choice, Saphsa. I mean, if you were exposing me for money, at least there would be something to respect. But, this? You think this is a chance to change your life? I'm sorry, Saphsa. But, this is just a new way for your world to come crashing down.

—I beg to differ.

—Is it too late to stop this?

—I sign my publishing deal tomorrow at the Hardaway Building.

—This isn't a fresh start.

—Please.

—This is nothing.

—You think I am nothing? I am trying to be filled with graciousness and forgiveness here while you are filled with hubris and judgment.

—And jokes. Don't forget the jokes.

—I'd say it's quite easy to forget your jokes.

—Hey! No ragging on my jokes.

—*Your* jokes? I didn't realize you wrote any of them yourself.

—Ha. Ha ha. Nice angle. Making light of me just because I didn't get here on my own.

—Oh. I know you didn't.

—Whoosh.

And there it was. From the moment they made eye contact, J. Aaron knew the fuse was being lit. He now understood where the bomb was intended to drop: in his own lap. This deranged woman—this performer (clearly in stage two) has deluded herself into believing that she knows him and that he owes her. Now, the ploy was clear. Ha ha. Ha ha ha. Earth to unfamous person: you will never get what you are after.

—You listen to me, Rhonda—if that is your real fake name—doors have been opened for me, but I funnied my way through them. I force-talked and lampooned my way into opportunities thinner than the space between this table and my spleen. I did it. I! I! I! It's *my* turn! *My* stage three! The third is the best. I love third things! They *rule*. They are the best part of life. The best jokes—and you will not take my third thing away.

—You know, famous people die in threes.

—Don't ruin my third-is-awesome speech!

—You really think you can talk your way out of a guilty conscience?

—Who said anything about a guilty conscience?!

—You just did.

—What?!

—Here.

She showed him her MiniPowerPad 3.6 (wow, she has the new one) and revealed the latest blah attributed to J. Aaron Epsom:

```
Dinner   is   not   going   well.
Feeling quite guilty.
```

Nausea set in. J. Aaron was certain that he never wanted to smell the scent of deep-fried cubed ham again. He scrambled for his own MPP to confirm this crisis. There it was. Words he had not written—attributed to him alongside another update:

```
You have 1738 followers.
```

Disaster. Clearly, twenty minutes had passed and blahblah had blahed J. Aaron's second blah for him in his absence. He plopped his forehead upon the table, flushed red and narrowly missing his fork tines. The vibration of it shook Saphsa's 64-oz. unsweetened tea. He was perplexed. A random choice of second blah for blahblah to make on his behalf. Also startlingly insightful.

—I did not write that.

—You didn't have to. Blahblah profiles you psychologically by observing your habits and then reflects them in subsequent whatchadoins. Some say it is truer than what you would write yourself.

—How is that possible?! I wrote *one* blah! One!

—It was snarky, derisive, and self-serving. That's a lot of information.

—And now everyone has seen it.

—Perhaps everyone should.

—What is that? What sort of threat is that? he said with venom and wildness in his eyes.

—Go ahead and talk, Saphsa countered, unhinged. —That's what you do. Your precious funny famous voice. You just keep talking.

—You are mean and you take up far too much booth space. There. It is said.

—Another fat joke. Keep talking.

—I'm going to call the concierge and have you escorted out.

—Whales English Eatery doesn't have a concierge.

—I will have you life-flighted out with a hospital helicopter.

—Talk.

—I will ask my twenty strongest friends to roll you back into the ocean.

—Orvin, if you go any further, you won't be able to take it back.

He was waving his water glass in front of his face now, on a tirade loud enough for surrounding families to hear. He was calling her all known categories of dirigibles, insisting that entire herds of cattle could be saved in a flood by using her as a flotation device. At one low point, he compared her appearance to an entire family of border collies melded together into one gooey yipping orb. He was on a roll, the venom flitting from the end of his tongue like so much pent-up insecurity. He was hurling insults, not of his own making, but every one he could remember being used against him in his childhood. His pain became hers because how dare she— how DARE she for one moment think of taking away what he had earned ...

—Stop it now, she insisted.—This is your last chance.

He prattled on ... his voice. His precious, famous, hilarious voice.—This is less than a pound of fact and more than a pinch of opinion—

—Orvin. Take it back before it is taken from you.

... it was a miracle, a salvation of the modern airwaves, the antidote to his anxiety. It was his wit, his tongue, his beloved and sovereign voice!

But Saphsa silenced him with a stare. The stare like her Uncle Howard's. The stare that melted peace. Her insistent gaze burned into the bridge between his nose. He would have skittered away had he not been wedged betwixt the booth and table. The silence hushed the restaurant. All eyes were on the celebrity and this behemoth. She bared her teeth first, and then with a whisper slowly hissed the same word three times:

—*blah. blah. blah.*

She burst into tears and stormed out of Whales.

Saphsa was gone.

The chatter reprised from the customers in the eatery as if no fracas had occurred. J. Aaron pushed the table away from his abdomen. There were fumes of fried ham cubes lingering in the air. Discombobulated, he brought his water glass up to his mouth.

tik.

What the—? Something had fallen into the bottom of the glass. He fished it out. It was a tooth. A human tooth. His own.

J. Aaron ran like he had not run in a year. Of course, he hadn't actually run in a year. The show had runners to do that sort of thing for him. He ran with one hand cupped under his chin, the other holding his MPP where he could read it while sprinting. Should it hurt this much to sprint? J. Aaron couldn't remember, but thought nothing should hurt this much. Especially while your teeth were falling out.

(phing)

It was the sound of another blah coming through. An interesting sound like whoosh or poom. He made a mental note to remember it. This was all, of course, before he read the blah in question:

A fourth tooth is falling out.

Where are they getting this information? And is blahblah actually considered a they or an it or perhaps a collective? J. Aaron did not know what a collective was but he belonged to several. And furthermore, this information was inaccurate. Only three of his teeth had fallen into his cupped hand.

pamp.

Okay. Now it was accurate.

In different seasons of J. Aaron's life, he held prevalent what he considered the single pivotal question in life. The question in question changed, of course, as he matured. What began as *where did I come from?* soon became *where did all these other people come from?* Later, *why do I have to have a name like Orvin?* gave way to *is this lazy eye operable?* Soon after, *is there a higher power?* transformed into *can the higher power get me a hotter girlfriend?* And finally, *can a live show go into syndication?* became *why are all my teeth falling out?*

Why indeed. It was not the normal comeuppance for a bad date, except perhaps one that ended in fisticuffs. Had Saphsa cursed him? And if so, how would that be plausible? She's an actress, for crying out loud—worse than an actress: a comedienne. And an unmemorable one at that.

tik. pamp. tiktiktik.

The teeth were falling out in pairs now. Chunks. Some hitting his cupped hand, most spilling to the concrete. He ran harder, scrambling to get to the studio as if all solutions would become clear inside.

He slammed the writers' room door three times before Barry Gooz awoke from his siesta on the casting couch.

—What?! What! Is it showtime?

—I'm bweeding fwom my mouf!

—What time is it? What are you talking about?

—I had a bad ebening ad I'b bweeding fwom my mouf!

—Aaron—you're bleeding from your mouth!

It was the first time J. Aaron had attempted to say something out loud since the incident at Whales. (*tik. pamp.*) It had not dawned on him that the absence of teeth would (*tik.*) deter his pronunciation. This was going to be a problem.

—Did you get mugged?

—I need teef!

—Did someone punch you in the mouth? Was it Rojeta? *No*—I bet it was Stonefaced. He's engaged to Rojeta. You can't go on the air looking like that.

—Da's why I NEEB TEEF!

—What you need are some teeth.

—YEJH! TEEF! TEEF!

The two of them scurried to the makeup department, J. Aaron dropping the few teeth he had caught like marbles, kicking them inadvertently into corners and crevices.

```
(phing) Now, my lips are going
numb.  Is  this  my  recompense
for  so  much  bad  behavior  gone
unpunished?
```

He stopped cold in the middle of the hallway, blood dripping from the slits between his fingers. He stared at the message. It was truth. Not the bad behavior, because J. Aaron would not call his habits something so derogatory, but the numbness—the numbness was true. He had not even noticed until he read it. His mouth was deteriorating fast, eliminating his ability to speak for himself. It became clear that the only words the public was going to hear from him tonight would come from this machine—this blahblah. These words that his followers

(phing) You have 3468 followers.

would assume were coming from his precious mind.

Barry Gooz doubled back down the hallway with Facial Enhancement Artiste (the moniker she preferred over "makeup lady") Felicia Schulman. Felicia was carrying several sets of dentures in a Ziploc freezer bag.

—Wow, sweetheart. You weren't joshing, Felicia opined, interrupted only by the smacking of her bubble gum.

—Why would I lie about J. Aaron losing his teeth?

—I assumed it was a euphemism for being really really drunk.

—No, we call that stonefaced.

—Oh. That explains Steve. Goodness. Mr. Epsom looks like a baby or an old man or someone in-between with gingivitis.

—Can you fix it?

—I can fix anything in the facial arena. But, I've never had to replace all of the teeth at once—not on such short notice.

—Will it work?

—Oh, I can fit him with a new set, but only if they're ALL gone.

—What?! We can't wait for that! He's on the air LIVE in five minutes!

—Okay, sugar. I'll run go get my pliers.

He lay there on the hallway linoleum. To have made such a fortune. To have wooed so many fans. All with the wit and savvy of his tongue. And now—now—it would all disappear in an instant. In an evening. In a single broadcast. This, he imagined, was terrible irony.

Yes! Of course. That was the solution. Irony! Convince his followers that this was all an act—all part of his beloved smarm. He could actually perpetuate the unsightliness of this deterioration and milk it for all it was worth. He would make this tragedy appear to be intentional. A—what do they call it? A statement! Yes! He would make it appear as if his inability to speak was merely a statement. He couldn't say anything because he was saying something—perhaps a criticism of other talking heads. It was brilliant. Genius. But, how to perpetuate the idea?

He lay prone as a pool of his own saliva and mouth-blood warmed the back of his neck. He pulled out his MPP. *The pain. The pain. Oh, the excruciating pain.* He would blah. He would blah like blahblah had never been blahed before. (phing) (phing) Two more whatchadoin's had just been added:

```
Why am I being so vulnerable
with you followers? I trust you
least of all.

You have 7982 followers.
```

ARGGH! He'd better blah quickly—before the blahblah out-blahed him. But, what to type? How to best illustrate irony? It was a formidable *thepainthepain* challenge. J. Aaron was not an irony fan because you could never be certain that the intended target would catch on to the ironic nature of the irony. J. Aaron did, however, rather enjoy ironing, which is ironic.

He crafted what he considered a top-notch self-deprecating sort of entry:

```
All of these blahs have been
ironic. Or have they?
```

Ha ha. He thought about adding LOL, but did not because he only laughed internally and did not want to lie. Instead, he added a blushing emoticon. He was just about to click "submit" when he realized it wasn't a very good joke. Too obvious. "Or have they?" No. He would delete that portion. Much better. Of course, now it wasn't a joke at all. It was merely a statement. Yet perhaps that is the joke. He wished he could send two blahs before this so that this would be the third. THEN it would be funny. He clicked the "submit" button anyway and read what appeared on the screen:

```
All of these blahs have been
iconic.
```

Iconic?! That's not what he meant to type! Curse these clumsy thumbs! Well—iconic and ironic are almost the same thing—right? He couldn't remember, but the nausea building within insisted otherwise. Or maybe that was the pain from the exposed nerves in his mouth *thepainthepainkillmenow*.

Barry and Felicia rounded the corner with Howard Howard in tow. Felicia held pliers and Barry clutched a bottle of alcohol. They rushed at him like a triumvirate of bullies smelling a freshman.

J. Aaron wasn't certain which was worse: Barry Gooz scrubbing blood off of his face with rubbing alcohol, Howard Howard screaming at him for rejecting Saphsa, or the wrestling match Felicia was having with his remaining teeth. She was much more robust than she appeared. That girl had the strength of a farmhand, and as she planted her boot into J. Aaron's sternum to leverage herself, a molar was set free with a trajectory toward the ceiling tiles. J. Aaron felt himself begin to pass out, his face being rubbed raw and the yelling and screaming all merging into a single monotonous hum.

The hum continued and became a drone.

The drone persisted and became a whoosh.

J. Aaron was out cold.

All was silent, save the whoosh.

J. Aaron felt as if his eyes were open but all about him was blackness. There was a lone illumination: the soft blue glow of his MPP. He reached out for it, but it seemed to no longer be in his hand. He stepped (Was he standing? He did not remember climbing off of the floor) toward the glow. It appeared close. (phing). No. The sound was far off. J. Aaron walked briskly, reaching out for the glowing light. He found himself trotting, then sprinting, the pain a phantom memory now.

And then the light grew larger and larger until J. Aaron found himself standing at the foot of his own MPP, now the size of a monolith before him. J. Aaron stared up at the blinking icon, uncertain of what to do next.

—Speak to me.
It blinked. Seven, eight times. Mocking him.
—Speak to me, blahblah. Tell me what I really think.
And then,

       All of these blahs have been
       iconic.

—That's not what I meant to say. That wasn't the real me.

       All of these blahs have been.

—How can you say that? I haven't even written most of them. You—the blahblah machine. You've been generating them for me. Not that they weren't true. Some of them—okay, all of them—were truer than my own blahs. Truer than my own words—maybe even than my own thoughts. Perhaps I haven't been completely honest.

       All of these blahs have.

—Listen, I'm in the entertainment business. Yes, many say it's the news business, but the moment I make that funny, don't I open the door for it to just be my own perspective? And isn't that the point, that we each have our own perspective and mine is more important because I have so many followers? Doesn't the number of followers reinforce the fact that my perspective is the one that is correct? Can you really give me one piece of evidence to the contrary?

All of these blahs.

—Touché. But again—they weren't all me. Some were true, some were you, some were fabrications, some were deceptions, and at least every third one was a joke. What I need to know is which of these is the real me?

All of these.

—Not possible. I can't be all of these things. I would implode if I were all of these things. I know. I used to be a truer person and it didn't really work. Back with the Hordelings. We used to sit on the roof of our apartment building for hours on end, improvising scenes that weren't funny at all. They started funny with a suitcase of unicorn dolls or a man giving birth—you know, ideas the audience had thrown out earlier that evening. But, the scenes always ended up playing out what was in our head—or rather, deeper than the head—behind the head. The soul. The transition from laughter to pain was always subtle and surprising. The sort of thing you want to slam the door on, but in those moments, the momentum was a force of nature all its own. I don't know where so much overflowing truth came from. Those moments didn't have a fence or a rule to hold back the unexpected. It became a therapy or life force for us. At first, I engaged in it all to be the funny one, but whenever it would turn—that's what I called it when it got personal: the turn—that's when I would leave the circle and sit cross-legged on the roof ledge. If you left the circle, you couldn't be tagged in. I liked to watch. I discovered a weird calming that would come over me when the others would get raw and weep or lash out or throw something off the roof. One time, I didn't sit far enough away from the circle and I was tagged in. I didn't know what to say, so I started rambling about this road trip my Dad took me on for his work when I was nine. He thought I was asleep and never knew I saw the bad things he did there. You'd think I would remember which city. But, what I did remember was that it had been the first day in my life I had felt unwarmably cold. Those were the only words I could come up with to describe the feeling and I immediately regretted saying it out loud. The Hordelings all wrapped around me like a blanket and started smothering me. Just this sense of people an inch from me—overbearing people. They thought it was affection, but the only reason I had said the thing I said was so that I could throw the trash can off the roof. Is that so bad? It was true. Just because I'd rather throw something than feel something—what does that make me? It doesn't make me anything. It doesn't make me anything good or bad. It just makes me no thing. It makes me a comedian. One rather beefy set of arms was wrapped around me most tightly and I forced my fists up through the embrace and shoved the arms off, knocking the girl in the forehead. Yeah. It was a girl. Funny, huh. I said something witty about the size of the arms not realizing it was a girl. Some girl. I forget which girl. Large girl. And no one laughed and I thought—isn't this why we all came together? To laugh? Isn't that the purpose in finally finding others who crave what you crave? At least I thought that was what I had found. Up until that moment, I thought I had been looking for a group of people who all craved their own success. But, in that instant, as they shunned my joke and rallied around Rhonda—got it. That was her name—as they rallied around Rhonda, I realized that I was not looking for a group of people who all craved their own success. I was looking for a group of people who all craved *my* success. That is when I left the Hordelings for good and begged Howard Howard for an internship with the network. I left the second stage of a performer's career behind and I went to great lengths—and I mean *great lengths*—to make certain that I never remembered it again. Everything after that was one fist to the rope at a time—one strenuous pull of my entire body upward— and it has been agony. Sheer agony. And this aloneness—not just aloneness, but an unwarmable aloneness—grows everyday. I think what I am doing is taking care of myself. I reject others for the sake of my own success because I need that warmness—or what do they call it, warmth? I am desperate for that warmth and I will find it, either through the laughter of a studio audience or a trio of dateable sisters or the sheer volume of followers. I will use my snarkiness and my wit to dodge the conversation every time it turns and I am at risk of being tagged in. I will instead redirect with the blahblah and the audience will love me for it. That's how you get a top-rated show and a best-selling book— a best-selling life. I fully understand what it makes me. I fully understand that I am less than human and less than warm. But *I will achieve warmness*. Oh, I will achieve warmness yet. Because, as you have said to me time and time again, some of my blahs may be ridiculous—but all of these blahs have been iconic.

Nothing. No response. He waited.

Still nothing. Absolutely nothing. Until—

He regained consciousness abruptly at his news desk, the camera blinking before his eyes. He caught a glimpse of Barry Gooz running off stage, having just snapped a pellet of smelling salts under J. Aaron's right nostril. The live audience was aflutter with applause, urging him toward another scathing late-night program. He sat and stared, wide-eyed, not yet fully abreast of his surroundings. His right palm was just below the note cards his writing staff had written, yes, the same as usual. His left hand tapped his ring against the water glass. All was ritual. He at least appeared alert.

He felt the enamel of his teeth against the inside of his lips. A full, shiny, smooth set. All crises had been diverted. Felicia had provided a miracle.

His vision barely fresh in his thoughts any longer, J. Aaron gave the briefest hesitation. Would he change things now that his life had been so rattled? Would he speak truth tonight or just another set of verbal blahblah?

The intro narration came to completion:

—*He's a pound of fact, a pinch of opinion, and you can keep-a-change! It's J. Aaron Epsom Tonight!*

The music wrapped. The spotlight landed—and J. Aaron smiled a wide, perfect grin at the studio audience, his teeth perfectly white.

Perfectly artificial.

And as J. Aaron attempted to lick his lips in order to sink his teeth into the next comedic victim, he discovered that he could do nothing more than grunt.

The audience, hushed, stared in puzzlement.

His smile persisted. The teeth were whole—but his jaw was clenched. J. Aaron swallowed hard with the understanding that his teeth were not going to separate.

His mouth was not going to open.

The artificial teeth were stuck together.

Oh. He thought to himself. *This.*

This is ironic.

    (phing)

Fear of his audience mounting inside of him, J. Aaron Epsom took one last glance down at the device in his hand.

    Or is it?

THE WHIPPERSNAPPER

Conrad Reed knew better than to pick at the whisker that was beginning to grow back into his neck. Of course, if it were sense he were minding, he would have shaved backward this morning to begin with, removing the irritation altogether. Instead, the throbbing ache just to the left of his Adam's apple was adding a whole new torture to this typically overlong meeting. But, there it was. Digging it out would simply make the matter worse.

Speaking of things that need to be removed, he now officially loathed Rod Perk, assistant marketing director at XtraX and Conrad's immediate supervisor. Rod coddled his own turns-of-phrases as if they were new lovers, each a ripened plum. But the words thrust out of Rod's mouth across the room smacked Conrad in the face, each reeking of lukewarm halitosis. Come five o'clock, this hypocrite, this—this *ape* would no longer have the power to tell Conrad what to do. Conrad had interned here as a junior in high school, transitioning into an assistant's job at nineteen. Eight years later, he was both invisible and overtrusted. Tonight, he would finally say good riddance to the only place he had ever worked and move forward to a far more significant future—if all went well.

As dull as Rod Perk's droning had become, Conrad knew better than to fall asleep. A few years back, he dozed in a braintrust meeting with his arms folded and unintentionally said *Eleanore* out loud in his sleep. He never lived that down. He, of course, did not really know anyone named Eleanore. Just the one imaginary girl in his dreams. That was a better world anyway. Happy endings and whatnot. He wished terribly that just once he would remain asleep long enough to see Eleanore's face. One of the many downsides of imaginary love. Conrad did not allow himself the luxury of romance in real life.

He should be teeming with anticipation, but instead, his fingers tittered nervously, aware that today he would be the focal point for the first time, his resignation the only instance he had drawn attention to himself. But, he only needed to sustain a modicum of normalcy for seven more hours. He tapped the hard object in his right pocket with his ring. It made a sound. Bad idea. He instantly removed his hand.

He rolled a bullet of paper he had created by winding his gum wrapper tightly and licking it closed. He was able to make it pass over all five knuckles before drumming it back to the start—over and over. Rod's diatribe was in its second trimester now, and Conrad could see that he wasn't the only individual who heard their supervisor as white noise. Conrad's eyes drifted, and he noticed Selma Ripkin on the other side of the plexiglass conference room wall. She was waving to Conrad—not a hello as much as a warning. She pointed toward Conrad's cubicle where he could clearly see a terse and well-dressed woman wondering why he was not at his desk.

Conrad stood up so quickly that his notepad fell onto the table, knocking someone's cold coffee onto a nearby laptop. The ensuing melee covered his exit quite nicely.

—Are you Conrad Reed?

—Conrad I am.

—Is that supposed to be cute? she asked in a tone that seemed to disapprove of cute things.

—Not necessarily.

—Today is your last day with XtraX.

—Is it? Time sure does fly.

—Follow me.

He wasn't certain if he was supposed to gather his belongings. He had never ended an occupation before. He had expected some sort of exit interview, counted on it, in fact. But now that it was time, he wasn't certain of the protocol.

She welcomed him into the executive elevator. As the doors shushed closed, the fancy girl pulled an ID tag from her waist. It was attached to a tiny retractable zipline. Neat. She waved it in front of a sensor and the elevator began to rise. She released the tag.

Zhhhooop. Back to her beltline. Fancy.

She kept her back to him, facing the doors. Conrad considered the nape of her neck attractive. Not quite Imaginary Eleanore attractive, but appealing nonetheless. He attempted to slowly shuffle himself 45 degrees to at least face her cheek, but she made the same subtle pivots as he did, allergic to eye contact.

Conrad had not realized how high they had risen until sudden sunshine poured into their little motion cube. The rear wall of the elevator was see-through, but having never ridden it above concrete slab levels, he hadn't noticed before. My goodness, they were high. It made him feel queasy. Conrad considered using his inhaler but thought it would make the fancy girl pivot extra and he did not want to give her the satisfaction.

Ding.

The doors shushed again and Fancy remained unmoved.

—Um. Shall we?

—We? Not we. Only you.

—Excuse me?

—Straight down the hall. The last door on the right.

He stared at her, mouth open and skull at an odd angle. Her eyes nudged him away from her. Tentative, he shuffled out the doors. They attempted to close on him.

—Move along.

Yep. She was one of them.

Conrad slipped out as the elevator doors made their resolve. He peered down the long schmancy hallway before him, noting that the ceiling was at least twice as high as it deserved to be. His steps echoed, as did his knock when he finally reached the door. A voice resonated from the other side.

—Enter.

Conrad stepped inside and immediately regretted it. The room was vast and opulent. Higher ceilings than the hallway and a billboard-sized window behind the desk.

A young man—younger than Conrad anyway—smiled large while speaking into the tiniest of headsets attached to his face.

—Substantial. That is a substantial concession on the part of Dr. Rathbone and you would be remiss to disregard the offer. Uh huh. Uh huh. Um huh. Huh.

Conrad didn't see how there was time for the person on the other end of the phone to be replying between this young man's *uh huh*s. And yet he twirled his laser pointer in his hand like he was escorting a parade into the city.

—Uh huh. Um huh. Yeah. Yes, he droned on—Of course. Of course not. You can't be serious. You shouldn't be. You won't. You will. She did. I'm putting you on hold. And you are?

Eight awkward seconds went by before Conrad felt the heat of the laser on his forehead and deduced that the young man was now addressing him.

—I—I'm—My name is—Can you not point that at my face?

—It's a pointer. It's made to be pointed.

—At my face?

—I'm pointing it above your face. At your forehead.

—Can you not do that?

—Um huh. And you are—Conrad Reed. Third floor.

—Second floor, actually.

—We include the basement.

—There's a basement?

—Dr. Rathbone will see you now.

—I'm not here to see Mr. Eeley?

—Excuse me while I laugh. No one on the third floor gets to see Mr. Eeley.

—Second floor.

—No one on the first through ninth floors gets to see Mr. Eeley.

—I can't even knock on his door and thank him for so many years of employment?

—Mr. Eeley's door has remained closed all day today. Even so, it would not be permissible to knock.

—Permissible?

—Advisable. Dr. Rathbone will see you now.

—Who's Dr. Rathbone?

—The person who will see you now.

The laser pointer was now aimed at another door, a new realm on the north wall. Or rather, the door itself *was* the north wall. It opened on its own, Conrad assumed through magic, until he saw the young man put the remote control back in his desk drawer. As Conrad eased in, he discovered the room in evening darkness, though it was midmorning outdoors. All windows were deeply shaded and a single lamp illuminated a portion of the large desk that someone was seated behind. As Conrad moved deeper into the room, the doors closed behind him and he could hear the distinct sounds of an albatross on the beach.

—I find the ambient sounds soothing to the work environment.

—Dr. Rathbone?

—Yes. And you are Conrad Reed, she stated as if it were news.—A shame we have never met, though I assure you I know a great deal about who you are.

—I wasn't aware of a Dr. Rathbone working for XtraX.

—Well—I don't exactly work *for* XtraX as much as I work *with* XtraX.

—I don't understand the difference, Conrad said.

—You needn't. Please sit. I've had the chair warmed.

Conrad sat, his glutes confirming her declaration. He was afraid to ask exactly how this had been accomplished.

—Would you care for a milkshake?

—A what? A milkshake?

—Or sandwich? Energy drink? Protein bar? Shark steak? Fried cheese? Some clams? Or a frittata left over from brunch? Perhaps just coffee.

—I'm fine. I just finished breakfast.

—We never really finish breakfast. It's what makes us human.

Yep. She was one of them. It was the shes of XtraX (not to mention the hes, especially the hes) who had brought Conrad to his decision. The decision not only to resign, but to move forward with the precarious circumstance he had planned for this evening.

—What I mean to say is that we are never full. Never sated. Never finished wanting things, she waxed philosophical though it was all rehearsed.—It is that same characteristic that makes us never finished *not* wanting things. Am I clear?

—I am fully aware of the XtraX vision statement.

—You don't even know how to say it. You call it "Extra X" as if referring to an additional *X*. The *a* is short and it is all one seamless word.

—I know. I was making a joke. And, no, it's not supposed to be cute.

—You say you know the vision statement.

—"To rid humanity of the one thing they each must live without."

—Accurate. I would expect no less from someone who has worked here as long as you have.

—Thank you. Conrad nodded.

—But, I do have to ask—because there is one thing different about you, Conrad Reed. One detail that makes this exit interview necessary.

—I never used the discount.

—Exactly.

—You need an exit interview with me because I never used my employee discount.

—There are waiting lists, Mr. Reed. Individuals who wait three to five years for an XtraXion availability window. You work here for well over a decade at an insignificant salary, the only real perk that you may jump the line at a reduced price and you never—*never* seize the opportunity?

—Did you consider that I don't want anything removed?

—We all want something removed, Mr. Reed. You don't strike me as the sort who has never considered the fact.

—Exactly what is it that you do here, Dr. Rathbone?

—Please. Call me Ariel.

But he would not avert his eyes.

—You're in public relations, Conrad guessed.

—Well—no flies on you.

XtraX was nothing more than a local upstart back when Conrad was six years old. It had been a heightened time for him as he was overcoming a stutter. His teacher assumed the problem was lack of brain capacity and called him a dullard. She had no genuine idea what was going on inside of the Reed home. Conrad wasn't old enough to know more than the singular detail that his mother had a mass—that was what all the aunts whispered when he passed doors slightly ajar. The only mass Conrad knew of was the colored clay he played with that smelled like salt and hardened if he left the plastic lid off the can. To this end, whenever he caught his mother asleep with her mouth open, he closed it for her so the mass would remain soft.

His moments with his mother in those months were fleeting. He would come in before school and kiss her on the cheek. She would wipe his forehead so that his hair would part on the side, a style he did not prefer but neglected to comb out. She would look at him with those tired eyes, barely open, and call him her little whippersnapper. He didn't know what it meant, but assumed it was something old people incorrectly think young people want to be called.

Back then, the organization was known as Extraction Specialists, Ltd. They specialized in a radical overnight weight-loss that required very little of the patient other than a fat chunk of change. No dietary modification, no exercise program, no scars or soreness. Customers would simply show up one day and emerge from the facility twenty-four hours later with their unpleasing excess absent.

News coverage was swift. Conrad's town was touted as the thinnest in the nation. An influx of insecure nomad chubsters took residence and the local economy catapulted to the stratosphere. After taking heaps of criticism for pandering to only one demographic, Extraction Specialists, Ltd. attempted to diversify. They tripled their staff of medical professionals and applied their secret extrication technology (a secret held by only two individuals at the time, one now surviving) to disease. It seemed logical. Eradicate fat and you should be able to eradicate cancer, right? A plea was made for test subjects.

Conrad's aunts enlisted his mother.

It was a brutal three weeks away. Silence pervaded the halls of his home. There was no news. Literally nothing. The only details Conrad heard were the rumors his teacher would spill to the classroom, unaware of Conrad's situation.

But then, on a Sunday morning, two men in white showed up on the Reed doorstop. They were pushing a wheelchair. In that wheelchair was Conrad's mother.

The mass was gone. She had survived.

—I am, of course, aware of your mother's history, Dr. Rathbone offered.

—I thought those files were private.

—For anyone who doesn't work for XtraX Executive, yes.

—With, not for.

—Pardon?

—You said you work *with* them, not *for* them.

—You listen well.

—So I've been told.

—And your mother is still alive? Thriving?

—Yes.

—All the more inexplicable.

—What?

—That you have a first-person emotional connection with an XtraX success story and yet you have purposely—

—Who said this was intentional? Conrad took a breath. This was clearly not going to be an easy out.—Have I done something wrong? Am I required to utilize the opportunity?

—Of course not. That isn't really the point.

—I'm waiting for the point, Dr. Rathbone.

—My point, Mr. Reed, is that my superiors don't even know you exist. They don't make an effort to notice your sort. I, however, make it my mission to notice. There is a continual, ever-dwindling list of employees who have not yet taken the plunge, so to speak. That list is larger than you alone, I assure you. But, the names alongside yours on that list are neophytes. New employees, still frightened by the prospect of what the procedure may entail. You are the only one who has worked here for a decade.

—Eleven years, actually.

—Yes. Since you were sixteen. You experienced our work with your mother and years later joined our mission. What is unsettling about you, Conrad, is that you appear on the surface to support what it is we do here while never committing to take part yourself. That seems, if you will excuse the term, nothing short of intentional.

—You are accusing me of—let me get this straight—seizing less than my fair share here.

—I'm not accusing you at all. I'm here to help. And I would be remiss to allow you to set foot out of those doors at five o'clock this evening without giving you the opportunity to purge yourself of whatever haunts you.

—Nothing haunts me.

—Something haunts everyone, Conrad. It is why XtraX exists.

Soon after the test subject triumphs became publicized, the line wrapped around the Extraction Specialists, Ltd. building for days. A despairing campsite of individuals with the desperate hope that the wait for this miracle would not outlast the days they had remaining to survive. Conrad had to walk past the line every day in order to get to school. It was strange. The attitude of the people in line as a whole never really felt like hope as much as desperation, like someone pulling the arm of a slot machine over and over though their bowl of coins is nearing empty.

The company could hardly keep up with the clientele. Demand was extraordinary. So again, diversification became necessary. They changed their name to XtraX (less procedural, more accessible to the common man) as they simultaneously hired a more complicated series of experts and began to utilize their secret extrication technology on, well, *everything*.

If an individual wanted an addiction removed, that was possible. An anger issue. An out-of-control emotion, a memory—if you could pinpoint it with their team of professional counselors, XtraX could remove it. The procedure, however, was too psychologically and emotionally taxing for anyone to undergo its breadth more than once. That was the limit. If you were human—if you were alive, you had one and only one shot at XtraXion. One thing to be extricated. It became the ad campaign: *what do you most desire to live without?* And the customers flooded in. The town boomed. And Conrad Reed counted the days until he could become a ground-floor employee.

—Have you been all that unhappy here? She asked it knowing the answer.

—Sometimes.

—Perhaps we could remove that.

—Remove unhappiness?

—Why not?

—Because if you removed unhappiness, I wouldn't know what happiness feels like any more.

—You would know it well. You would feel it all the time.

—All the time. Really. Elation and euphoria—all the time? Isn't the whole idea of elation that it is more—*more*—than whatever I felt right before?

—Dissatisfaction, then. We could remove whatever you prefer.

—I prefer having nothing removed.

—Or we could remove your fear.

He stared at her. Now would be a good time for that frittata.

—You think I'm afraid of the extraction process.

—Of course you are. Isn't that the heart of what is at hand here? You first came to work for this organization because of what happened to your mother. True?

—True, Conrad admitted.

—So many individuals apply and are rejected, but you gained entrance because … well, why don't you finish the story?

—I'd rather hear your version.

—Let's have that coffee now. She tapped a button on a device affixed to her temple.—Dijon, bring in a cup—make that *two* cups of espresso. Conrad heard a brief *um huh* muttered faintly in Ariel's ear and attempted unsuccessfully to keep his nervous ring finger from tapping against the hard object in his pocket.—Where were we? Dr. Rathbone persisted.

—You were trying to remove my unhappiness.

—No. You were going to answer my question.

Conrad tilted his head in thought.—I'm curious, Dr. Rathbone. All I've done is save your company money by not taking a bonus. Where is all the antagonism coming from?

—Antagonism?

—You have to agree you're coming on a bit strong.

—Well, many say I'm a strong woman.

—I suppose you're certain what you want in life.

—This meeting isn't about me, Conrad.

—I'm just trying to figure out why you think you need to bring me down a notch to get whatever it is you want.

—I would think it clear that all I want is the truth.

—A little kindness might get you there quicker.

—Not in my experience.

Conrad relented.—It was a gift.

—That's right. This job offer was a gift—or rather, a prize. At your high school. A raffle on behalf of XtraX. Your name was drawn, but you declined the prize of a $25,000 college grant.

—You could say I had it removed.

—Cute. You asked for something else instead. You asked if you could exchange it for something of equal or lesser value.

—An internship.

—Exactly. You willfully gave up a substantial head start on a college education—a start at life—for a chance to get your foot in the XtraX door. The press was marvelous: a local boy whose mother was one of our very first test subjects. A miracle—the one of our own creation—healed her and you desired to repay the gratitude. It was delicious. Of course, I knew there was more to it. I knew there must be something you were desperate to have removed.

—Is it too late to get cream with that espresso?

—You grew up with a stutter, a nervous child. You didn't expect that sort of emotion to kick in when it came time to have the procedure done to yourself. So, you stalled. You neglected to choose—which is a choice in and of itself, of course. All these years, remaining in a menial job, getting very little compensation, all the time waiting to have your mother's miracle happen to you. But, you never could do it, could you? You never could summon the courage. It all would have made perfect sense.

—Would have?

—I was stuck on that theory for years—for a decade. And, then suddenly one detail disproved the fable.

—I resigned.

—Yes. And no one was more disappointed than I was. I wrote the news story that completes your journey years ago, waiting for it to come true. Waiting patiently for the little stuttering boy who gave up his schooling and career in a trade of gratitude for what had been done to his mother. Waiting for that young man to follow through with his own miracle. Now, that would have been quite a story.

—A story is a good word for it, Conrad said.

—And then you resigned.

—Sorry to disappoint.

—You don't disappoint. You confuse. But, I am nothing if not eagerly adaptable.

Dijon entered, carrying in a small tray with two tiny espresso cups. He was engaged in a phone call and stirred up the tension in the room with his lack of candor. He threw some significant and well-rehearsed hand gestures her way. The clatter of the tray appeared to agitate Dr. Rathbone and she bid him exit with a motion of her hand. He set the tray down beside Conrad and exited in a similar whirlwind.

—Go easy on the cream, she instructed Conrad.

—You want me to fix your coffee?

—I believe you are still an employee, are you not?

He didn't hide his distaste for the request. —How many sugars?

—Surprise me.

Begrudgingly, Conrad stepped over to the small table and began preparing both cups. He felt like an eight-year-old in the kitchen with his aunts.

He would stand, stirring milk into their tea, and the yelling would begin. The yelling that would cause his stutter to flare, the yelling that would make him retreat to a corner of his bedroom and face the wall while imagining a better life with an imaginary girl named Eleanore. Days were rife, filled with all the hurtful words that could be mustered. Needless to say, Conrad did not like to stir things.

—You didn't ask what I meant when I said that I am adaptable, she stated self-congratulatory.

—That's because I knew what you meant.

—Of course. Because you think you know what I really want.

—I think you've decided that I—like everyone else in your world—am some sort of enemy and that you cannot win without me—or again, everyone else—losing. The world isn't your enemy. I don't think the whole world is anyone's enemy.

She smiled. He set her cup before her and returned to his seat. She assessed him without moving her head.—I wouldn't say that I consider everyone an enemy, Conrad.

—No?

—But, I am certainly on the fence about you.

—Because?

—Just this morning, I had an unusual headache from all these years of preposterous thinking concerning your story.

—My story, Conrad stated deadpan.—That is preposterous.

—And it suddenly dawned on me.

—Perhaps the whole story is a lie?

—Exactly.

—Not that any of it is untrue, but the heart of it, the motivation you assumed was behind it. Perhaps it was never true, Conrad said.

—Precisely my thinking.

—Aren't you clever.

—I assumed you came to work here because you wanted something removed, but then grew fearful and couldn't follow through. But, I had it backwards. You never wanted the procedure to begin with. Am I correct?

—You are.

—I knew it. You've never wanted anything removed.

—Oh, Conrad said—I've wanted something removed.

—The love of Eleanore?

He almost spit out his coffee.—What?

—Rod Perk spoke of a time you mentioned her name. Who is she?

—There is no Eleanore.

—Ah. So it is love indeed. The pain of a broken heart.

—No. You don't understand. She isn't real.

—You spoke her name while asleep. That seems fairly real.

—She's real to me.

—She's a delusion? A psychosis?

—She's—she's just a thought. Hope I'm holding on to. Just a single idea that I certainly do not want removed.

—Then, I don't understand, Conrad. I legitimately do not understand. If there is something you indeed want removed, when did you plan on having it eliminated?

—Isn't that obvious, Dr. Rathbone? I'm having it removed tonight.

The look on Dr. Rathbone's face was astounding. She was completely perplexed. Of course she was. She didn't know. How could she? How could any of them know? Wasn't that the point? They were all so consumed with themselves that they couldn't possibly notice the truth. They were in the business of recognizing the one thing each individual wants removed. They were not trained in the art of revealing what filled in the gaping hole its absence left behind.

Mrs. Reed remained in that wheelchair for a year, not out of necessity but of paranoia. The things that had been done to her, the extrication process, had seemed to her less than human. Yes, she had wanted the thing—the mass—out, but it had all been so disruptive, so brutal. Conrad would ask her if they hurt her. She would always answer the same—*not my body.* But, she had been changed. Gone were the warm touches to his forehead—the very thought of him at all. She didn't even call him by name any more—only the meaningless *whippersnapper.* The name meant nothing because it is what Conrad had become to her: nothing. She was no longer a mother, but a thing. When they spoke, Conrad considered his voice landing upon her ears as a diversion might, an echo. She always seemed elsewhere.

And the worry, oh the worry. The knowledge that she had used up her one chance to have something removed made her paranoid that she would grow ill again—or go mad. She could not bear the thought of a second sickness. She obsessed over the thought that perhaps she had made the wrong choice—had the wrong thing removed. She could have had them extract her fear—or her pessimism—or her hopelessness—or a thousand other things than just the cancer—only the cancer, not the cause.

And the paranoia turned to anger and the anger rage. Her words were short, her eye contact slim. She was pervasively disappointed in Conrad, and why wouldn't she be? She was disappointed in herself. The company thought they had removed his mother's sickness, but they had in fact removed his mother completely.

Conrad knew he must leave the house. In the middle of the night, he shoved his meager belongings into a pillowcase and began to work his way through the streets of town. And then, just as he was crossing Mobrigger Bridge, he saw it: the top of XtraX tower. The highlife being lived by those who did this to his family. Those who did this—this awful thing to their town—to their community. That night, Conrad raged against the establishment, shouting platitudes into the night nothingness. Screaming so hard in the cold mist that he eventually coughed up blood.

Within an hour, he knew that it was not his mother that he hated, for his mother had at one time been the only one to show him love. No. He hated those who had changed her. Those who had taken her one thing away.

That night, he forged a plan.

—You would hold us accountable for attempting to do good?

—Who said anything about good? Your motive was profit. Always profit.

—Our bottom line—yes, but our motive was to extricate wrong.

—There it is, right there.

—Oh? Enlighten me.

—You can't extricate wrong. You can't rub it out with an eraser or wish it out or yank it out with a chain. Wrong must be kneaded out. Slowly, persistently, intentionally, painfully. It's got to be worked out like a muscle wedged between vertebrae.

—And how do you propose we do that?

—*You* don't do it. Only I can do it for myself. But that's not what you're really after.

—And what am I after?

—Who knows? Power—security—vindication to correct something someone labeled you when you were young? Maybe you're just trying to convince yourself you've won. But whatever it is that you are at war against mankind over, it's a phantom—and you are making things worse for others *and* yourself by your continual unconscionable actions within this company.

—You are angry, Dr. Rathbone stated.

—I've been angry for a very long time.

—We can have that removed.

—Oh, you're funny.

—You think you're our first dissatisfied customer? Get over yourself, Mr. Reed. We have done mountains of good for humanity.

Mountains. You do not have a full grasp on the importance of what we do here. It would be a shame for you to waste your efforts, not to mention your career, on attempting to bring us down. You would have very little impact, I assure you.

They stared, eye-to-eye. Dr. Rathbone took the smallest sip of the cooling espresso, and then Conrad finally played his hand—allowing himself the smallest wrinkle of a smile.—I don't know. I think perhaps my impact will be significant.

—What could you possibly mean?

—You'll know soon enough. If Dijon is thorough enough with his search of my bedroom, he'll find the blueprints to this building taped underneath my T-shirt drawer.

Espresso went up her nose. She coughed a hot, sputtering cough.—That's—that's absurd, Dr. Rathbone said.

—It's all right. I've expected it. Planned for it, actually.

—Planned for what?

—You've removed enough, Dr. Rathbone. Please don't add my dignity to the list. You called me into your office to keep me busy the exact same hour that my mother has her monthly health review by your doctors. You know my home is empty—and your gestures to Dijon gave him the go-ahead to scope out my room—to uncover my plans.

—Why on earth would I imagine you have plans?

—Because it is what I have wanted you to imagine. It is why I have encrypted emails and buried strange blueprints deep in my hard drive. I know I'm being observed. I know how to make you paranoid. But, I assure you. Everything you have found has nothing to do with what I really want.

It was Dr. Rathbone's turn to smile.—Nicely played, Mr. Reed.

—Thank you, Ariel.

—But, if it all means nothing—if it is all a manipulative ruse—then why would you need the stolen keycard in your right pocket?

—In my—you don't know what you're talking about.

—You think all we are capable of is a backdoor into your hard drive—of searching your bedroom? We have intercepted several off-site calls, garbled though they were, where you clearly expressed interest in obtaining a high-level security keycard.

—That's why you brought me up here.

—I don't know what you have planned, but I know that you have a very skewed perception of what this company has done for you. So, here is what is going to happen. You are going to hand me the keycard and I am going to have security escort you out of the building forever. No need for us to press charges. You'll just be on your way.

—And where would I keep this keycard?

—As I stated: your right pocket.

—You mean this?

He pulled out what was clearly a metal flask of some sort. His ring finger had tapped against it repeatedly, scratching the side.

—Empty your pockets.

He did. Nothing but the flask, save some coins and a mint for later.

—That's it? That's what this is all about? You're drinking on the job? You're merely depressed?

—Oh, I would never drink what is in this flask.

—Why?

—Because it's only for you.

She stared. He continued.

—If I were to drink this, I wouldn't be able to move my legs, then my arms, all the way up my body until I couldn't even yell for help anymore.

Dr. Rathbone squinted in bewilderment. Understanding did not become clear until she glanced down at the espresso that Conrad had prepared. She attempted to stand—and could not.—What have you done to me?!

—Surprise.

Her arms were immovable now. Panic set in.—You—what have you—what have you—

—Relax. You'll be able to move again come sunrise.

—But, the security card—

Her voice began to trail off, her vocal chords numb.

—Yes. Thank you for reminding me.

Conrad slipped around the desk and carefully removed Dr. Ariel Rathbone's security keycard from the zipline on her belt.—My apologies, but I didn't expect you would see things my way. You see, you're one of only three people alive who have the kind of clearance I need. And before you panic, I'm not going to rob you. I'm just going to walk out of this building and fetch my friends. Then, tonight, we're going to come back and use this card to get into the third sub-basement while you sit immovable in your office closet.

Her eyes were fried eggs.

—I know. I had to hack the system for ten years before I finally learned about the third sub-basement. But, it makes sense. I was just trying to bring XtraX down—find some sort of incriminating evidence that what you are doing wounds people deeply. I just kept obsessing about my mother and how you robbed her of a true healing. You jerked her problem away, and she came up on the other side wanting, lacking. She's never been the same—because though she wanted the thing gone, she didn't realize how much she needed to push it out herself. I would weep—I'm telling you, *weep*. And then, it dawned on me: if there is a gaping hole left in my mother, then what used to be there must have *gone somewhere*. I mean, these XtraXions. They can't possibly just evaporate. These cancers, these infirmities and addictions and thorns and sins—they must be *stored* somewhere. That became my new mission. And I've found them. In the third sub-basement. I gathered the support. I made a plan. All I needed was a key. And that meant I needed to get close to you. And that meant I needed you to invite me to your office. So, I resigned. The irony is that it took leaving this job to accomplish what I took the job for in the first place.

Dr. Rathbone no longer had the ability to speak. A tear ran down her cheek as Conrad quietly wheeled her into the closet atop her office chair.

—Like I said: sunrise, you'll be fine. Until then, the hallucinogens in this concoction should grant you some thought-provoking dreams— a real deep dig into your psyche. Same with Dijon. My friends were waiting for him. Don't worry. I know you've had your grief removed. I would hate for you to suffer all of that again—even though losing it this way made you half a person. But, I'll make certain it is destroyed.

Conrad gripped the closet doorknob as he gave her one last linger.—As for the rest of it—a decade-and-a-half of sins never truly dealt with? Simply shoved in the basement while leaving gaping holes across town? This company is going to have a lot of explaining to do for never killing all of its extracted transgressions. Especially tonight—

—when I let them all loose into the wild.

SKULLDUGGERY

—*aftermath.*

    —Son, I can't help you right this moment.

    —But I dunno what *aftermath* is. I dunno what it means.

    —I'm on an important call.

    —Does it have anything to do with gym?

    —Why would it have anything to do with gym?

    —On Tuesdays and Thursdays, gym is after math.

Earl Senior gave his son the look.

He knew that every time he did, his son died a little bit inside. It wasn't his intention to hurt Earl Junior—it was rather a necessary by-product of getting the child to respect the privacy of business. It wasn't his fault that Junior had waited until tonight to complete his definitions list any more than it was Junior's fault that he had a business call. Nevertheless, Junior was going to need to wait to discover the definition of the word *aftermath*.

His own father had referred to this process as the chisel. Sculpting, scraping away excess character flaws with discipline until all that remains is the man underneath who has not been able to inhale beneath all that plaster.

The moment Junior disappeared down the hallway, he felt a pang of regret. He was, after all, on hold. He had been on hold for a very long time and had no earthly idea when he would be asked to rejoin this call. But it would be tremendously embarrassing if his publisher beeped back in while he was in midexplanation defining *spelunking* or *cornucopia*.

All was quiet. Earl Senior loved the endorphins that flooded his body during a successful negotiation, but they were too often replaced quickly with parenting guilt pangs. Tonight, it seemed the two would comingle. Perhaps just one definition.

—Junior?

He called Earl Junior "Junior," much to Earl Junior's chagrin. It was the same reason family called him "Senior." He had named his son after himself so the name would live on and ironically it prevented either from being able to actually go by the name. Two Earls equals no Earls at all.

Well, not everyone called Earl "Senior." At the office, they called him Sir, as they should because he was a man of means, a man of business. An owner. A success. The esteem had been the one thing he had truly been after—and lookee here.

—Now? Can you help me now? Can you?

—Just one. Maybe a few.

—I have to do the whole rest of the page.

—"The remainder of the page." Not "the whole rest of the page."

—What are you talking about? Junior squinted, bewildered.

—You're going to lose your window with me, Senior said with mounting frustration—if you don't get a move on.

Junior rifled through pages.—When you get back on the phone, can I play with the Chinese box?

—It's Japanese. And you know the answer to that question.

—But, I won't look in it! I'll just peek, maybe.

Junior never failed to ask to see what was in the Japanese box. The item was precious to Senior, untouchable. He had made that clear to Junior as far back as he could remember. What he could not remember was why the item inside the box was so precious. But, the boy's insatiable curiosity reminded him of himself. It always came as a surprise, the realization of how utterly similar he and his son were. Such complex emotions. Pride that someone exists who takes after you in the smallest nuances—and yet that slight revulsion, knowing what bad tendencies will grow out of those nuances. How do you love the best of a son without loathing the worst parts of yourself you see brewing within him?

—*pragmatist.*

—That's a very good word. An interesting word.

—Okay. What does it mean?

—You know I can't do all the work for you.

—Gimme a hint.

—It's what I am. A *pragmatist* is what I am. Tell me what you think that means.

Junior squirmed a bit in his own skin. He clearly did not want to answer.—A—a father?

—No. It describes me. It is a word that describes me.

—Does it mean that you're really serious?

—No. Well—yes, a little. But, there's more.

—I dunno. Can you gimme another hint?

—Okay. It's something your mother was not.

—Oh. Does it mean angry?

He was beeped back into the call. He waved Junior away.—Yes—well, when will Mr. Hardaway be back on the call? I would consider this a pressing matter as well.

Junior stood beneath the doorjamb and cocked his head, studying his old man. He had never noticed Junior observing him before. He wondered if his appearance changed, if his demeanor thickened like a Halloween mask without the rubber band. Senior knew Junior couldn't hear the exact words of Mr. Hardaway's assistant on the other end of his father's phone, and yet he stood there, unnerving him for a solid two minutes until he placed his palm over the phone receiver.

—This might take a while, son. Maybe you should go down the hall.

—I can wait.

—It wasn't a suggestion.

—Oh. But you said maybe.

—Go down the hall now.

—That's not a maybe.

—Now.

—Could I take the box? Just one peek?

—Go.

Junior slipped away, expelling an exasperated breath loud enough for Senior to roll his eyes at. He pulled his hand away from the phone and attempted to reengage Mr. Hardaway's assistant—only to find he was on hold once again.

He stared at the phone.

This is what he had a tendency to do when perplexed. Stare at the thing. Force it with his gaze to boil or be answered or grow up. Never worked. But, the staring gave him a moment to think. He felt a strong skip in his heartbeat. It ached. Odd. Was that a tremor? Last physical, his heart was in tip-top shape. Tip-top. That was what his doctor had said and Senior remembered because the phrase felt like pandering. Certainly he was only stressed. He pressed the speakerphone option and laid the receiver on the cradle. He drummed his fingers rhythmically on his mouse pad as the small speaker played a tune he had never heard.

He needed this deal to go through. Mr. Hardaway owned several institutions around town, most notably a book publisher. Earl Senior had spent a great many of his days away from his family securing their future and he wanted his story told his own way. Mr. Hardaway, however, preferred someone else to chronicle his exploits.

But Earl Senior trusted next to no one, so he was going to be difficult to convince. It certainly didn't help that whenever he became belligerent, Mr. Hardaway would put him on hold. He was not used to this sort of treatment, especially from someone who had not accomplished as much.

—I still don't know what a *pragmatist* is.

He had forgotten about the definitions list. Junior had appeared in the doorway again. But, goodness—had he aged? He seemed somehow older. Appeared older. Even spoke as such.—Why do you wait until right before something is due?

—You're never able to help me until right before.

—Stop sassing.

—I'm not sassing. I'm being honest.

—You're being belligerent.

—Hey! Thanks. That word's on the list.

—A *pragmatist* is someone who is very practical.

—Okay. And that's what you are?

—I only make decisions that fall in line with logic.

—*delusional.*

—*You will not talk to me that way!* He felt the rage boil inside of him. The rage he hated—yet it was there. That sort of disrespect always pushed his precarious emotions to the hilt. He hardly realized it as he raised his right hand in a manner as if to strike the boy. The boy tensed up and threw a sentence in between them as a shield.

—The next word!

He caught himself as his son spoke, stopping his arm midmotion, still seething.

—*delusional* is the next word! The next word on the list. I wasn't sassing, his voice choked.—*delusional* is the next word on the list.

He stared wide-eyed and teeth-clenched, uncertain how to best save face as Mr. Hardaway's assistant piped back in on the call. He scrambled for the receiver as Junior skittered out of sight. He took a moment before responding, but he barely listened to the next exchange. All he could consider was the terribleness. The terribleness he had just felt so strongly. It was this sort of silent outburst that he could not risk an outside writer chronicling. He must tell his own story on his own terms. Otherwise, it would all be for naught.

Earl Senior had spent his life fortifying the future. He was one of two original founders of a pharmaceutical company known in the early days as Extraction Specialists, Ltd. It went by a modern, more marketing-friendly moniker now that Earl Senior hated. The company exploded into a phenomenon and carried the good and bad that accompany such territory. He knew his exploits would go down in history if told right—and infamy if told askew. He was desperate to write his own life, desperate for his legacy to be one of healing and wholeness as opposed to the garbage that his opposition continually threw his way.

He fingered the top of the Japanese box. Why couldn't he remember? Was it reward for a business dealing? No. That didn't feel right. It was something more bittersweet than that.

The voice on the other end of the phone blathered on about it being extremely irregular for a public figure to write his autobiography unedited. The whole idea of an autobiography was that the first-person account brought a deeper truth to the proceedings—but truth unchecked is merely opinion. A good three minutes passed before Earl Senior realized he had been nodding instead of speaking and that the voice on the other end of the phone could not surmise his take on the matter. Misunderstanding his silence as absence, she put him on hold once again.

Earl Senior swore. Why was this particular evening so stressful? He could not put his finger on it except to consider that there was an anger inside him aimed both at his son and himself. He did not know where it came from. He found himself calling out, not in anger, but roving as a hook in a carnival game.

—*delusional* is a state of being.

Junior peeked around the corner, waiting closer than Senior expected.—Of what?

—It means you are deceived. What you think is real is not real. What you think is true is actually false.

—So, it's another name for a sucker.

—Basically.

—I would never call you that. It was only the next word on the list.

—I know. I know that now. What's the word after *delusional*?

—Um—*palpable*.

—*Palpable*. What do you think *palpable* means?

—I don't know. Able to palp?

—No. Funny that word is after *delusional*.

—Only on my list.

—In a way, it's the other extreme.

—The other extreme of what?

—Of *delusional*.

—So, it means that what you think is real is actually real?

—More than that. It means that there is proof handy. *Palpable* means you can touch it or see it or hear it and that is how you know it is real or true.

—So, you can't have both?

—Both what?

—You can't have *palpable* and *delusional* at the same time? They're opposites?

—Well—no. Not quite opposites. I suppose there could be proof of something very near and yet someone could be *delusional* about that truth at the same time.

—You mean like, somebody could hold a bird and look at it and yell, You're not a bird!

—An extreme, but yes.

—Sweet. I'm gonna try that.

—No, you're not. You'll catch a disease if you hold a bird.

—Unless it's not a bird.

—How many words are left on the page?

—Three. Why is your phone playing music?

—It's a speakerphone. I'm on hold. When you're on hold, the phone plays music.

—Why is it bad music?

—Because it wants us to know what hell will feel like.

—This is what hell will feel like?

—I'm joking.

—I thought jokes were funny.

—Stop sassing.

He saw it. It was subtle, but he saw the boy wince, as if the mention of the word "sassing" always preceded a blow to the head at the hand of his father.—I'm not going to hit you.

—I'm sorry. The fear was in Junior's eyes now.

—Why would you do that? Why would you inch back? You act like I would hit you.

—I'm sorry.

—Why would I hit you?!

—I'm—

—Stop apologizing. It's weak. My son is not weak.

—I'm not—weak.

—You do these things in public. The rearing back as if I will strike. The weakness. People see these things, you know. They see them and they define for themselves what these things mean and then they write about it in the press. It's the reason we struggle for good publicity. It's the reason I must write this book.

—I am the reason?

—Not you exactly—but the things you do in front of the cameras, yes.

Junior stood with his mouth slightly open, as if the orifice had been emptied of words and was grasping for a consonant to latch onto.

—Oh, don't look at me like that. I have to be able to tell you the hard truths. I'm your father. It's my job.

But Junior had turned the corner. He wanted to round on him with a fatherly chastisement, but bit his tongue instead. He had never talked back to his own father like that, even though his father had given him plenty of reason. His father was all business all the time, giving very little regard to the young nuisance of his son. It was what launched Senior into this business world. He longed to prove his father wrong—that he could not only survive but also thrive in this cutthroat world. His father had never actually said that he would amount to nothing, but their interactions always had that flavor about them, of disappointment and condescension. His father died when Extraction Specialists, Ltd. was rather small. It was his deepest regret; he had wanted to give his father palpable truth that Senior was worthy. But his father had only ever seen him as delusional.

The assistant was back on the phone.

—When will I be able to actually speak with Mr. Hardaway?

The voice explained that Mr. Hardaway was currently involved in a significant crisis of the utmost importance, and that the assistant had been authorized to negotiate this particular circumstance, seeing that it was a less-than-significant matter.

This sent Earl Senior over the edge. A less-than-significant matter?! She couldn't be serious. This was his life. His entire life on the line.

She continued to explain that though his life was obviously of great significance, he would be wise to not think the same of his book. She then promptly put him back on hold.

Earl felt a pain creep into his temple. Like a bubble working its way across his brain, throbbing until it popped, which would mean both relief and something deeply unpleasant.

He stared.

He picked up the Japanese box gingerly and studied the foreign lettering and artwork. It was very pretty. Not so much beautiful—but pretty. Like a flower that doesn't match the room it is in. Curious, he shook the box and felt something light inside, it sounded of marble. It didn't stir a recollection.

—Can we do another word? I'm getting tired.

Junior appeared in the doorway again. This time, he was certain of it: he was taller. His voice had changed to that of a young man. How was this possible? Senior considered how quickly it all passed, how much of Junior's life he was missing waiting on this one phone call. And he only now noticed how much he and Junior were the spitting image of one another.

—Go ahead, son.

—*remission.*

—You know that word.

—Why would I know that word?

—Because your mother died of cancer.

—*remission* is cancer?

—*remission* is when the cancer goes away.

—That happens?

—Sometimes.

—But, not with Mom.

—No.

—Oh. I don't think I want to think about that.

—Then don't.

—But, I have to write it down.

—You could write down another definition of *remission.*

—It has more than one definition?

—Most words do, Senior offered.

—Here it is.

—Where?

—In this dictionary.

—You have a dictionary on your cell phone?

—Everybody does.

—Then why do you keep asking me what these words mean?

—Because I have to learn them. I don't remember anything when I just read it. But, you explain the word in ways I'll remember.

—Like how?

—Like when you got mad at me for saying *delusional.* I'll remember that.

—Oh.

—Or when you said *remission* is what didn't happen to Mom because she died.

Too much silence. Too much muzak.—Forgiveness.

—Huh?

—That's what *remission* means.

—Thanks, Dad.

He didn't intend to be terse, but it had been a lousy day. He knew that much. The details were a bit foggy, which was odd because Senior always took his gingko biloba and therefore remembered everything. There had been a phone call. One of his many enemies. And an angry exchange. No, a threat of some sort.

Wait a second.

More than a threat. There had been blackmail. Yes, blackmail.

It had been very upsetting.

Why was he just now remembering this?

There had been a phone call and a terribly unpleasant photograph and the discussion of a sum of money that Earl Senior would deliver in a cardboard box somewhere across town at 3:17.

Or else the photograph would be shown to his publisher.

What time was it? It was evening. Where had the day gone?

This must be why Mr. Hardaway would not take his call. Why he was eternally on hold. He had missed the exchange and now the photograph had been given to Mr. Hardaway. But that made no sense. Without the photograph, the blackmailer would have no leverage.

A surge of electricity poured through his chest.

His sight went black, his eye sockets hot. What was going on?

As the pain ebbed then subsided, he caught a mammoth breath and his thinking began to become clear once again.

Wait. He sent a man.

Yes, he remembered, he sent a man. A detective he trusted, though you couldn't call him trustworthy. He sent a detective to the drop in order to get photos of the blackmailer, beat him at his own game.

He began to calm down.

But, that would have been hours ago. Shouldn't he have heard news of some sort?

And where had the day gone?

An automatic attendant voice piped in on the on-hold line, its directness startling Earl Senior out of his stupor. He was remembering things. That was good. The day was less of a blur now—though he was curious to know what was in that Japanese box. Still, something kept him from opening it. Some clear-minded foreboding that he chose to heed.

—Is your phone call over yet? I'm getting tired of walking back and forth to my room.

—I'm sorry my role as provider is requiring that you walk a few yards.

—I'm just saying.

—Can we get through this list please?

—*albatross.*

—What?

—*albatross.* The next word is *albatross.*

—Like the bird?

—I don't think so.

—No, son. An *albatross* is a bird.

—But it must be something else, too. A bird isn't the sort of thing the words on this list are supposed to be.

—I don't think so.

—You said words usually have several meanings.

—Words, yes. Not birds.

—Unless this is that bird that is not a bird.

—Which would make you delusional, remember?

—Oh yeah. Junior laughed a little and Senior liked it.

—Funny.

—What?

—The albatross sandwich.

—That sounds disgusting.

—It's a riddle, Senior mused.—There are two men on a deserted island. They've been there for a long time because they were sailors and they shipwrecked. All of the other crewmates died. One of the men was blinded in the accident and the man who could see nursed the blind man back to health by feeding him albatross. Eventually they were rescued and years later—many years later—the blind man walks into a pub and orders an albatross sandwich.

—Why?

—I don't know. To remember their survival. The blind man takes one bite of the albatross sandwich, leaves the pub, and then kills himself.

Junior gasped audibly.—This is a guy you know?

—No, no, son. It's a riddle. Don't you see?

—Don't I see what?

—I've already given you more clues than I'm supposed to. Why did the man kill himself?

—I don't know. Because albatross tastes disgusting?

—No. You're kidding around and I'm trying to teach you a lesson here, son.

—I thought it was a riddle.

—If you're not going to really listen when I'm attempting to give you instruction—this is why you are failing at so much.

—Failing? At so much? Where did that come from?

—You stand here, hovering, desperate for my help and then when I freely give it, your mind wanders. It's no wonder you screw up.

—I'm sorry. Geez. I'm sorry.

—Don't apologize. It's weak.

—I'm sorry. For apologizing. Sorry for apologizing.

—Don't—I'm not—forget it. Maybe we should take a breather before I say something I don't want to say.

Junior gave him that same open-mouthed stare.—Something you don't want to say?

—Yes.

—So, everything else you've said. You wanted to say all of that.

The pain resumed in Senior's temple. He picked up the receiver of the phone as if some phantom progress was suddenly being made on the call. He averted his eyes from Junior as he did when he wanted Junior to slip silently away. But Junior stood his ground, typing feverishly into his cell phone. After a moment, he recited to his father.

—*A seemingly inescapable moral or emotional burden, as of guilt or responsibility. Something burdensome that impedes action or progress.*

Senior wasn't quite following Junior's point.—What is that supposed to mean?

Junior revealed the proof on the screen of his phone.—That's an *albatross*. I guess it does have two meanings.

Junior slipped down the hallway again, chin up and defiant.

Senior threw a stone paperweight across the room, shattering a side of the aquarium. Water and stench and a few living things flooded onto the hardwood floor, but Earl Senior didn't care. He was up to here with this child and his—what was the word?—sassing. If the boy was going to be ungrateful, then he would feel the sting of retribution. He rolled up his sleeve past his right elbow and pushed his roller chair away with the back of his thighs. He was just about to move down the hallway when the muzak came to an abrupt halt.

She said Mr. Hardaway would speak with him in two minutes.

He stopped and reconsidered his temper long enough to mutter a thank you. He prided himself on his ability to regain perspective quickly. He took several deep breaths and worked his way back to his chair, his foot squishing on the sopping wet area rug near the door. He folded his hands on the desk, weaving his fingers together like a wicker basket. He took several more breaths, pausing for a moment to press his index finger against the pain in his temple. He calmed himself.

—Junior.

Nothing. Not even footsteps.

—Son.

—I'm sorry, Dad.

—I understand.

—I'm so sorry. I'm—

—Stop—just sit down and let's finish the list.

—I don't want you to do any more of the list.

—Only one word remaining.

—Yes.

—Then, let's get to it and just be done.

It didn't seem to motivate Junior the way Senior had hoped, but he unwrapped the tattered page he had been clenching in his hand for the last hour. Senior watched Junior's eyes scanning the page up and down, up and down, the way Senior did when he double-checked and triple-checked his work. Well. Perhaps there were more similarities yet to discover. Finally, Junior spoke.

—*subterfuge*. Is that one of those boats that can go all the way underwater?

—No. What do you think it is?

—I think it's one of those boats that can go all the way underwater.

—What else do you think it is?

—It sounds like a spy word.

—You're on the right track. It's a deception.

—Then why don't they just call it a deception?

—Because it's more specific. It's a deception to escape a consequence. Like *skullduggery*.

—Like what?

—*skullduggery*, Senior repeated.

—That's not a word. You're making that up.

—I'm not. It means a single deception.

—I don't like that word.

—Why not?

—It sounds deadly.

—But you like *subterfuge* because it sounds like one of those boats—

—That can go all the way underwater, yeah. So, I'll just say *subterfuge*.

—Well, they're not the exact same thing.

—You said—

—I said *subterfuge* is deception. But, it's actually many deceptions over time. *Skullduggery* is only one.

—Just one trick?

—Sometimes, it only takes one.

—And that makes it more deadly?

—Well, what do you think? Would you rather be deceived slowly over time in many, many ways—or would you rather put in a life of hard work only to have one act of *skullduggery* trip up your existence?

—I would rather not have either.

—You'd be the first.

His eyes roved the page. He crossed out the word slowly, sadly. He looked up at his father—or rather, toward his father. His eyes met the phone receiver before they met Senior face-to-face.—I guess that's it then.

—You best go to bed.

—I will.

He paused, pensive, his eyes glazed and stuck toward the floor. After a beat, he arose from the chair, crumpling the paper in hand as if he had never heard of folding.—To bed.

He gave a half-smile and rolled around the doorjamb. Senior could see his shoulder lingering, resisting the march toward slumber. Senior knew the moment. He was reasoning something through.—It didn't taste the same.

—What didn't taste the same, son?

—The albatross on the island and the albatross sandwich. They tasted different from each other.

—That's right.

—And the man was blind.

—Keep going.

—Which means on the island, his friend wasn't feeding him albatross at all. He was feeding him his dead friends. The blind man figured that out and couldn't live with himself.

—Exactly.

—That's *skullduggery*, isn't it?

—I believe it is.

—One bad moment messed him up for good.

Senior leaned back in his chair, self-satisfied. His son indeed had his father's brain after all. Junior was lost in his thoughts, troubled. He asked one last question.—Who would do such a thing?

—Well, it's an ethical conundrum, son. His friend didn't know how long they would need to make the food last, so he ate albatross while the other man ate—well—something other than albatross.

—Not that. Who would do such a horrible thing?

—What horrible thing?

—Who would kill himself?

Fire. An explosion in his torso. As Junior rounded the corner to head to his bedroom, he thought his heart would enlarge and burst from his rib cage. A tumultuous firework of a surge had awoken pain he had never experienced. He groaned, clutching at his sternum, gripping the edge of the desk as if to snap a chunk off. A cold, cold sweat emanated from his hairline and he found himself unable to cry for help. Just as he began to regain his voice, the pain swept away again like an undertow, gone as quickly as it had become unbearable.

He rested his forehead against the cool leather ink blotter in the center of his desk as a soft but commanding voice interrupted the muzak cacophony.

—Mr. Eeley?

Earl abruptly lifted his head an inch off the desk and swallowed the blood left over from where he bit his tongue during the surge in question.—Yes. Mr. Hardaway?

—My assistant says you have an urgent need.

—Yes. I know you have very strong opinions on this matter, but I must vehemently insist that I—and only I—pen my autobiography.

There was a lengthy silence. Had there not been an absence of muzak, Earl Senior would have assumed he had been put back on hold.

—Hello?

—Is that your urgent need, Earl? Is it really?

—You don't understand. This book must make a significant impression—

—An impression? Really?

—I am the only one I can trust with truth.

—I didn't realize you were attempting to achieve the truth.

—What else would this book attempt to achieve?

—*Skullduggery.*

Senior sat with his mouth slightly open, as if the orifice had been emptied of words and was grasping for a consonant to latch onto.—I beg your pardon.

—Forget the book, Earl.

—Excuse me? Do what?

—Forget the book and open the Japanese box.

—How—how could you possibly know about my Japanese box?

—Open it. It's for your own good.

—So, you're going to take the kid's side. Open the box? All will become clear if I just open the Japanese box? This day—this peculiar, maddening, forgotten day will all spill out of the Japanese box? I'm supposed to take your word for that? That if I do the thing that I fear most, it will be for his own good?

—It's for *your* own good. I never said his. I said yours. There is no his.

Senior sat. Stunned.—What did you just say?

—You heard what I said. Now, I must be off to other matters. Pressing matters. Farewell.

And the other end of the line went dead. Mr. Hardaway had hung up the phone. What on earth was that supposed to mean? There is no his? That's all Earl Senior needed: for his publisher to fancy himself some ethereal potentate of life skills. He eyed the Japanese box.

Wonderful.

Just get it over with.

He opened the lid carefully and reached into its darkness. A tender strand met his thumb and forefinger and he lifted out a precious jade necklace, ornate and tasteful. He held it and gazed.

It was familiar.

It was the shape of a tear.

A tear. Sadness. Heaviness. When his wife died?

No. That didn't make sense. He pictured this teardrop on his wife, pressed against the soft spot above her chest. It had been hers. Yes. She wore this necklace. He was beginning to remember as he rolled it around in his hand. It was hers. It was a gift. A gift from him. He had chosen the teardrop specifically to remember something.

In remembrance of something.

He turned the teardrop over and felt the inscription on the back. Only a few words and numbers. A date of birth. A date of death. And the name Earl Eeley, Jr.

He began to shake. His son. His only son.

His son had died before he had even turned a month old.

There were no more children after that. The battle had been too painful. There was no Junior.

So, why did all of this feel so familiar? Earl could recall with great emotional accuracy the fights, the disappointment and disapproval, the distance and the sting of the father's hand. The father's.

His father's.

It was Earl Senior's own father who had treated him this way. Treated him harshly and with great pain. He had hated his father for all he had put him through. It played a significant part in the decision to not father another child after Earl Junior's passing. It was the influence that had caused Earl to become so cold and calculated. So distant.

But, if there was no Earl Junior—and if Earl Senior was playing the role of his own father—then where exactly was he?

The memories began to flood.

The blackmail. The photograph. The phone call. The money. The pills.

Earl Senior had taken the entire bottle of pills early this afternoon quite intentionally.

—Dad?

The voice of his son startled him from the doorway. Or was it his own voice? Senior looked up to see that Junior was fully grown. A man. Junior was Senior. Junior was himself. It took Earl Senior several moments to gather the epiphanies of the past two minutes into a single syllable response.

—Yes?

—You never did the first one.

—The first what?

—The first word. You never defined the first word on the list. What does *aftermath* mean?

Earl Senior gazed into the hopeful, wounded eyes of himself and suddenly understood more about himself, his father, his son, his world than ever before.

—It means—what comes next.

Fire. An explosion in his torso. Earl Senior thought his heart would enlarge and burst from his rib cage as he filled his lungs with an enormous gasp of air, his eyes focusing and settling on the EMT who was inside the ambulance with him, removing the paddles from his chest.

99 PAGES
(SOMEWHERE NEAR THE MIDDLE)

The ding of the opening elevator doors startled Liliana. Her mind had wandered, but not too far to fetch. She inhaled deeply as a lesser girl might on her first morning at a new job. She stepped out and into the hallway, knowing that somehow today would be different. Different from what, she could not quite recall, but butterflies filled her stomach. Like nervousness. Or anticipation. Or love.

It was here that her life would begin anew. The sixth story.

It was the sort of morning where one arrives where one was headed so lost in one's thoughts that one doesn't quite recall the specifics of how one traveled there. Liliana Vega was that one. It was 8:27, and she paused just inside the sixth story hallway of the Hardaway Building to take a deep breath and settle herself. In that moment with her eyes closed, she recognized the void inside—the emptiness that she was desperate to fill. Something about this opportunity—this day—tasted of epic grandeur. She was finally here at Shrub & Sons Publishing, filled with equal measure of hope and dread.

The two kindly security guards at the front desk of the first floor had been surprised by her presence, having not heard her enter the building. They were, in turn, courteous (the larger younger one) and curmudgeonly (the shorter one with the limp), scanning a clipboard for her name and turning the key in the elevator so that she could travel to the sixth story.

Her palms began to sweat at the very idea of becoming a publishing neophyte. Never considering herself a writer, she would find joy in the binding and design—in the tactile feel of the pages. To handle those pages while still warm, smell the ink while still wet, seemed to her as close to euphoria as one ought to expect within the permission of a workday. And, Shrub & Sons—well, Shrub & Sons simply felt exact, as if there were a secondary and secret purpose for her being here.

She wandered her way down the newly carpeted hallway toward the faint cacophony of busyness—or, in this case, business. She could feel the electric nausea of nervousness building, that fleeting thought of *will I fit in This Time?* She did not know why she capitalized "This Time" in her thinking, but it felt necessary.

She walked in on the morning lecture. The pep talk. And the harbinger of the pep was none other than the company's CEO, Miss Shrub.

—You will quickly acclimate, Shrub insisted —to the understanding that I am not the sort who needs support. I will, however, stretch that truth from time to time. Most likely when I discover someone with the editor's gift of taking my words and turning them into action. Not the words I say. The words I mean. The words behind and beneath the words that come out of my mouth. Consider my instructions a Berlin Wall between you and what you actually should be doing. Perfect that and you will go places. Of course, if you fail at that, you will also go places, but they will be less pleasant places.

Miss Shrub gave her own rib cage a hearty thump with her balled fist.

—My gumption embraces your gumption. Earn it. In the meantime, I am entrusting you with my red pens. You will use them to transform the message on the page. You will chop, massage, and massacre these sentences into submission and oblivion. And when you are finished, you will have bound a book that is completely you, whether or not that is what the author had in mind at all. The red ink is permanent. Please take one pen and pass the others around.

As Liliana observed the back of this woman's head and reveled in her ability to motivate so many others to greatness (or rather, to augmenting someone else's greatness), she coughed. It startled Miss Shrub, who did not realize the new hire was standing three feet behind her. She turned her head just slightly enough to catch that muscle in her neck that ruins the whole day and winced—the first expression Liliana would ever see her make. Not that Miss Shrub's face made many pleasant expressions. You don't get to the top of the publishing game by smiling like a gagging goat. And you don't get to the top of the publishing business by calling it a game and insisting it be played by goats who don't chew their food properly. This is wisdom. And it is what makes Frances Shrub both successful and the grandest of buzzkills.

—And you are? Shrub eked out as she turned just enough to glimpse Liliana in her periphery.

—Liliana Vega. The new girl.

—You were just born?

—No. I was just hired.

—Then, don't call yourself new. Call yourself recent. Did you receive one of the red pens passed about?

—Looks like you're out of red pens. All for the best, though. I prefer blue.

The room gasped.

—My, aren't we full of the unexpected, Miss Vega. You're clearly a leader, so why don't you follow me. Miss Shrub led Liliana to her new desk while handling a book as if it were a plate of hors d'oeuvres.—I like a proactive woman, and I can see that you are neither, so let us begin with the basics: while you are in my employ, you will have three secondary duties and one primary. You are to proofread for the purposes of spelling, grammar, and clarity. You are to make red ink changes accordingly. You are to manage my schedule. But, most importantly, you are never to open Archive Box A.

—I—I'm to what?

—Not to what. You are *not* to what. *Never* to what.

—Open Archive Box A?

—Ah, you are a fast learner, Terri.

—My name is Liliana.

—Yes, but you will go by Terri because it is less ethnic. That's life, or as my mother always said, *c'est la vie*, which is French for something.

—I don't even know what Archive Box A is.

—I would think it obvious that it is the box to the left of Archive Box B.

—Oh, am I allowed to open Archive Box B?

—Of course! Why would I forbid something as silly as opening Archive Box B? And why would you ever be so inclined? You are an enigma, Terri: a leader, yet a rebel. Like Thomas Jefferson or Mr. Hardaway. What is this television doing here?

The mention of the name Hardaway punched Liliana in the brain, like a milkshake sipped too quickly or a cat too long in the microwave. A three-syllable tsunami. Yet, Liliana could not exactly place the name. But before Liliana could ask precisely who Mr. Hardaway was, Miss Shrub had become distracted, staring at a television monitor mounted on the wall beside a camera affixed to a tripod. To her, it was clearly a new item in the room.

Liliana, having been thus far transfixed only by the brazen aura of Miss Shrub, looked about the room for the first time to determine exactly whom she expected to answer her. There were only three options. The first: Isaac Portense, had been here the longest—or so Liliana surmised from the rows of "employee-of-the-month" certificates adorning his cubicle. They were stapled to the burlap-covered partition in a fanned manner, like magazines at the dentist before the first patient's toddler ruins the pattern. His eyes darted and fingers drummed. Liliana assumed Isaac the scattered sort who might change his tie twice daily in order to distract from the fact that he had worn the same shirt all week. For someone with a receding hairline, his skin appeared extraordinarily supple. Even milky. Like a laxative. Liliana wanted to reach out and touch it, but did not as she thought it would be a most awkward icebreaker.

The desk adjacent Isaac's had a name placard teetered upon its lip: Miss Quidnose. As far as Liliana could tell, the woman didn't have much need for a first name, what with her fondness for skirts with no curves or pleats. Her dress looked more like the bag you store a nice dress inside. Her cubicle smelled of hand sanitizer and room-temperature corn tortillas. She merged all her words into one lengthy, mumbled whisper as if speaking secrets to a companion living deep in the pocket of her tartan blazer. Her words were not responses as much as asides, as if her mouth resided between parentheses.

These extremes were balanced out by the executive assistant in charge of bulk sales. His name was Bump Rinderhart and, from what Liliana could assess, he merely existed. Separated from Portense and Quidnose by a single vacant desk, he did not instigate conversations as much as he thumbtacked his verbal blurbs onto opinions already being conversed. There was no way for Liliana to know for certain, but she imagined him a desk calendar sort of person: one clever thought per day. He sat—even now as Shrub asked him a question—with phone tucked securely beneath chin as if he were just about to begin a new sales call. He wasn't. It was a way to avoid the conversation that Shrub persisted.

—I repeat: what is this television doing here?

Isaac answered first. It appeared that Isaac regularly answered first.—That television there?

—Of course this television here, Shrub spat.—Do you see any other television here?

—I believe—I mean to say, it is my understanding—though it might be a misunderstanding—that we received a memo.

—A memo?

—Yes Miss Shrub, continued Isaac, it says that it is from the higher-ups. I mean—it *reads* that it is from the higher-ups. The memo did not speak—not saying it couldn't if it were a voice memo—but it is at the moment on paper.

—Well, I am the only higher-up. I am the highest-up. Why was the memo kept from me?

—It wasn't kept from you. No one kept it. It's for you.

—And if it is for me, why do I not have it?

—You were busy with the new girl.

—The recent girl.

—Um, the recent girl, I mean. Her. Not to exclude any other her. You understand—not to assume you do. Here it is. Not her. The memo. On paper.

—Thank you, Isaac. "This is a notice that the delivered monitor and camera are being installed in the sixth story for purposes in conjunction with the announcement." There's a camera?

—Miss Shrub, what is the announcement?

Liliana knew from her research that Miss Shrub was a leader among women. Her bio boasted of being the youngest graduate in the history of Montpelier Beauty Academy to simultaneously acquire the Assistant Manager position at Casa del Pancake. By sheer force of will, she could cut an onion without crying and steer a motorcycle using only her knees. Liliana knew all of this.

What Liliana did not know about Miss Shrub was that Miss Shrub didn't have the foggiest idea what the announcement was—or for that matter, who wrote the memo. Well, that is not exactly true: Miss Shrub had one foggy memory, and the sudden recollection of him persuaded her to take an altogether different approach to handling this predicament.

Downstairs, Wit stared at the two security guards he would need to work his way past. He was told by his companion (Colin, the leader of this particular mission) that the security guards could not see them when they stood on this side of the glass. Considering both guards had guns, Wit thought this a mild consolation at best. He and Colin observed and waited. The moment would come soon—and from what Colin stated, would only last a few seconds.

The larger, younger guard's name was Burke, while the shorter one with the limp went by the moniker of Travis. It was more of a nickname—apropos because nicknames are what security guards go by these days. Travis had lost his real name thirty years ago, but in all that time, had never been required to give a nickname to anyone else. That pattern would end today: Burke's first day on the job.

Travis thought and thought and thought while Burke filled out the paperwork and Travis introduced him to magnetic chess darts.

—Why does this say I will be working for Hardaway Corporation? Burke said, puzzled.—I thought I was going to be working for Shrub & Sons Publishing.

—Shrub & Sons is only the sixth story and it's a division of Hardaway, Travis said.—It's why you have to pay attention and memorize the pages.

—It's all very confusing. Is it supposed to be confusing?

—Chess darts or the paperwork?

—Yes.

Their desks were separated by the room. One on either side of the walkway that led to the elevators. It was a divide-and-conquer sort of intimidation that didn't require either of them to be in decent shape in order to stop intruders. Travis held his magnetic chess piece (white rook) aloft, considering the best of three moves. The chess board itself sat atop a rolling table, which became just another way the two men could interact without having to rise from the chairs in which they were seated.

With a minor epiphany, Travis overtook the black bishop and palmed it in his hand. He then hurled the game piece across the room toward Burke, where it stuck abruptly to a magnetic dartboard. He then shoved the game table with his foot. It glided effortlessly along the linoleum flooring toward Burke as Burke glanced up at the board and announced Travis's score.

—Triple six. That's sixteen more points.

—Three times six is actually eighteen, Burke. And it's your turn.

—So, just like that, she hurls my jujitsu memorabilia collection out the breakfast nook window and kicks me off the duplex property, changes the locks. So I was pretty much forced to get this job.

Travis retorted—My third wife did the same thing.

—Uh huh. I'm talking about my mom, though. And I looooove chess darts. I'd-a applied for this job months ago if I'd-a known about chess darts. I'm having trouble memorizing these. I don't think I'm gonna memorize them.

—Well, they're the rules of the premises. If you're gonna enforce 'em, gotta know what you're enforcing.

—Did you memorize them?

—Oh, years ago.

—And you still remember them?

—When it's necessary.

Then, a squeak. The revolving door leading to the outside of the building moved. Only an inch. But, it moved. It was enough to cause both Travis and Burke to do the unthinkable.

They stood.

—Are we expecting somebody? Burke asked.

—We've never expected somebody before, Travis answered.

In all his days as a gun-carrying employee of Hardaway Corporation, Travis could not remember anyone utilizing this revolving door. Ever. He had not been certain that the door actually revolved, assuming the name Revolving Door was intentionally ironic like a Lazy Susan, which actually works quite hard. He had become accustomed to the door as nothing more than a unique window to the outside world. A sort of proof that it was out there waiting.

It moved again.

—It moved.

—I know it moved. I have eyes.

—What made it move?

—I see the same nothing you see, Burke.

—You think it's the wind?

—The wind's never been all that interested in coming inside.

And both Travis and Burke found themselves instinctually reaching their hands over their gun holsters.

—If there was someone on the other side, Burke said philosophically —wouldn't we be able to see that person through the glass?

—That is a very good point. A very good point indeed.

It was the first time that Travis thought Burke might actually add something to this team. That was sound reasoning. It caused Travis's trigger finger to uncrook and relax. Nonetheless, he and Burke each found themselves inching slowly toward the center of the room between the elevators and this perplexing door.

And then.

The door spun. Faster and faster. A literal whirlwind, ruining the tuft of hair Burke had spent twenty minutes taming with pomade. Neither Travis nor Burke knew what to think of the anomaly, partly because it was absurd and partly because the door had never moved at all. It was one of those moments that came and went so fast, there was hardly time to make sense of it, much less make a decision toward a proactive ensuring of the building's security. Travis had always prided himself on his ability to remain abreast of all circumstances so that nothing took him by surprise.

This was an exception, so much so that Travis was no longer reaching for his gun when Wit and Colin burst through the door, stealing the keys right off of Travis's belt. They disappeared up the fire escape, locking the door behind them.

It was over in ten seconds.

Burke stood there, staring at the keyless belt adorning this man who had been his role model one moment ago.

Travis flushed red.

Wit was breathless, clutching the keyring he had snatched off of Travis's belt. Colin cradled what appeared to be a well-worn book of some sort, the binding peeling off and the pages the brownest sort of yellow. He was calm and collected, having not broken a sweat.

Wit palmed his knees, leaning over in a gasp, keyring looped around his left index finger. On the other side of the door, Burke's newly copied, unlabeled keys were being inserted into the door one-by-one as both security guards fumbled to find the one that would actually grant them entrance.

Colin hugged the archaic book and waited patiently for Wit to catch his breath.

—Don't look at the ground, Wit. Look at me.

—I'm looking. I'm looking.

—Are you prepared to do this again?

—Again?

—Forget it.

Burke's keys chattered furiously against the metal door. Colin took the moment to sit on the stair and gingerly take a tattered napkin out of his shirt pocket. He fondled it gingerly and studied words written on it that Wit was unable to discern.

—Colin? Don't you think we ought to—run or something?

—We've got eleven more keys, Colin mused, before we have to run.

Liliana sat and gazed upon the beauty of the slick rectangular object in front of her. A desk. *Her* desk. Her *first* desk. The adjectives kept coming, and with them, a groundswell of internal gratification. She had made it this far. She opened her purse and retrieved the only office supply she had brought with her: a cube of rainbow Post-its. She had whiled away many sad moments picturing herself seated at her own desk at an actual publishing company—but in the vision, there was always a cube of rainbow Post-its. Green on the top. That was the way she liked it because she had a predilection for green. It seemed the lonely color, with the fewest friends to call it a favorite. She had to search seven stores before she found green on top. See? Lonely. She admired the cube, setting it in the far right corner of the desk as it was in her vision. It was the first piece in her jigsaw puzzle of happiness—of filling that long-felt void. She was so lost in admiration, Shrub's current tirade had not yet begun to register.

—I have been persuaded, Shrub insisted —to take an altogether different approach to this predicament. An unusual sentiment from the usual Miss Shrub; at first her employees did not understand the meaning of the sentence. Quidnose spoke first.

—This, um—what now? Hm?

—Do not mumble, Miss Quidnose. THIS predicament.

—The—the—mm—camera?

—What other predicament has been presented?

—I dunno, Quidnose offered —mm, not sure. The girl?

—The new girl?

—The *recent*—

—Yes, well, how would she know what other predicament has been presented?

—No. I mean—she. That is, mm, the girl—I thought maybe she—you know, SHE was the mm, predicament.

—Of course not. Honestly, Quidnose, I don't know why you try to say things. The camera—the *camera* is the predicament.

—So—um, what …

—What what?

—What is your altogether different approach—to the camera?

—Oh, yes. We shall destroy it.

There was a light back-and-forth of consternation and hubbub, though the two were indistinguishable from one another.

—I don't mm, understand, Quidnose said, puzzled.

—Why would I want that camera to remain?

—Why wouldn't you?

—Well, Miss Quidnose, it does seem that you and I have rather differing opinions on the what and the why of this particular camera. Do shed some light for me.

—Well … Quidnose hesitated for a moment, having never verbalized her actual opinion to Shrub.—Perhaps it is a means to communicate with, you know, the higher-ups. To share what we, um, think. You know: feedback. Mmhm?

—Oh, well thought out, Miss Quidnose. You are a veritable cornucopia of reason. But—say! For what explicit purpose do you imagine that information might be utilized?

—I don't—know what you mean.

—Certainly, you are accurate that the camera and the monitor are for the purpose of gathering our thoughts. But once those thoughts are bundled, what use do you suppose the higher-ups will make of them?

—I wouldn't—I dunno. I—I've never been a higher-up.

—No, Miss Quidnose. You most certainly have not.

Mr. Rinderhart raised his hand.

—You don't have to raise your hand, Bump.

—Sorry.

—Do not apologize.

—I didn't mean to apologize. Forgive me.

—Stop it.

—My bad. I mean for apologizing. Question: if raising my hand is frowned upon—not to say that is bad. But, how—how shall you then know when I would like to speak?

—Because you will *speak*!

—Oh. Sorry.
—Do so now.
—Never mind.

Liliana bristled as Miss Shrub sermonized of the need to pro-
tect one's information—of one's perspective and skills and opinion
and private life. These—what some naive individuals might call
"strengths"—would inevitably be gathered and loaded into a machine
gun by the higher-ups and used against the individual while he or she
wore a blindfold. Bump cowered. Isaac nodded. But Liliana was most
intrigued to observe that Miss Quidnose did not hear a word of it.

Miss Quidnose was in a trance. She was fixated on a young
handyman who had entered the floor via the elevator some time during the camera brouhaha, his rugged hands chalked black with toner.
His fingers roughened from many a healed paper cut wound.

He was Froman.

And he was here to repair the photocopier.

His work was his everything with the exception of the occasional
miniscule glance aimed the direction of one Miss Quidnose. Liliana
watched as Quidnose edged the red pen off of her desk, reason
enough to saunter away from Miss Shrub's diatribe and into the wake
of Froman's teeming testosterone. She followed him into the office
supply closet. Though Liliana knew it was bad form, she could not
help but follow and eavesdrop through the door, which remained
ever-so-slightly ajar.

—Careful, Froman began —it locks from the outside.
—Mm, hello. What brings you, um, to the closet?

—I'm here for the toner. The copier needs toner.

—I understand. I understand needs.

—You have lovely eyes, Miss Quidnose.

—D'you think?

—And I know my perspective is accurate because your grotesquely magnified lenses enlarge your pupils forty-seven percent from this angle. But your lipstick could use a touch-up.

She self-consciously retreated a half-foot to perk up her lips.
—So—is the thing—uh, copier doing its job?

—It tries. But, a machine is nothing without a human to love it.

—Your hands. They've a lot of toner on them. Very masculine. She pronounced the word unusually, as if it rhymed with muscadine.

—It is well soaked into my fingerprints, now. I must be careful not to touch the glass, Miss Quidnose, and yet …

—Mm, yet?

He handed her a piece of sixteen-weight paper.—I must check the toner all the same.

—This is a picture of a hand.

—My hand. And it's not a picture. It's a photocopy. An exact replica, Froman offered.

—Your *hand*. Quidnose mewed.

—I know there's a danger in touching the glass with soiled fingers, but I didn't want to subject my buttock area to the ultraviolet rays. You know that photocopiers are the number one source of buttock cancer.

—I did not know that.

—It was a joke. But, since you didn't laugh, I shall attempt to disguise it as a factoid.

—I was staring at your—at this—your, um, hand.

—The real or the copy?

—What's the difference?

—On the real, the cuts are deeper. I blame the caliper.

—I don't know what that is either.

—I know you don't, Miss Quidnose. And it is charming.

Quidnose peered quickly out the door's lone square window. Liliana ducked silently.—Can I, um, keep this?

—It would be an honor, Froman replied in a rapturous whisper.

—You wouldn't be breaking any tonerman ethics?

—They're meant to be broken.

—Mr. Froman!

They responded quickly. Miss Shrub was shouting for Mr. Froman from the other room. It was an intentional interruption. Liliana scurried into the coffee nook. Quidnose scampered into the elevator vestibule. Froman skittered to Shrub's side.

—Yes, Miss Shrub?

—Might you fetch a box, please? Something large and in the cardboard milieu? I'd like this camera placed into storage.

Froman was quick to retort.—Anything you ask, Miss Shrub. Anything you ask.

And with that, he was gone, on to other floors with other machines and, Liliana imagined, other Miss Quidnoses.

Wit's thighs were aching.

He and Colin swung precariously from separate harnesses within the bowels of the elevator shaft: far above the two security guards pursuing them, but far below their intended audience.

Wit could hardly remember now why this mission was so vital, why he considered Colin at all trustworthy. The recruitment, the details—they were all a blur. Wit knew that the pages in his hand held the balance for those who worked on the sixth story. Especially the girl. So much hinged upon the girl.

Supposedly.

Perfect. Now, his thighs were going numb. Why now? Why is Colin on his cell phone NOW? Wit began to grow impatient. He eyed the manuscript embraced in the crook of his armpit, the one he had been instructed to guard with his life. It seemed an unreasonable demand. He thought to himself: just a peek. Why not just a peek? In the meantime, Colin finished his call.

—Farewell.

And with that, Colin hung up the phone.

—Wit? What do you suppose you're doing?

—Me? Nothing. Aren't your legs numb? My legs are numb. Shouldn't your legs be numb?

—You were looking at the pages.

—I wasn't. Just a glance.

—Which was it? You weren't—or just a glance?

—I don't understand why I can't …

—I didn't bring you here to understand. At least not yet.

—You didn't bring me at all. I followed.

—What is it that you would prefer, Wit? Would you suppose that all would become clear if I would only allow you to read 99 pages somewhere near the middle? Would that make sense of everything? For you to read it alone here in an elevator shaft?

—I wouldn't be alone. I would be with you.

—There is a time and a place for understanding. Patience. Not much longer.

Colin's cell phone rang again. Perhaps it was the echo in the elevator shaft itself or perhaps it was the overall numbness of Wit's extremities, but the ruckus of it startled Wit so heartily that he dropped the manuscript.

Pages separated and flittered and flew every whichaway—down, down, wedging into crevices, disappearing into darkness.

Wit stared at Colin as if he had just been accomplice to a murder.

Colin did not let his gaze break from Wit as he flipped open his phone.

—I'll have to call you back.

Shrub had retreated to her office where the vibration of the windows made it clear to Liliana that Shrub was blaring Tchaikovsky's 1812 Overture. Precisely when the cymbals began to clash (and Bump's pencil holder began vibrating itself off his desk), Liliana noticed a little thing.

—Why is there a blue star on the calendar?

It startled them all. Bump's coffee overturned and began to waterfall down the front of his desk.

—Coffee spill! Oh! So sorry!

—Oh dear. Where's my purse? I always have a few spare, um, napkins.

Isaac, always attuned to the word blue being bandied about, practically leaped to Liliana's side.—What star? What calendar?

—This calendar, Liliana offered —here. Today. A blue star.

—Well, it's certainly not a blue star, Isaac declared.—No one has a blue pen but Shrub. Allegedly.

—What do you mean allegedly? You think there are more blue pens?

—I don't actually believe Shrub has one.

—That's silly. Why wouldn't Shrub have a blue pen? Why shouldn't anyone have a blue pen?

—*Oh, should they*?! Should *anyone* have a blue pen, recent girl? I'm willing to wager nine employee-of-the-month certificates that you have never held nor seen a blue pen yourself.

Liliana laughed, betraying the lack of specific memories currently catching in the cogs of her wheelhouse. She squinted incredulously at Isaac, awaiting the punchline, but her misunderstanding egged his ire. His stare smelled of vinegar and brimstone. She winced in surprise and stumbled for her response.

—Have too.

—Describe it, Isaac persisted.

—What?

—Describe a blue pen.

—You're insane, it's just like a red pen, but there's no red in it. Only blue.

—And what does the blue look like?

—What do you mean?

—I mean for you to search your memory. Not the words free-flowing from your mouth.

—I don't understand.

—I mean, search for the truth—not the words! Every moment, you say things. Just groups of letters you can't really see (Isaac was rambling now, gaining momentum). Where do they come from? My words spill out like pages unjammed from the photocopier and I can't seem to stop them—but if I hold them in, if I swallow them and force them to knock around the sides of my brain, I find that I begin to taste them. And the taste—the taste is—

—Is?

—It's—foreign. I ramble on about my stepmother scrapbooking in the corner of my condominium sucking down her gin fizzes, but I cannot actually picture her or the details. I chatter of blue while I don't know what blue looks like. I say it is the color of the sky but what—what exactly is that other than a thing on the other side of this glass that surrounds us? How can the sky be blue when it changes color all day long and then disappears at night? I think I know how blue feels. Right? But looks? It is foreign. As foreign to me as the name Albert C. Hardaway and yet …

—Something changes inside when you speak his name.

—It does. It legitimately does. Like warm chocolate pudding.

All of their eyes were stuck, pondering. Liliana admired a spider weaving a web and thought it a more pleasing arrangement than the room she was standing in. Bump chimed in.

—But that would make Miss Shrub a liar.

—I would think that obvious, Isaac retorted.

—An absurd thought: Shrub never having handled a blue pen, Liliana said.—How could she come to own a publishing company?

—She can sell books. She can *edit*—for that is the power of the red pen. The RED pen. To command the blue pen means one stops editing and begins writing. Original thoughts. Would we be in this business if we had the ability to write books ourselves? Would she?

—Then where did the books come from?

—Not from her.

—Preposterous. If Shrub had no blue pen, there would be no Shrub & Sons?

—But, there are *no sons*! Isaac ranted.—Do you see any sons?

Bump intervened. —We only ever see her *here* at the office.

—That is because we only exist *here*, Isaac said.

—What? No.

—Think about it, Rinderhart. Describe another place in the world. Any other location but this building.

—That's where you're wrong, Isaac. I could describe a hundred places: the Murrumbidgee River weaving like a snake between the Australian Alps. The Eiffel Tower. A pride of lions roaming Swaziland. The Gaza Strip, Tel Aviv, an aboriginal rainforest, New York City! Mobrigger Bridge—

—You've actually *been* to those places?

—Of course not, but I've read—

Bump gaped. He found himself unable to close his mouth. Happiness began to drain from the folds in his brain that were not already overstuffed with sales minutia. He had not, in fact, actually *been* anywhere. He was stunned he had not realized this. But, Isaac was relentless.

—Bump.

—Yes, Isaac.

—Name this city.

—This city?

—The city that you call home.

—I—I can't.

There was a fire of some sort. An open flame. Wit could smell it as he felt his way along the moist concrete floor of the elevator shaft. Not sulfurous or propane. It was rather the scent of a campfire. Burning wood. Or paper. It was a meager enough glow for Wit to stumble upon the dropped pages. One page, another. He had lost count. Wit could hardly understand why he was involved with this mission, why he felt such a depth of commitment to the mission. That was curious. How could one feel meant to accomplish something so vague? As if the steadfastness itself were pivotal, regardless of the details still to come.

The heat was stronger here, on the north wall. Wit knew what this must mean and felt about tentatively, not wishing to burn his fingerprints off. Here. A crawlspace. Wit wriggled his way through and, within yards, was birthed out a vent into an open hallway. Colin's call was echoed, as if within a seashell.

—You alive down there?

—So far, Wit answered.—I'm on another floor. I think the third story.

—Quiet.

Quiet? What was that supposed to mean? Wit wanted to ask, but realized it the sort of impertinence that would deliver Colin's glance. That glance. It was like a scolding. And then, on the other hand, Wit found himself consumed with gratitude for the man. So bizarre. This building must be rife with black mold, because something about it seriously infected the mind.

Wit saw the source of the heat. An old oil drum, flames licking almost to the ceiling, sparks flittering about like kamikaze gnats. Something inside Wit wanted to put out the fire, but he couldn't manage any emotion further than the desire to gaze into it, approaching it slowly with the pages outstretched. He managed a half-turn before the hand on his shoulder startled him outside of himself. It was Colin.

—So, you have the pages?

—You're very stealthy.

—The pages.

—I have all I could gather.

—All you could gather?

That glance.

—Wit, do I need to be explicit?

—Please don't.

—About the importance of this manuscript?

—You haven't been explicit about anything, insisted Wit.—You haven't even leaned toward the upside of vague.

—I don't say explicit to mean detailed. I say explicit to mean crucial. This isn't some casual gathering.

—I get it.

—This isn't something you muster. These pages are important. Each page equally important. One page even more so.

—What?

—Hm?

—Never mind, Wit exasperatedly replied.—Here. Here are your life-altering pages.

—I didn't say they were life-altering. It is not the lives that will be altered. It is the *perception* of said lives.

—So, basically, these people—the ones we are delivering this to—they are already doing important things.

—Things of the utmost importance.

—But, they don't know they are.

—Correct. And therefore …

—Therefore what? I don't get you.

—Never mind, Wit. Utmost importance.

—Let's just get upstairs already. All the pages should be there.

—And yet they are not. Not all.

—How could you possibly know that?

—Wit, if you had the slightest inkling how long I have carried these pages—how many days, how many times—you would be certain of that which I am certain. That there is one page missing.

—One page? You can tell by the weight that it is missing one page?

—The last one.

—Let me guess: utmost importance.

That glance.

At this particular moment, Wit wanted to do a bevy of things. He wanted to run. He wanted to scream rational ideas into Colin's glance-happy face. He wanted to crumple and swallow each remaining page of the manuscript. He wanted to weep and laugh and apologize and embrace Colin or kill him. But, none of these were what Wit wanted to do most. Right now, more than anything, Wit wanted to answer the cell phone he heard ringing down the darkened corridor behind him.

The cell phone that Colin did not seem to hear at all.

By now, Quidnose and Bump had gathered at the calendar in question and were staring in concert at the indeed blue star hand-scribbled on today's date. All but Liliana came to the same conclusion at the same moment. However, Bump was the one to verbalize it.

—Perhaps it is her birthday.

—Whose birthday? Liliana offered.

—Miss Shrub's birthday.

—But, Bump, didn't Isaac just establish that Miss Shrub could not have drawn this blue star?

—Isaac established nothing, Liliana. Isaac merely doubted.

—Merely doubted? I would say he did more than merely doubt. He made me think. Isaac made me think in ways I don't believe my brain smiles upon.

—Only an open mind can leak, Lilly. It's why I wear hairplugs.

He had called her Lilly. It was an accident, but a lovely one. She wondered why it felt so familiar. It turned her.

Quidnose interrupted the moment.—Then, um, who did?

—Who did what? Liliana said, puzzled.

—Who could have drawn the blue star?

—Who among us would have a blue pen?

—I dunno. No one. Albert C. Hardaway.

The name fell out of Quidnose's mouth as if it had always been lodged there, awaiting use. Like a chipmunk's lunch. Quidnose seized her own lips shut with her newly painted fingernails, smearing her cheeks with patriotic glitter along the way.

—What name did you say?

—I did not intend to, uh, say any name.

—But, you did, Liliana said, persistent.—You said Albert Hardaway. Do you know Albert Hardaway?

—I dunno. What do you mean by "know"?

They stared at one another, believing each to have the answer that neither was certain existed. Liliana witnessed a gleam in Quidnose's eyes that would have been indiscernible, had they not been transfixed on one another. There was clearly more to this woman than her cankles would attest.

Both lifted an eyebrow to the other as if to ask a question they were not yet willing to postulate. Then, startled, they turned to the scraping of Mr. Rinderhart's desk chair against the linoleum.

—What are you doing, Bump?

—I'm going to say something, Bump offered.

—I don't understand.

—To Mr. Hardaway.

After a pause of understanding, Quidnose and Liliana skittered to Bump's side.

—You can't do that, Quidnose eked.

—Why not?

—Because you—you dunno how he will react to what you might say. He might, mm—get angry. He could fire you.

—Then why put a camera here in the first place?

—Well—we aren't certain it was Mr. Hardaway, are we? Liliana made the observation.

—Then, who did, Liliana? Who placed a camera here pointed at our little world? Someone who hoped we would never use it? Seems unlikely, don't you think?

—It does seem unlikely, Quidnose urged— but, nothing else seems likely.

—That isn't true.

Until Bump shook them off, neither realized they were gripping his forearm so intensely. Bump straddled his chair in reverse, resting his chin on his folded arms. The ladies retreated for the moment, willing to hear him out if it would stall pushing that record button.

—One thing seems very likely: placing another hundred sales calls. Manipulating another hundred customers into purchasing more than averages prove they can sell. Thumping my wedding ring with my forefinger, causing it to spin precariously near the edge of my desk: my only thrill in hoping it will settle before dropping off. Being distracted by the light peeking out from the slit in the photocopier as I imagine smaller people living in there. Drinking this coffee until it cools and the cream makes a cloud at the top. Imagining that cloud resembles an ouroboros. Staring aloft, as if a fluorescent bulb is missing, so as not to be pulled into Shrub's arguments with Isaac. Consuming my lunch in a handful of painful swallows only to bite my tongue, taste the blood, and imagine I'm momentarily alive. Fearing every human interaction. Pretending here is anywhere but here. Wishing. Wishing. Wishing any of it mattered. That seems likely.

The women stared.

—I'll take a stab at unlikely, please.

—How did you get this phone number?

—That depends, Wit. How did you get this phone?

—You know my name.

—I know. I'll bet you think that's impressive.

—Are you one of the security guards? I have your keys.

—Sheesh. Do I sound like a security guard?

—A little.

—Great. Now, I'm insecure.

—It's hard to hear you. What is that in the background?

—Tchaikovsky. And you didn't answer my question about how you got this phone.

—The phone was in the third bathroom stall.

—Interesting. Different place every time.

—What do you mean every time?

—Wit, the next decision you make is going to be the single most important decision of your existence.

—I find that very hard to believe.

—Which is why you are going to do what I tell you.

—And why would I do that?

—Because I am going to inform you of details and nuances that you have neither experienced nor felt before they actually become true. Isn't that swell?

—I suppose. Sort of.

—Beautiful. You're decisive. This will prove to you my power. You will be very impressed.

—I'm not impressed so far.

—And yet I have caused a cell phone to appear before you out of thin air.

—You didn't make it appear. I found it in the bathroom. And you didn't even know where it—

—Blah, blah. You're majoring in the minors here, Wit.

—I'm going to hang up now.

—Is he coming?

—He who?

—He Colin. Oooooooh, *spooky*! I know who you're with. Impressive.

—I'm not *with* Colin.

—*With* has a whole list of definitions. At least one of them fits. What is he doing right this moment?

—Probably obsessing over that old napkin he carries around.

—Napkin? Hmm. Perhaps it contains his quickly scribbled missive to make his way to the sixth story.

—Is that where you are?

—Let's not make this about me. Here is what I need you to do—

—Let me guess. You want me to keep him from getting to you.

—On the contrary. Get here as soon as you can.

—So you *are* on the sixth story.

—Pssh! You know, if I wrote down what I was going to say before making these phone calls, I wouldn't slip so much with the spoilers.

—You want Colin to succeed in his mission?

—Now, I didn't say that.

—But, if we make it to the sixth story, he will tell them.

—Yes, he will, Wit. But, who's to say that telling them completes his mission?

—You don't think they will believe him.

—Believing him has no negative effect on my plan. Only what they each do with that belief. Or do not do. It's semantics. So, you will help me?

—I don't know what helping you looks like.

—And yet you will say yes.

—What makes you think so?

—Because you know what helping Colin looks like.

Wit considered the offer. There was no reason to trust this individual. And yet, Colin seemed to simply assume Wit would do whatever was asked of him. His brief relationship with Colin certainly had its extremes—at times, Wit considered him an irritant, in other moments, he found himself ready to confide his deepest unspokens. It had the taste of control about it. Combine the fact that Wit was certain that details had disappeared from his memory, important details that had somehow been squeegeed clean like a missing last page. It was a bit nefarious, and someone outside of Wit himself was pulling the strings. This buffoon on the phone was clearly not the one to blame.

Wit responded— What do you need for me to do?

—Do you still have the phone? asked the voice on the phone.

—Are you serious?

—Oh yeah. Right. I do that all the time. I'm like, "I can't find my phone! Gaaaa!" And I'm speaking right into it. Wow. Ironically, I seem to have misplaced my phone right now.

—Why do I need the phone?

—Just bring it with you.

—That's all?

—Well—you did mention having the security guard's keys.

Burke knew full well that the two culprits' trajectory was upstairs. And yet, here he and Travis were. They had spent the last half hour downstairs, in the basement, rummaging through row after row of archives. Burke was annoyed. If he was going to be out of his chair, he thought he should at least be shooting someone.

—These shelves don't look very sturdy. Maybe we shouldn't be standing betwixt them.

—You don't even know what betwixt means, Travis argued.

—I do so. It's fancy for between.

—Then, just say between.

—I like betwixt. It makes me think of candy bars. Let's go get candy bars.

—We're not leaving. We haven't found—*wait*!

—Waiting is all I've ever done.

—Archive Box D, Travis said, staring.

—So?

—So, these—

Travis used the cuff of his sleeve to wipe what must have been years of dust off of the labels designating the boxes to the left of Archive Box D.

—would have to be Archive Boxes C … B … and. Oh.

—I'm gonna guess A.

—It's not here.

—Archive Box A?

—Not here.

—Is that bad? asked Burke.

Travis gazed at the empty space where there should have been a box. He did not blink.—Do you have your gun?

—I don't know that I actually wanted to move here permanently. My mother didn't think it was an appropriate place for a twenty-two year old to be on her own. But I didn't really think it was appropriate for my mother to have any say in the matter if she isn't going to actually mother me the rest of the time. A couple of days before my aunt called saying Mom had died, I received an envelope from her. Not a letter. Just the envelope. Mother had forgotten to put whatever she had written inside of it. But it was definitely from her because there was no return address. She didn't believe in return addresses. She said it was just one more way for your past to find you.

There was a hush of understanding about the room. And then Bump, closest to the camera Liliana had been speaking into, turned the record button back to the off position. Isaac stared. Miss Quidnose was in tears.—That was not what I thought you were planning to say, Quidnose offered, after more than a beat of silence.

—I didn't have anything planned. Right before Bump hit the button, I was thinking: what do I possibly have to say to the man who owns this building? And then the light went red and it was as if my whole world was in that little convex glass lens. I could have told it anything.

—I didn't know your mother died.

—Funny. I don't think I knew it either—until I said it.

—How is that possible?

—I don't know that it's possible. I only know that it's true.

Miss Quidnose turned, her left hand to her temple as if in pain or thought.—This is the strangest sensation.

—What is?

—So funny. I normally think of me. Even when I talk about you. But, while you were talking about you, I—um—found myself thinking about you. And feeling for you. And then these.

—Tears?

—Yes! Thank you, stated Quidnose— I had lost the word. It's like a sadness that fills some of the happy needs as well.

Then: a ding.

Much like any other ordinary ding—except something about it gave the group pause. They each stopped what they were doing, glancing nowhere and everywhere, but acknowledging something significant about the ding like a sunrise or a backache or a new flavor of ice cream.

Another ding. It came from the elevator.

Tchaikovsky ceased.

Miss Shrub peeked out of her door. Isaac broke his gaze out the window. Froman stopped assembling the box he had retrieved for Miss Shrub. Shrub gazed at the gathered group.

—You used the camera? Shrub asked, wide-eyed.

Another ding.

The six of them made their way toward the hallway where Liliana had first observed the back of Miss Shrub's head.

The elevator door was blocked open by a large metal box. As Shrub approached it tentatively, she was within three feet before realizing it was open and empty, and labeled Archive Box A.

—This cannot be happening.

Liliana spoke up.—What cannot be happening, Miss Shrub?
—No. No. This cannot be …

Following Shrub's lead, the others wandered back into the room where they had just been. And there, seated in front of the camera with his feet propped up onto the desk, was Colin.

—Why don't we all sit down?
Wit stood behind him like the Secret Service, intently paranoid regarding what might happen next. But, it was Shrub who spoke first.—You are not the higher-up.
—The higher *what*? Colin retorted.
—Up. In fact, the tattered cuffs on your jeans make you look more like a lower-down.
—I'll take that as a compliment.
—What right have you to call an impromptu meeting?
Colin was direct.—This right.

Colin plopped the archaic volume he had carried throughout this building onto Isaac's desk. Its spine broke and the pages fanned, practically tumbling off the edge—like mail after too long a vacation. Shrub, knowing books, scoffed at the craftsmanship.

—Pfft. That's not a very sturdy book.
—It's not a book, Frances. It's *the* book.
—Oh. *The* book. Is that supposed to mean something?
—Every word means something.

MARK STEELE

Liliana felt there were more important issues not being addressed.—Excuse me. But, who exactly are you? And how do you know Miss Shrub's name is Frances? We didn't even know her name was Frances.

—That's because she didn't know her name was Frances.

Miss Shrub quickly transitioned from moderately amused to cross.—I beg your pardon, she exploded.

—I assure you, there will be no need to beg.

—Of course I knew my name was Frances. When you said it, I knew exactly who you were addressing, didn't I?

—Yes, Colin offered— when I said it.

If it were possible to triple-take, a bonus take beyond a double-take, Miss Shrub proved the prospect.—I don't think I like the tone of your voice.

—That's ridiculous, Frances, because the tone of my voice is perfectly simpatico with what you deem pleasant. I know because I have studied you for many years and refined the vocal timbre that is most likely going to ease you into the news. I'm afraid it's not the tone of my voice you find offensive.

—Oh, then what is it?

—Your own thoughts.

—My. Isn't that a maddening way of seeming to say something while saying nothing at all?

—I have a way with words.

Liliana jumped in rather abruptly.—What news?

—The news of the day. Of the moment, in fact.

—I don't understand, Liliana continued.

Colin held it as he said it.—The book.

—You came all the way here to deliver this book?

—I have come much farther than you could possibly imagine for more reasons than I really should explain.

Wit chimed in.—Oh, for the love! Would you clarify just one thing?! Help us understand *one thing* instead of answering every question with a mystery?

The excitement of Wit's statement startled almost as much as his presence. Colin was such a mesmerizing, fully-realized soul that it was unfortunately easy for the others to miss Wit standing in the corner.

—You have something to add, Wit?

—I agree to this mission and all you do is hide the details from me and now you do the same to the very people who you insist must know?

—Oh? Did you actually agree to this mission?

—Of course! I'm here, aren't I?

—Being here in person doesn't really have much at all to do with being on board with the plan.

—I risked the security guards with you. I sat in that harness. I climbed down the elevator shaft—

—Yes, you've informed me several times.

Isaac was ready to come out of his own skin.—*Clarifying*, Isaac belted.—You were talking about clarifying one thing!

—Hello, Isaac. Didn't realize you were listening.

—How did you know my name is Isaac?!

—Missing the point as usual. That is so Isaac.

—You're the higher-up, aren't you? AREN'T YOU?!

—There's no need to speak in all caps.

—I WILL YELL IF I WANT TO YELL!

But, the remainder of the room was beyond perplexed. Liliana stared at this gentleman.—He didn't say yell, Isaac. Liliana eased into the uncomfortable idea. —He said speak in all caps.

—Well, Isaac retorted— what's that supposed to mean?

Liliana was transfixed on Colin.—I do know you. Colin, is it? I do.

—Do you, Liliana?

—I'm asking you.

—It didn't sound like a question.

—I don't remember anything before here. Are you—before here?

—I like your cube.

—Wh—what?

Colin wandered to her desk, handling the Post-it notes she had brought from home. He thumbed through them like they were pencil sketches coming to life.—Green on top. So it's less lonely.

—Wha—how? How could you possibly know that?

—It must have taken you a long time to find green on top.

—Um. Seven. Seven stores.

—Name them, Colin said.

—I beg your pardon?

—Okay. Name one. One store you visited to attempt to find green on top.

—I—*can't*. Why can't I?

They were practically nose-to-nose now. The sort of argumentative streak one can only achieve after intimacy.

—How—how—these feelings. Liliana stumbled to find the words.—Where are they coming …

—I can only answer questions that have answers.

Liliana stared into his eyes.—What did you mean by speak in all caps?

—Ask Miss Quidnose.

Colin nodded to the corner. There, enraptured in her own world, was Miss Quidnose. She had gathered up the pages of the archaic volume while no one was noticing and she was leafing through them one by one. Backward. She started every book at the end to make certain it would be worth her time.

—There's no ending, Quidnose declared. She hugged the pages to her chest, some held in place with her chin. She appeared to be confused by more than merely the absence of narrative closure.

It was Bump who first peered over her shoulder.—What good is a book with no ending?

—It seems to have an ending, Quidnose continued.—The ending is simply not attached. As if a page is—um, well, lost.

—I'm not going to waste the time reading it if there's no ending in sight, Bump added.

—Yet—it's almost familiar, Quidnose persisted.

—What do you mean, familiar?

—I don't know exactly what I mean, Bump. The way certain foghorns are, hm, familiar or the turnip-green smell from the house you were born in.

—Oooh. I want to read something familiar. Can I peek?

Colin interjected —Take any page you like, Bump.

—But, that's not how you read a book.

—I know.

And all eyes would have been on Bump Rinderhart slipping a random page out of the manuscript, had they not been distracted by the gun aimed their direction.

—Nobody move.

It was Burke. He had both shaking hands on the gun, but it was clear he was intending to aim at Colin. Travis put his hand kindly on Burke's shoulder.

—Whoa, son. That's a smidge premature.
—But he opened Archive Box A.
—Circumstances lean to that, but we've no way of knowing.
Colin, clearly intending to speak on his own behalf, did.—There's one way of knowing.
—You shut your key-stealing mouth! Burke bellowed.
—But you'll have to ask someone else. Because I didn't open Archive Box A.
—Well, it's open! And you stole the keys.
—I didn't steal your keys. You're welcome to have them back.
—Then hand them over, Burke demanded.

Liliana turned quickly to Miss Shrub, who was being pummeled so furiously by this rapid-fire barrage of information, she kept shifting her intense gaze from Isaac to Liliana, even to Froman—hoping for someone to clarify even a single thing. Liliana needed a few answers of her own.

—What was in Archive Box A? Liliana said it to Miss Shrub in a voice she considered hushed, but its harshness bandied instead about the room.

—I don't know, Miss Shrub stammered.

—You told me never to open it, Liliana whispered.—You must know!

—I know the *rule*. That doesn't mean I know the *why*.

—I'd settle for the what.

Burke, privy to their sidebar, persisted.—Well, I'm interested in the who. And the who is you.

—Colin.

—Is that your name? Burke asked.

—Yes.

—What was in it?

—What was in what?

—ARCHIVE BOX A! Burke was red-faced now.

—I didn't open Archive Box A. I'm not here for Archive Box A.

—You're here for the book.

—No, I brought the book with me. I'm here to show you what is inside the book. Or, in this case, who.

Miss Quidnose piped in.

—Everyone stop interrupting and just let the man explain! Colin, please.

—Not yet.

—What?! Why not yet!

—You're not quite ready for me to explain myself, Colin stated. —It will only frustrate you more. I need to give you just a few more minutes to come to that understanding on your own.

—Are you kidding? You sit there so smug, withholding the answers we need—

—Are they, Miss Quidnose? Are answers what any of you truly need? Is information going to fix anything? No. What you actually need ...

And then, terrible.

Wit, considering the banter tiresome, lunged forward as a gesture toward curtailing Colin's enigmatic nature. He had no physical intent. He was not going to wrestle the truth out of Colin, nor would he be likely to prevail if he made the attempt. But, the lunge itself—the shifting of his body six inches forward toward Colin—

—was enough to sever the tension thread that was keeping Burke's trigger-finger at bay.

Blam.

Blam. Blam. Blam.

Burke fired his gun four times, emptying most of his ammunition into Colin's chest.

And like the pages before him, Colin fell spread eagle upon the desk.

—What did you do? Liliana shrieked the words while grasping her mouth.

—I—I didn't mean to ...

—Burke? Why did you pull the trigger? Why did you pull the trigger four times?!

—I hardly realized I did. It was like—like I tried to stop myself—force my finger the other direction—but I couldn't tell east from west—

The others stood immobile in the moment, gaping, their arms forgetting what arms do. Travis's hand didn't leave Burke's shoulder. Burke broke down as a result of his first kill. Shrub, Quidnose, Isaac, and Liliana formed an arc around the body—a barrier between him and Froman, who warmed his fist on the copier like a security blanket, his other hand ticking nervously against his pant leg. Wit was simply frozen in his tracks. Only Bump focused elsewhere, the page in hand intriguing him so.

—This is great. You should read this.

Liliana knew she should be falling headfirst into a solution regarding the tumult in front of her, but her brain tumbled instead backward as if off a precipice of which she had been unaware. This man. This Colin. He had brought such confusion. Yes, such feeling as well: a sudden spring of emotion but also upheaval. Liliana would not consider it chaos, as he had not brought *noise*, but, it was as if her life had been a series of jigsaw pieces set aside one another so closely that she had never realized it was unfinished. Into this jigsaw puzzle Colin had come like a gust of wind and jumbled those pieces out of pattern. Now the gaps were more noticeable. Her day, the mishmash of emotions from the elevator at 8:27 to the camera moments ago, seemed less random than before. Her memory before this day more eradicated. Colin had arrived with a stack of pages and a larger stack of nebulous platitudes. All reason would label him an intruder and urge her to find relief in his demise. Yet, seeing his crumpled body before her, Liliana could not help but feel she had lost more comfort than gained through his omission. A matter of moments ago, she was ready to throw herself in front of Bump to shield him from this intruder. Now, Bump's detachment from the tragedy boiled ire inside of her she had not seen coming.

—Bump, now is not the time.

—I think it is exactly the time.

—To read? Could you please put the page down?

—Why would I put the page down?

—Do you not *see* this body? Do you not *see* what has happened here? This Colin who has been shot and killed a few feet from you?

—Shot, not killed.

—What?

—He's fine.

GAAASP.

Colin sat up so suddenly that Shrub screamed, a banshee-like shriek to wake the dead. Those who had the wherewithal to step backward lined the wall, palms inward. Liliana's eyes bulged, as did Froman's (who had otherwise remained silent).

Colin clutched his chest and seized enormous gulps of air. It was not until Colin braced himself and sat upon the edge of his desk, palms on his knees, that Burke realized he was still aiming the weapon squarely at the man's torso. Shrub must have been attempting to speak because her mouth formed a silent O.

Bump kept reading.

It was Miss Quidnose who broke the silence.

—Mr. Froman, run and get Colin a glass of water.

To which Froman replied— Anything you ask, Miss Quidnose. Anything you ask.

Froman was out the door before Miss Quidnose finished making her request. Liliana approached Colin suspiciously, palm outstretched—she did not know why. As she came upon him, she felt for his chest. Reached to touch the bullet wounds.

There were none.

No holes or bullets or bullet-proof jacket.

—What happened to the …

No one interrupted her but reason. Her fingers lingered at his collar, like a mother preparing the son for school. Colin gasped and answered.—They're not real.

Liliana met his eyes for the first time.—What aren't real?

—The bullets, Colin added— they couldn't have killed me. They were never real.

—How could they not be real?

—Because *he* did not make them.

—I don't understand. Security guards don't make their own bullets.

—Not the security guard. Mr. Hardaway. Mr. Hardaway did not make the bullets.

Stunned, they found themselves glancing about the room as if everyone was in on the same secret but no one knew every detail.

—You know Mr. Hardaway?

The pain clearly subsiding, Colin sat upright with full breath.—
We all know Mr. Hardaway.

Isaac Portense had remained silent for some time. A tirade had
been building within him up until the moment Colin seemed to
have died. A death in the room can cancel anyone's tirade. But, with
this newfound correction, Isaac found himself bubbling anew. He
was done—absolutely done with cryptic proclamations.

—How dare you, Isaac protested —how dare you portend
who we know when we clearly don't? I know what you are. Oh,
yes. I know what you are because I have attempted unsuccessfully to be you myself. You are the superior. I don't mean the
boss. I mean the attitude. Sure, you ease into the room and pose
everything in such a way to be deemed friendly, dropping bombs
like Mr. Hardaway's name—but it's the *what* that you say that
defines your hubris, Mr. Colin. You don't actually speak *of* things.
You speak *around* things. You don't think I can do it, too? I can
drop a cryptic earth-shattering platitude that is actually nonsense.
You're not the only one who can impress through ridiculousness.
Here goes:

And what Isaac said next was not, in fact, nonsense in and of
itself. However, the room indeed gasped in concert.

—The paper clip will save us all!

The gasp was not due to the nature of the statement. Rather,
the group was both sucker-punched and flummoxed by the fact that

Bump Rinderhart said *The paper clip will save us all!* at the exact same time as Isaac.

The exact same words.

The exact same time.

Isaac's eyes were daggers.

—How—did you know I was going to say that?

Bump's hand was shaking, the page rattling like a baseball card in a bicycle spoke.—It says it—right here—in the book.

A beat. The room heaved. Quidnose crumpled her nose.

—I don't get it, Quidnose said, puzzled.—It says *The paper clip will save us all?*

—That's what it says.

—How could Isaac quote a book he has never seen?

—We're all quoting the book, Bump said— even you—right now.

Isaac marched aggressively to Bump, ready to seize the page.—It doesn't say that in the book. That's impossible.

—It's possible.

—Where?! Where does it say that?

—Right here, Bump said— on page 201. Just before, "Bump continued reading as Isaac grabbed the page and uttered—

—inconceivable!"

He said it as he read that he said it.

Liliana's eyes darted about the group. This was nonsense.

Nonsense.

Ridiculous nonsense.

Or ...

Or had everything else been?

Liliana retraced herself. The day had begun at 8:27. There was nothing in her memory before that. Nothing. Like the inception of a chapter. Every bit of knowledge that would have existed prior to that had unfolded through monologuing, each character discovering who they were at the same moment as the rest. Could it be? These people—that Liliana herself—thought they were in the business of outputting books. Of correcting the thoughts of real writers. What if they were not truly makers at all? What if they were, in fact, being made? She felt her hairline burst into a cold sweat as the thought escaped her lips, convinced it must be written on a page somewhere scattered on the floor.

—That book—is us. Liliana glanced about the room.—We aren't real. We're characters in a story.

Miss Quidnose bent down on hand and knee and began flipping through the pages, clearly hell-bent on finding something specific. Bump looked at Colin, bewildered.

—Not real? Bump protested.—How can I not be real? My mouth is ultra dry. That's real.

—I didn't say *you* weren't real, Colin finally spoke— I said the bullets aren't.

—How is a Bump any better than a bullet?

—Because you are an invention of the author.

Miss Shrub was stone. She held Colin prisoner in her embrace.

—Is this the truth? Is this why none of us can remember before this morning? Frances was on a tirade now. —Did our story begin unfolding just then? Are you the cause of the memo and the camera on this so-called blue-star day? All of this just to expose the contents of Archive Box A?

Colin met her gaze sympathetically, still reeling from the impact of the unreal bullets.—I already told you. I did not open Archive Box A.

—No, but you were certainly eager to share its contents.

She held a fistful of the pages as if they were a grenade or an unwanted cheeseburger wrapper. It was Wit who was first to correct her.—Frances.

Startled, she caught her neck searching for him in the shadow of the corner.

—The book wasn't in Archive Box A. Colin brought the book with him into the building at the very beginning—before we had the keys.

Isaac broke his own silence, flailing his arms around the gravity of Colin's head.—You—you've been outside the building?

—Of course.

—So, some characters are let out while others …

—You're missing the point.

—Missing what point? That some of us are—what? More well-developed than the others? I know how narratives work, Isaac declared.—The hierarchy is topsy-turvy: dominant individuals become supporting characters because they don't have the traits of an ingénue. It no longer matters who's the boss or the employee-of-the-month or the copier guy or the recent girl. It's suddenly all about the story.

—It's not all about the story, Colin protested— it's all about the characters.

—Says who?

—Says the author.

At that moment, Miss Quidnose seized the page she sought in the pile of random manuscript detritus. She stood silently with the title page firmly in hand, her knees popping as gravity fought her.—"99 Pages (Somewhere Near the Middle)."

—Near the middle of what? asked Miss Shrub as she leaned in.—I don't understand.

—That's the name of our story. "99 Pages (Somewhere Near the Middle): a short story written by Albert C. Hardaway."

It was as if they were each thumped by an enormous thumb.

—Mr. Hardaway?

—Our author.

The truth had been floating around the room for minutes, but it only just now settled on their shoulders. The weight of it caused them each to be seated. Colin was the last man standing.

—I've been trying to reach you—to tell you this for the longest time—but every time I get close, something happens—and the story begins all over again.

—Like an ouroboros.

—Yes, Bump. Like a snake swallowing its own tail. Now, listen to me. Because I know our lives can be the makings of a beautiful narrative—but you have to believe me when I say that one of you is not who they claim to be. One of you is the snake—and I believe that snake in question opened Archive Box A.

Miss Shrub was done.—And how do you intend to convince us of that?

Colin did not answer. Instead, he stood—still clutching a rib—and allowed his eyes to probe the floor. When he found the object of his search, his eye wrinkles relaxed, but his jaw clenched.

—Security Guard Burke? Colin entreated tenderly.

—I'm so terribly sorry.

—You needn't be.

—Oh, I need be, Burke hedged— I need be.

—All you actually need to do is hand me the page that you are currently standing upon.

Burke did. Colin gripped the page with two fingers as if it were a soiled diaper and handed it to Miss Shrub. Her eyes did not instantly travel to the page number: 196. Nor did her eyes instantly travel to the sentence that referenced Burke replacing his gun into his holster, unfired. Instead, Shrub's eyes grew wild at the appearance of handwritten changes made to that sentence. It had been crossed out and replaced with words describing Burke firing the gun into Colin's chest four times. Words that had been scribbled onto the page—in blue ink.

Miss Shrub gasped aloud. It was enough to attract both Liliana and Miss Quidnose to her side.

—Archive Box A didn't contain this story, Frances. Archive Box A contained a single blue pen. Might I ask if any one of you recognizes this handwriting?

—I don't, Miss Quidnose answered. Then, tears filled her glasses as she pointed to the bottom corner of the page.—But I recognize that.

Colin looked at the telltale sign Quidnose had discovered: a distinct fingerprint. Every fingerprint is unique, of course, even for characters on the page, but the truly betraying nature of this smudge was that it was clearly made with the toner from a photocopy machine.

—You are as complicit in this as I am!

—Now, hold on, Wit protested.—You just asked me to get you the keys. You didn't tell me you were going to shoot Colin!

—I didn't shoot him, Froman protested on the phone. —I just wrote the words down on the page that said the security guard did it.

—It's the same thing!

—Yes, Wit. It's the same thing as you giving me the keys to open the box. It all led to the same conclusion. Each action has an ultimate reaction and it is often more costly or painful than we had anticipated. It's why I'm hiding. Details evolve unexpectedly. For instance, how was I supposed to know it wouldn't kill Colin? How was I supposed to know the bullets weren't real?

—You didn't know?! Wit was aghast. —Didn't you read ahead?!

—It's complicated. Every time, he scatters the pages and I always pick up a different one. This is the first time I was able to get actual bullets in him, so I guess I should be thankful for small victories.

—Wait a second. What do you mean "every time?"

Froman laughed out loud on the other end of the cell phone. A less sinister laugh than Wit would have expected from a snake that eats its own tail.—Are you really that thick?

—I beg your pardon?

—Oh, no pardons forthcoming. You really don't see it?

—See what?!

—There is nothing new in this enormous glass box, my man. You and your friends have lived this single hellhole of a day over and over ad infinitum. You never remember. But, Colin and I, we remember. Boy, do we ever. And that fella has got a tenacity you wouldn't believe. Sometimes, I'd like to take a carrot peeler to that voluptuous top lip of his and—

—The story—our story—it changes?

—Well, the details, sure. But, it always ends the same.

—

—That's a little too much dead silence for my taste, Wit. What's rolling around in that noggin of yours?

—Whose ending wins?

—Pardon?

—If the story always ends the same, whose ending has always won: yours or his?

—If you wanted to know that, you shouldn't have lost the last page.

—Do I always help you? DO I?!

—Let me put it this way. You don't always intend to.

Again with the laugh.

—I'm sorry! I don't mean to be snarky, but you're so predictable. You're aiming your flaring nostrils at the wrong target. I would blame your lack of backstory. You're a bit thin, don't you think?

—At least I have enough sense to not think I can hide.

—Pardon?

—Oh, no pardons forthcoming.

The door to the bathroom burst open. Colin was on Froman like hydrogen peroxide on a cotton swab. Froman barely had time to squeak out —How did you find me?!

Wit replied—I just read the next page.

Liliana stood several yards away from the office supply closet where Froman was locked away. She did not want him to see her through the lone square window, and yet the man had gravity about him she could feel pulling her within his orbit. She began to understand Quidnose's attraction. And yet Quidnose herself was currently balled up on the floor just down the hallway.

Colin had searched Froman thoroughly but found no blue pen. Certainly, he had stashed it elsewhere while obeying Miss Quidnose's request to fetch a glass of water earlier. Still, he did not have it on his person. This was made clear by the incessant rap-tapping that Froman insisted upon syncopating against the secured door. If he held possession of the pen, he would simply scribble his way out. Liliana watched as Quidnose winced at each percussive sound, as if her duped affection had empowered the nefarious plot to which she had recently been witness.

Why Quidnose? Why had the author chosen her to be fooled by this fraudulent fondness? It seemed cruel.

Froman was yelling something, his face pressed against the window, but it was indiscernible.

Surely, a writer who had taken such care in crafting her would not build her up only to tear her down. It seemed an inherently false idea. And yet, there she was: frumpily dressed and bespectacled. For Hardaway, it was only words on a page. Liliana understood that Quidnose was going to have to live with it. A woman no man could love—and yet one almost did. One.

Liliana turned back to the main room. It would be much later that she would realize Quidnose had been unconsciously moving closer and closer to the office supply closet.

Shrub had retreated to her office while Colin moved intently about the room, set out to accomplish clear goals. The others scampered around him, pages in hand, wowing themselves with this newfound narrative magic.

Colin was taking large strips of duct tape and securing plexiglass cubicle dividers with them. Like storm windows. Liliana simply couldn't accept the vagueness any longer.

—Where did you get the book in the first place? She whispered it close and forceful, startling Colin.

—What do you think it was that made you want to turn on that camera and speak into it?

—What? How did you know—

—I told you. I live this over and over. I've read the pages. It's always a little bit different, but you're always drawn to the camera—among other things.

—Other things?

—Help me move this.

Colin began dragging Isaac's desk across the room as Isaac, Burke, Bump, and Travis approached with the pages in hand.—Adjacent to that table there, Colin's instruction continued.

—You've read the pages, Liliana restated.

—Often.

—That doesn't explain how you found the book to begin with.

Bump pointed at Wit and stated incredulously —And now he's going to say, "No, it doesn't. But I can't get ahead of the story. As you would imagine, there would be consequences."

And, of course, Colin did. They walked away, circus monkeys. Liliana palmed Colin's face, a little too familiar.

—Listen to me, Liliana softly demanded.

—You couldn't understand, Colin said. —I know my mysteries frustrate, but I've done this enough to know that when I tell you anything before you discover it, it makes it all the harder for you to believe. If any of this is going to stick, it has to be birthed in you first.

—Then why sneak up to the sixth story at all? If we're the ones who have to find the answers, why go to the effort?

—Because if you didn't meet me, you wouldn't start looking.

Liliana felt overwhelmed with sadness. This was maddening to her, because she simply should not have known this character well enough or long enough to feel as full as she did right now. Colin unrolled more duct tape, securing other partitions, as if preparing for a hurricane. Liliana seized his arm.

—This is an enormous—an enormous thing. This. You bursting in here and making this announcement as if it were true—

—It is true.

—*If* it is true, not knowing anything that can be done about it. She was short of breath, though there had been no heavy lifting.—I'm asking you, Colin. Please. If Mr. Hardaway cares about his characters, what do we do—what do I do next?

He seemed genuinely flustered, perhaps even unprepared. It gave Liliana hope that she had not asked these questions before.—You're going to have to pursue those answers. It would not be fair.

—Fair? Fair. You are the one who finds a copy of this book and marches—

—I did not find it. You wouldn't understand.

—*Stop it*! Found it or not, you brought it here. You welcomed it into our lives like a nuclear missile. And then you wave this disastrous news like it's just a normal day's to-do for you.

—I didn't realize you considered the news disastrous.

—And then you expect me—*me*—to make the next call?!

—That's because it is you, Liliana.

She looked into his eyes and forgot her next line. He had those kind of eyes.

—I've been through this narrative enough times to know that it is your decision that holds the outcome of the story in the balance. Your thoughts. Your words. Your choice. The end. The end comes down to you.

He broke his gaze and moved on to his duties. She interrupted him midstep.—But, it's already been written.

He doubled-back, more intense than she had seen him.—Is that what you think?! That once created you are imprisoned to serve one direction, one pattern, to one end?! Look around you!

—But—ugh—Answers! She screamed it like sanctuary.—You have them! I need them! Give them to me!

—That's it then. That's the goal, is it? To get answers. And then what?

—What do you mean then what? Then I'll—I'll *know*.

—And what then? Think about it, Liliana. And I mean think about it like you've never thought before. Is it truly *knowing* that you desperately need? What happens when you get your answer?

—I don't understand.

—Think! What happens—what happens to *you* when you *get* an answer as opposed to what happens to you as you *pursue* an answer?

—The—the same thing.

—Oh. It's not the same thing at all.

—You have no idea.

—I have no idea? You think I'm not pursuing something? Why do you think I return to this story over and over and over? You don't think there's something here that I've lost—that I'm chasing?

—You had a life outside the building—outside the story! What could you possibly be chasing?

He grew silent. She deflated.

—You can't be serious, Liliana persisted. —You can't even explain that much to me? Fine. I've got secrets, too. Secrets outside this book. Things you'll never know.

—You think you have secrets, but you don't. I've read it all.

—You haven't read what I'm thinking.

—I have.

—So you're telling me that even if I improvise—if I tear these little Post-it notes off one by one and write down whatever comes to mind, that you've already read it—even though I haven't even thought it?

—I'm saying that your improvising is all a part of the story.

—How?!

She grasped the Post-it cube from her desk and began ripping off the green, scribbling on each square one by one, allowing the thin paper detritus to flit about her desk.—How can this possibly be part of the story? Here's something about me you do not know. And another. And—wow—not even I knew that one and yet I know somehow it is true. Another. And another. Secrets about my thoughts. And about my fears. She scribbled like a hurricane.—And about where this deep deep heartache comes from. How the news you've brought makes me feel. And about my mother.

The notes floated aimlessly, some landing readable, some drifting into the garbage can. Others curling and taking trajectories no aim could have predicted. Before she paused to realize the length of her tantrum, all the green was gone. The Post-it cube was now yellow on top. Liliana did not like yellow at all. She gripped the cube like a vise until the touch of Colin's hand upon hers released her fingers.

—How can this—these scribblings—this randomness—be part of this story?

—Trust me, assured Colin.—It will matter.

—It's nonsense.

—Just because you don't know what purpose these green squares could serve doesn't make them nonsense. Maybe they will matter to you. Maybe they will matter to someone else. All I know is that you say they are random, but you would have never scribbled them down if I hadn't shown you the truth—and that isn't random at all.

—Maybe I should have written them with the blue pen.

—You mustn't think that way.

—I musn't think *what way*? That it might be nice to write my own life? He's a writer, a craftsman. It was my very first thought on page one of this narrative to beam with pride over having the tiniest involvement with an original story. He wrote that thought! He moved me. Certainly, Mr. Hardaway would be proud to see me make that same attempt.

—Oh, he is proud, Liliana. But the blue pen is not the way he wishes for you to craft your own story.

—Why not?

—A character does not seize the blue pen because he thinks he can impress Mr. Hardaway. A character seizes the blue pen because he thinks he can replace him.

—Then how do I move on? Please tell me there is some way to take part in the writing of my life. If it's already permanent ink, I think I'd rather just die.

Colin glanced about, searching for the metaphor. He seized one of Froman's soiled papers and began folding—and folding—and folding. He was the tinker at work buried into his creation. Liliana sidled up to him, resting on her knees aside the desk. She found him finished with his handiwork. He held it up. Liliana was flummoxed.

—It's a monkey.

—You say that as if you are mocking me.

—It's just—we were having a fairly heated exchange, finally getting somewhere real, and you take a hiatus to fold up a toy simian.

—It's the only origami I know how to make. It's for kids' parties.

—Still not getting the point.

—The point is I just made this myself. Follow me here.

Liliana stared at the jovial thing dangling midair between his thumb and forefinger.

—I made it. I could build a square block where it will reside. A park and a swingset. The sort of place I assume a monkey would embrace as home.

—Okay.

—So I made it and I made its home and now I choose to let go. Tell me, Liliana. When I let go, what happens to the paper monkey?

—You tell me.

—I can't.

—Why not? You made it.

—I can't because of the wind.

—The what?

—Not the what. The wind. I made the monkey—and for argument's sake, let's say I also made the wind. But, guess what. I made the wind in such a way as to always shift. To move in ways that even I choose not to predict. And the wind that I made moves the monkey I made in ways that I designed to surprise me. He cannot move on his own. He cannot speak or walk—or even think. And yet the wind will take him on a journey. A journey not entirely of his own making, but a journey he will take part in nonetheless. How much more could the winds of this story carry you?

Liliana stared at him for a moment in pensive silence. Colin's eyes were almost pleading, sad—as if it broke his heart that she could not quite wrap her head around it all. Colin sighed and picked up a paper clip off of the desk.

—Here. He clipped the monkey to one of the memos adorning Liliana's cubicle wall.—Every time you look at this—consider what I've said.

For the first time in so many minutes, Liliana imagined that no one knew what she was thinking. Not even Albert Hardaway.—Colin?

—Yes, Liliana?

—So, what *is* the difference between pursuing an answer and getting one?

—If I told you that—you'd get your answer.

Isaac and Bump pushed open Shrub's office door tentatively. She sat on the floor, leaning on the front of her desk, slowly ripping books from their spines. She was methodical, low-key.

—Miss Shrub? Isaac asked. What are you doing?

She continued to rip. Taking many seconds per page. Meticulous. She then set each page into her wastebasket, where they would burn.

—Bump continued —Do you wanna see something cool?

—No, Bump. I do not want to see something that you think is cool.

—Why are you ripping up all your books?

—I'm clearing my mind.

—We can do that by ripping books?

—You can't. I can.

Isaac seized the damaged book from Miss Shrub's hand.—Frances.

—You don't get to call me Frances.

—You need to pull it together. Now.

—I don't need to do anything of the sort. I was special.

—We all thought we were special, Miss Shrub.

—I didn't *think* I was special. I *was* special. My name was on the door. I was the number one—the highest-up. And then I am notified that my life is artifice. That I am a supporting player. A recent girl. Merely story—and a short one at that. So, I will sit here and destroy books until mine is the only one left remaining. I have become a ruler in my own domain before by acts of sheer will. I will regain my specialness doing exactly the same. It is better to be third of seven than no number at all.

Shrub took the page of the book in her hand and tore it down the middle in front of her face, from top to bottom.

—By destroying the stories of others?

—Special has consequences. Get used to it.

She crumpled the page up into a loose ball.

—Your name on the door didn't mean you were exceptional, Isaac offered —It meant you were accountable. For every other soul and story that walks through that door. Tell me how that has changed. What does it say about you that the moment your leadership is truly needed, you become an island of one?

—I am responsible for *sons*. That is what the door says: Shrub & *Sons*. And I have *no sons*. It's a joke, you see.

Shrub threw the crumpled mass into the trash can. Into the fire. Bump observed the page sadly, flipping through his favorite of Shrub's books, guarding it, hoping it to be destroyed last. What he said next came almost as an afterthought.—Maybe we are the sons.

He closed the book.—Not actual. Rather, the sons in your care, Bump added —You know, just for this story.

—This story is all there is, Shrub said with despair.

—That we know of. The last page is missing.

—So? It's only one page.

—Maybe it says, "to be continued."

Shrub covered her mouth and stared out the window. A tear filled her left bottom eyelid. While she looked away, Bump seized the page she had just crumpled out of the burning trash, rescuing it. He smoothed out the page and set it gently on the bookcase.

—I knew, you know.

—I don't know.

—I knew, Shrub pondered —I was meant to know, *written* to know. I couldn't put my finger on it, because every time the reality would hint at itself, I would reject it and that intentional rejection would cascade over me into the ether of oblivion. It seemed so—out of character for me to be, well—the irony isn't lost. But,

I knew of Mr. Hardaway. I felt his name in my marrow, like he was part of me or perhaps vice-versa. Those two words: Albert Hardaway. They were on my lips when I saw the camera. When I read the memo. When I faced any question that seemingly had no answer. When I searched past 8:27 this morning—my true self. Each and every time, the two unspoken words that flooded my brain were Albert Hardaway. I knew it was the answer to every question posed even though I didn't know what to make of that answer. I knew. I knew. And all I did was deny it and try to manufacture a story of my own. That doesn't sound like someone whose name belongs on a door.

—No, it doesn't.

—Thank you for that, Isaac. Good to see you embracing your character.

—So, enlighten us. What other tantalizing tidbits do you just know, Miss Shrub? How else have you led us astray?

Shrub was offended by the question, accurate as it might have been. She gave Isaac a cold and dead stare as she made her way around the desk and pushed a button on her intercom.—Security Guard Travis?

There was a squawk of static, then words that melded together, as if the voice on the other end held both a walkie-talkie and a sandwich.—Yes, Frances?

—Don't call me Frances.

—Sorry, Miss Shrub.

—Is Burke with you?

—I can't get him to stop staring out the window.

—Then, make yourselves useful.

—How so?

—I need you to fetch something for me from the basement.

Liliana didn't understand why she was drawn to the lens of the camera without truly desiring to turn the machine back on. It seemed the answer should be here. Right here, where it all started. But, then again, Colin had warned about answers. That seemed a naive perspective. Perhaps Colin had been living the same story too many times. It had become the only tunnel through which he found a vision.

She glanced at him across the partitions. He stood alone, rolling a small napkin over and over in his hands, reading one side then flipping it, as if to experience the words scribbled on it fresh every few moments.

As Liliana approached Colin, she caught him noticing her in his periphery. He pocketed the napkin quickly. She had only one question this time.

—How do I become a character more like you?

And Colin's eyes brightened as a smile. But, before word one could be uttered, a terrible sound came from the elevator shaft. Colin's eyes closed resolutely. It spoke volumes to Liliana.

—This has all happened before. Colin opened his eyes slowly, sadness filling the space between them.—The end begins.

Colin hurried into the hallway, Liliana in pursuit. They sped by so quickly, Liliana would only remember after the fact that the office supply closet door had been opened.

Isaac, Bump, and Shrub stood staring out the window at the world at large, wondering how many pages needed to burn before they felt important again. Bump was just beginning to observe two men in business suits outside wrestling on the concrete when a familiar raptapping gnawed at each of them like a fever dream. Like mice to a piper, they stepped through the doorjamb into the partitioned area. There, with his feet up on Liliana's desk, was Froman. He was flipping slowly through the reassembled book, attempting to place it in chronological order.

—Why you insist on staring out that window is beyond me, Froman observed. —You people are like bugs to a zapper with that window.

—How can we not stare? It's the world outside our story.

—There is no world outside your story, Miss Shrub. You know what happens if you break that glass? The outer vacuum of nothingness. The end. Story over.

Bump argued —But, I just saw two men out there.

Froman laughed a bold "ha." —Are you going to believe me or what you're written to see? Oh well. I suppose you wouldn't be fiction if you didn't yearn for false things.

Bump seized the opportunity to address the obvious.

—How did you escape the closet?

—It's easy to escape with a blue pen, Bump. The closet door locks from the outside. That is, it does until I change a single word. Now, it locks from the inside.

—But, where did you get the blue pen? He searched you.

—Well—I wouldn't be a very good antagonist if I didn't have friends on the outside.

Shrub piped in.—It was Wit. Colin's right-hand man was actually your right-hand man.

—Wrong again. I'm left-handed. Wit was a red herring, Frances. Honestly, you'd think you had more experience with books. And would someone please rid this desk of these little green squares?

Bump picked up one and read it aloud:

—Miss Shrub is my mother.

But, Isaac wasn't interested in betrayers or Post-it secrets. He could not take his eyes off of the blue pen Froman tapped nervously against the book pages. Froman saw Isaac's obsession for what it was.

—I know that look, Isaac. You're curious. That's my favorite word. You want to know what I can do with this.

Isaac was salivating —Can you change the ending?

—No. I cannot make new pages. I can only mess with the ones I'm given, and only when one of you give me permission.

Bump interjected —We won't do that.

—You already have. And, as fate would have it, the end is always missing. So, I can't affect the end result. Irony. But, I can do better than change the ending.

—What could be better than changing the ending?

—Changing your minds. Behold the power of the blue pen.

Froman made a gentle blue X over the name Bump on the page and scribbled another name in its stead. With that gesture, Mr. Rinderhart was no longer seated in the chair between Shrub and Isaac. He had been replaced by Miss Quidnose, who had clearly been sobbing.

—Miss Quidnose?!

And just as quickly, Froman switched them back. Quidnose was gone. Bump looked on aghast.—Where was that awful place? It was cold and smelled of lilacs.

—That was the ladies room, Froman offered.

—Terrible, terrible music.

Miss Shrub was growing more disconcerted by the moment. She had always been drawn to power, but had never seen it wielded with such disdain.—What did you just do?

—It's a game, Froman teased —like puppets. And now …

Froman scribbled pointedly. Isaac's desk bursts into flame.

—Stop showing off! Isaac shrieked. —You're going to kill us!

—Calm down. I am in complete control.

This time, Froman wrote more fluidly—and rain began to fall, dousing the fire. Isaac, Bump, and Shrub looked about wildly, Bump staring the direction of the camera.

—Shouldn't we cover that?

—Oh no, Froman said, let it ruin.

—But you're destroying the room.

—I am destroying nothing. I am purging. Cleansing. Call it the creative process, call it regression, or call it failure. But, I can guarantee that this time around, the story will be distinctly different from the last.

He slashed savagely at the page, the rain pouring down now in torrents.

Colin and Liliana burst out of the stairwell onto the landing near where Wit had first dropped the pages. The wailing was definitely echoing from this floor. Liliana heaved in enormous gulps of air keeping up with Colin, straining to not lose him around each corner.

And yet, when Liliana lit onto the floor itself, Colin was nowhere to be immediately seen. Instead, smoke rose from a wastebasket filled with ashes. She stepped toward it, peering inside, not truly knowing what she hoped to find there. Something told her it was the final resting place of the last page of her story. She had little time to mourn, for behind her, a bathroom door thrust open. Colin carried a limp Wit over his shoulder and set him against the wall.

Wit lay, bleeding from his wrists.

—Wit?

—Colin. You couldn't understand.

—Wit. Look into my eyes.

—I'm sorry, Wit whispered out —I have to leave now.

—I won't lose you this way again.

A distant growl of thunder resonated. Liliana had never heard anything like it.—What is that sound?

Emotion boiled beneath Colin's steeled exterior.—That is Froman. Someone's let him out of his little room.

On the sixth story, puddles were gathering at their feet. Light fixtures were malfunctioning and shooting sparks across the room. Froman stood atop Liliana's desk and waved the pen like the sword of a gladiator, clearly waxing eloquent for the empathy of future readers. It was a spectacle to behold.

—I am the one, Froman declared —The one who has had to suffer the indignity of the copier man—feigning affection for the trollop in the ladies room! I have been forced to negotiate and manipulate version upon version of this literary device with no real control over the outcome. My hands have been tied! And so, the narrative has never concluded. But, now I—finally—after drafts and years—I have creative control. I have the blue pen. And, we will finally see who holds the real power to see this story through to the end!

But before Froman's platitudes could become decree, the rains stopped. Froman whipped around, slinging drops of water from his face to Isaac's (who could not help but grimace). Miss Quidnose stood at the edge of the hallway, having heard the disparaging remark. At the next desk stood Colin. Wit lay on the desk in front of him, bleeding profusely, just as Froman had written. But, the rub: Colin held a single page of the novel in his left hand.

—What did you do? Froman aimed the comment directly at Colin.

Colin crumpled a page into a tiny ball. Oblivion. Froman was about to come out of his skin.

—NO MORE! Froman was panicked now.—I've worked too hard!

—No more from you, Froman. You are done with the blue pen. Do you hear me? Done.

—Put down the pages, Colin. He will die. You can't crumple that reality.

—You know I won't surrender the pages.

—Then, we are at an impasse.

—You have to let me change the script. He's bleeding out.

—I know. I wrote it. Some of my best work.

Quidnose wiped her nose with her sleeve.—How could you? I was written to love you.

—You might want to touch up that makeup, sugar. The barn needs an extra coat of paint.

Quidnose threw her purse to the floor, makeup and contents spilling about. Colin was momentarily distracted by the scattered remains. Shrub panicked.—I thought you said he couldn't hurt us! He can't just stab Wit!

—He didn't, Frances. Wit gave him permission to change his story. He convinced Wit to hurt himself. We are all capable of hurting ourselves. It's why you shouldn't listen to him!

Liliana pleaded with Mr. Froman.—He's going to die!

—Don't look at me. Colin has the pages. He's the one with the power to make the deal.

—What deal?

—Ask him.

All eyes were upon Colin. He exhaled before retorting.

—Character for character.

Froman smiled at Colin's conundrum.

—You can change Wit's sentence, but you must surrender your own character arc to my devices.

It was crystal clear to Liliana that this was neither a good idea nor an even trade. After all, Wit had betrayed Colin—in essence, betraying them all. Certainly, Colin had the common sense to …

—Deal.

Before the room could muster a gasp, Froman hurled the blue pen at Colin, who flipped hurriedly through the pages. He found the culprit on page 227. The sentence read "The bleeding continued until Wit's cold body lay limp on the desk. He was dead." Sure enough, a pool of blood was sopping onto the page itself. Colin scrambled to craft a sentence..

THE BLEEDING STOPPED AS THE WOUNDS HEALED UNTIL WIT WAS STANDING NEXT TO THE DESK — VERY MUCH ALIVE.

And the blood retreated from whence it came. The pool shrunk to a pinpoint, life back into Wit's face. Oxygen back into the room. Wit gulped life.

And Froman sat on the edge of Isaac's desk, hand outstretched.

—The pen please.

Colin looked about the room, spectators wild with disbelief. He stepped over and placed the pen in Froman's hand.

—And the pages.

Colin obliged. Froman glared hungrily around the room.

—Leave them out of this, Colin bargained.—You have me. You have your deal.

—I can't help but wonder why you get all the questions.

—Pardon?

—It should be clear by now to all that we both have lived and relived this spectacle enough to have the answers. And yet no one comes to me. Curious.

—We don't trust you, beast.

It was, of course, Quidnose—and she spat as she said it. Froman gaped wolf-eyed, then leaned to her purse on the floor. He took one of her many collected napkins and wiped the spittle off the bridge of his nose.

—Just because I'm a beast doesn't mean I am an uninformed one, Froman offered —and it doesn't really benefit me any more to lie to you. You know you're written now, so you can feel it when you hear what is false. You always could. You just didn't want to believe lies are lies. Probably my best trick.

—There's nothing you could say that we would want to hear, Liliana said.

—Oh, but there is, Lilly.

He called her Lilly. It was an accident, but a horrid one. It repulsed her and made her wish it were not her name.

—The question should actually be quite obvious. Time after time, I am trapped here on the sixth story. Just like all of you. But, he isn't. He comes from the outside. And there is the question: why? Why does he subject himself to our hell over and over? Why is it so important for Colin to get himself to the sixth story? Why does he keep his agenda a secret?

—It's no secret, Liliana stated.

Colin closed his eyes, accepting the inevitable.

—Is it not, Liliana?

—No. Colin was very upfront about the fact that he has lost something here and that he keeps returning to chase it.

—Something. Lovely. And did he specify what said something might be?

—Well—

—He declined to answer.

—It's none of my business.

—It is very much your business, Liliana. For what Colin left here in the first draft—or rather, what left him—is not a what at all. It is a who.

Liliana had a few words left over to say. Words she processed midargument before this latest detail unfolded. But, the words stuck in her throat. She pushed to force them out but they wedged sideways like a cartoon bone. She blinked as if there were sawdust in the air and resisted allowing the information to register. All eyes in the room were on her. All eyes except for Colin's. Froman was right, Liliana knew a lie when she heard a lie. This was most certainly the truth.

—*You* are that who. It is you for whom Colin returns, Liliana. The fool is in love.

Liliana's thoughts stammered until she finally whisper-spit a rejoinder.—Wha—how? How can that be possible?

—Quite simple. Because you love him back.

Her eyes met Colin's as Froman spoke the truth as if it had a bitter aftertaste.

—You were written for each other.

Liliana stood several yards away from the locked office supply closet. Colin was inside because Froman's blue pen had put him there. She did not want Colin seeing her through the lone square window and yet his gravity pulled her within its orbit. Froman had reversed his blue pen decision and the door once again locked from the outside. He was a fickle sort of villain that way. Liliana could hear the man skittering about the partitioned room, preparing for his endgame as her once-great hero sat imprisoned among the staplers. How could he live this story over and over again and continue to lose? She could not help but be curious as to whether she was the cause.

She felt love. Yes, she did. But, did she feel love because the sentiment was true? Or did she feel love as a result of being told love was what she felt? Certainly her emotion tied to this man was strong from moment one, but she had never been able to pinpoint if it was the affection of lover, father, or mentor. She would never know. Circumstances being what they were, she would never be certain. She would never have her answer. Colin was correct. The not knowing drew her to him. But, now that she had her answer—she was more uncertain than before. She stood within inches of the closet window, knowing she had perhaps a dozen pages remaining in her existence and asked the question she supposed would define her.

—How am I supposed to know—

But, he could not hear her. She pressed closer, louder.

—HOW am I SUPPOSED to KNOW that—

He tapped his ear.

The moment was ripe, the question in her heart swelling to the point of rupture. She fumbled through the hallway door to the very first thing she happened upon: Quidnose's purse. She surveyed the contents on the floor and apprehended the lipstick and the napkin with which Froman had wiped his face.

She inscribed the message as best she could, grease color on the thin scrap—attempting in vain to make it readable without ripping. It was not a beautiful thing. But, the question was clear. She shuffled back into the corridor and pressed the napkin against the small square window. Nine words written in smears of plum gloss.

How am I supposed to know I love you?

Colin didn't attempt to answer. He merely pressed his fingers sadly against hers on the glass. But, his other hand reached for his shirt pocket, pulling out the tatters of the crumpled napkin he had cradled before.

He unfolded it. He pressed it against the glass.

How am I supposed to know I love you?

It was the very same note, the very same napkin—but weathered, aged—and blood-stained. Liliana gasped and covered her mouth, realizing the breadth of the cord tethered between them. Colin also stepped back from the window. He began to pull out his other pockets. There, spilling to the floor, were dozens of napkins.

Each saying the exact same thing.

Liliana stepped up to Froman with a hush. He was clearing a space in front of the camera, drying it off from the indoor monsoon.

—Remarkably resilient, this machine, Froman waxed —as if it's had a role to play in the end.

—I know it comes down to me, Froman.

Froman did not turn to make eye contact. He continued in his tinkering.—Told you, did he? Took him longer this time.

—He told me much earlier, Liliana admitted —but I didn't understand.

—And you believe that now, you do understand.

—I believe that you want this story to end.

—Obvious. Try harder.

—And without me, it won't.

He gave a crooked smile.—Sounds like the beginning of a bargain.

—I was told it is my decision. My thoughts. My words that make the difference.

—I concur.

—So, if I choose to end it, you won't interfere? You won't blue pen your desired outcome onto my actions? It will truly be up to me?

—I couldn't if I wanted to. Your words are your words.

—And you will release Colin.

—Within reason.

—What would you know about reason?

—I will release Colin, but he cannot touch you or speak until the deed is done.

—Agreed.

—So quick. So certain.

—There is one last caveat.

—There is never just one last caveat.

—The pen.

—Oh, this is new from before. Now it gets exciting.

—You will rewrite the lock on the office supply closet again. It will lock from the inside.

—I don't understand. I agreed to release Colin.

—And once you make that change, the keys and the blue pen— go inside.

—Inside?

—Inside the locked closet. No more changes.

—You deny me creative control?

—It is the only way you will get what you want.

—My dear, you know very little of what I want.

—I know you're going to get very little of it.

Their stares played chicken. Froman blinked.—Be careful of your caveats, Liliana.

—I am quite prepared for the consequences.

—Somehow, I doubt it.

—Enough. Decide.

His eyes smiled. Overconfidence or foreshadowing, she did not know.

—Deal.

Froman obliged every demand. The blue pen, the keys, they were locked securely away with no plausible means of retrieving them. Colin was out, but bound at the wrists. He was held against the wall at a distance by Froman, who seemed to prefer standing nowhere near the camera he had resurrected.

Liliana stood facing the convex lens—the one that had seemed like a form of home so many pages—practically a lifetime ago. It was now her only window to the higher-up. To Albert C. Hardaway. It was her one opportunity to plead the proper ending. To have audience with the instigating mind of her existence.

Travis and Burke remained in the basement on errand for Shrub, so only Frances herself, Bump, Miss Quidnose, and Isaac rounded out the cast of characters. Seven souls awaiting the contents of a lost page.

—Are you ready? Bump asked.

He steeled his forefinger against the lone red button, waiting for Liliana to nod affirmatively. She took a cleansing breath and complied.

She knew from the blinking light that she was finally being presented before Albert Hardaway.

—Mr. Hardaway? This is Liliana. I almost said "again," but I didn't realize to whom I was speaking the first time. I might have spoken very differently.

She paused to consider how to proceed.

—I knew somehow today would be different. I felt it the moment I stepped off the elevator this morning. I mean, yes—technically this is the only day I've ever experienced, but it seems that you have allowed us to experience it again and again—somehow differently. What I'm trying to say is that I feel I can be myself with you. Something I haven't necessarily been throughout this story. I mean—yes—before we knew we were written, we all moved forward with our stories as you had intended. But, the moment we discovered you—I think we revolted a bit. Pushed hard against your story. That's what is so peculiar. It is clear to me that you wanted us to know that you exist, but the knowledge of it set us on a tangent against you. I don't know if I've decided whether or not I'm going to like what you deem best for me—but I have determined to embrace the narrative. To go where you compose and add my intended flavor.

She glanced back. Both Froman and Colin appeared tentative.

—I am told that the next decision is mine—and that feels right, as if I was built for the moment. It gives me an idea of what it means to be both written and have words that are my own. So, here goes. Here is my decision—the only decision of which I am aware because it is the overflow of words from my heart. When I accepted the truth today, the one thing I couldn't bear was the idea that I was fiction. So, I only want one thing: the opposite of that. I want to matter. I want what we have done today, what we have lived—this short story of a life—I want it to be true. Actual. Nonfiction. With whatever repercussions and consequences that may bring, I want—we want to be more than characters. Everything about us—everything we have been and are now—

She stared into the blinking light and hesitated as her voice caught.

—we want it to be real.

KEE-RASH! The sound came from the office supply closet, which was impossible because the door was locked from the inside.

—What was that?

Froman scoffed.—Who knows? Maybe help just magically appeared out of the pen tip of Albert Hardaway.

—Why would we need help?

—You're about to find out why.

Liliana did not like Froman's smile. She did not like it at all. But what she liked even less was what she saw when she followed his line of sight and realized that Colin had gone white, life being sucked from him. He was beginning to bleed from the abdomen. He clutched himself and buckled to his knees.

—Colin!

She caught him, cradling him, as the others hurried to his aid. Froman kept his distance and held the smile. Liliana ripped opened Colin's shirt. Two, three, four bullet holes appeared. Blood poured.

—The bullet holes—I don't understand. You said they weren't real!

—They weren't, goaded Froman —until you asked for them to be real.

She attempted to sop up the bleeding, plucking napkins from Colin's pockets and making futile attempts to reverse this spiral. Colin gripped her hand, hoping to not lose their last moments together to her state of panic. His hand on hers caused her to stop.

—It's okay. I can change it back! Turn on the camera, Bump! Turn on the—
—Liliana.
—Bump, get off the floor and turn on the camera!
—Lilly. Colin said it with heaviness.

He called her Lilly. It was not an accident and was both wonderful and terrible. The tears were flowing now. She had not noticed feeling them, but saw them drip onto his chest.

—Is this what real feels like?
Colin heaved in between words.—You finally—have an answer.
—Oh, Colin.
—You did—good. It was the right—request.
—But I didn't—I didn't have time—to love you.
—That's all right. —I did.

His eyes were losing their light. They stared past Liliana for just a moment—into the invisible above her. His breathing became uneven. She squeezed his hand. One lone thick tear emerged from

Colin's right eye, forming a beautiful bead on his cheek as he spoke three last words.

—Wait. Not yet.

She gazed into his eyes as the blue left them.
Calm.
Colin was dead.
Liliana pulled her hands away like surrender. The room was silent save the drone of the photocopier. Wit broke the moment.
—He never told us where he got the book.
Froman was pleased to reply.—He didn't get the book, Wit. All eyes but Liliana's drifted to Froman.—He wrote it.

Liliana pulled herself up to a seated position, her back aching from the sustained hovering over Colin. She had never felt an ache before. She opened her palm, observing the bloodied and crumpled napkin in her hand.

How am I supposed to know I love you?

What had she done? The ending was all up to her. What had she done? Bump broke the silence.
—So, that's what the "C" stands for.
Liliana finally uttered the words to herself.—Albert Colin Hardaway. He loved me.
Froman waltzed over to the camera, light still blinking in recording mode. He tapped the red button elegantly to punctuate the fact

that everything that had occurred in the last five minutes had been observed.

—He always does, Liliana, Froman chided —And you always kill him.

Like a fury, Quidnose rushed at Froman with Burke's gun in hand.—You spoiled it all! You just spoiled it all!

Froman quickly reacted, seizing the camera off of the tripod and bracing it on his shoulder. He aimed it at Quidnose like a cannon. She halted midattack.

—Careful. You wouldn't want him to see what you've become.

She steeled herself, wiping her nose on her sleeve, keeping her aim steady.—I'll shoot the lens first, then you.

—Really? Froman was chiding now —You think that will vindicate your situation? Do you?

—I don't see him having a problem with offing the villain.

—It's called an antagonist, Miss Quidnose, and who exactly is it? I'm having a little trouble clarifying. Seems to me that I haven't physically hurt anyone. Burke shot the author himself before Liliana finished the job. Wit tried to kill himself. Now, you wave the gun at me. It's your tribe that is at war. Or so it would seem to the observant eye. I've wounded with words, sure—but who in the room hasn't?

—The gun is nothing compared to the blue pen.

—Which is securely under lock and key. I'll even check.

—Stand still!

—Certainly I pose no future threat.

Bump interjected. —Miss Quidnose. No.

She looked wildly in his direction, pleading for justice.—Do you understand who he is?

—I understand who you are, Bump added tenderly —And you are not this.

—We can end this by ending him.

—How do we know that's the right ending?

Isaac and Wit now entered the fray.

—Let's think through this, Wit insisted —We only get one chance.

—One chance until next time, Isaac argued.

—No, Isaac. We don't get a next time.

—Yes, we do, Wit! He said …

—Do you remember a last time?

—Well—no.

—Exactly. It's not another chance. It's a complete reboot. Back to chapter one, Wit implored. —We remember nothing. We learn nothing. That's not a next time. That's a *first* time. Over and over again. If we start over without remembering the last time, we won't get anything right! No change. No progress. Our story will just keep swallowing its own tail. That's not a second chance. That's prison. If we are going to learn from our mistakes, we have to get it right THIS time within the limited pages we have left.

—But, we've already gotten it wrong.

It was Liliana, face pressed against the window to the outside world. They each stopped where they stood.

—Whatever choices are left, we have already failed. I have failed.

—You don't know that, Wit persisted.

—YOU CAN'T TELL ME THIS WAS ALL PART OF COLIN'S PLAN!

A voice across the room settled the debate.—Well, of course it wasn't. The six of them turned. Froman stood, blue pen in his possession.—It seems the noise in the closet was something after all. Pity none of you checked before I did. Now, give me the gun, Miss Quidnose.

She didn't budge. Instead, she aimed the pistol at his face.

—Very well.

Froman scribbled words onto the remains of the book on Liliana's desk.

The gun vanished from Miss Quidnose's grip and appeared in Froman's hand.

—I suppose that's the easier way. No one move. Not even an inch.

They each stood absolutely still as Froman reclined at Liliana's desk chair. He exhaled.—This is the truly beautiful moment. Creativity can flow freely now. For the first time, I will write without resistance.

—For this draft, Miss Shrub declared.

—Yes, Miss Shrub. But if there's anything I've learned about you characters, it's that you will have no trouble forgetting whose side you should be on next time around. Which brings me to my two favorite words.

He said them as he jotted them at the bottom of the last page available.

The. End.

A distant rumble began to grow.

Froman sauntered over to a spot between a desk and a table. The spot between the desk and table that Liliana helped Colin move. It gave Liliana a moment of pause. Isaac noticed as well. He whispered.—Liliana? Didn't Colin …

Liliana's cogs began to turn. Her eyes darted about the room. She spoke in urgent hushed tones. Froman didn't notice. He was busy waxing eloquent in blue.

—And now that I hold the power …

—Wait a moment—Liliana realized Colin's plan.

—And I compose the story …

—Isaac, he taped the glass!

Colin had taped the glass. Colin had prepared them for this very moment. Each of them: Wit, Quidnose, Shrub, Bump, Isaac—even Liliana herself—were standing behind the only glass partitions he had secured many pages ago from this inevitable ending.

—I choose to finally go …

Froman aimed the gun at the outside window. In a split second of hope and wonder, Liliana's mind flooded with a myriad of details from 8:27 this morning forward. This moment had not caught Albert Hardaway off guard.

It was always part of the larger story.

—on the outside.

Liliana closed her eyes.—TAKE COVER!

She ducked as Froman fired the gun, shattering the outside window. The world disappeared in a flurry of cascading shrapnel and bright light. A rushing wind poured into the room. Before Froman could dart, the onslaught of wind shoved the desk and table Colin had positioned together, trapping Froman between them. This was clearly not what Froman had expected to happen. His eyes went wild. He screamed and writhed, attempting to force the desks apart as green Post-its flew through the air, a tornado of confetti, blowing around and around his head—and then up, a maelstrom of little green squares floating away into downtown and the world. Sunlight poured in and Liliana could not help but notice that the outside of the building was not at all the nothingness Froman had described.

And then, in the center of the chaos, everything slowed for the briefest of moments. All eyes in the room fell upon the same item. It lifted and wafted and rode the wind as if by design. Froman choked on his own silence, perplexed as he watched the origami monkey taken passenger by the wind, disappearing into the distance as a dot upon the skyline, traveling to who-knows-where for an adventure all its own.

The wind vibrated the room, the resounding bass threatening to burst their eardrums. The six whose hands were free clamped their ears shut, but Froman could see the trap. Window upon window and partition upon partition shattered inward like a tidal wave. Froman shoved against the desk and barely wriggled free as a large shard of broken glass caught him, lodging dead in the eye.

He shrieked in agony as a rushing whirlwind caught him up, thrusting him above the rafters into the sky, flinging him up and away, his cries echoes, out out out into the horizon of the wild outside.

Gone.

The entire sixth story was obliterated with the exception of the partitions that had been taped secure by Colin. Our characters were safe.

Isaac leaned over the desk and read the words on the page of the book where Froman had scribbled

The. End.

The blue pen was nowhere to be found.

Suddenly, a jerk.

The building was swaying around them, damaged beyond repair. It felt as if the floor beneath them was about to collapse. Liliana looked to Miss Shrub.

—What do we do?

Miss Shrub responded like someone whose name was on the door.—We follow me.

They ran. As wall joints ruptured and lighting fixtures exploded around them, they ran past the open door of the office supply closet—Shrub taking mere seconds to seize the keys from inside. They bounded into the elevator, Isaac kicking Archive Box A out of the way, it no longer seeming all that important.

—Aren't we supposed to take the stairwell in emergency scenarios?

—SHUT UP, BUMP!

It hardly mattered who said it. Wit thumbed the button to close the elevator doors as the hallway collapsed inward behind them. The elevator lurched downward a little too quickly. It felt as if it swayed with each stunted movement.

—This is not good.

—Really, Isaac?! Miss Shrub vented. —What clued you in? The building collapsing or the fact that we are almost to the last page?!

—Mother, please. Liliana put a kind hand on her shoulder. Miss Shrub recomposed herself.—Where do we go from here, Frances?

—To the basement.

Burke and Travis were working up quite the cold sweat as they heard the tumult on the floors above them. But, Shrub sent them to guard this item and that was exactly what they were going to do, even if they were crushed doing so.

The elevator door dinged and opened. Bump and Isaac were in midconversation.

—Did you see what all was out there? Isaac was boiling.

—You mean outside the building? Yeah. Pretty.

—Pretty?! Froman lied. He lied. He said there was nothing. Nothing but us. Nothing but here. I thought we were supposed to know when he lied.

—Maybe he wasn't lying, Bump insisted. —Maybe what we consider beautiful, he thinks is nothing.

Shrub marched directly to the security guards.—Did you find it?

—Yes, ma'am, Travis responded. —Archive Box B. May I ask why we needed to guard it if anyone is allowed to open it?

—Anyone is allowed to, Travis. That doesn't mean anyone ever does.

SHOOM. The elevator shaft caved in completely from the sixth story's tumbling rubble. It was no longer a means of escape.

Wit panicked.

—Miss Shrub, if you don't hurry, we'll be buried alive in here.

—Stay by the stairs. Over there: the fire escape. Let us know if you hear anything.

—Hurry!

Miss Shrub took the key in hand. She set Archive Box B in her lap, and she closed her eyes, preparing for the moment. Liliana interjected. —Miss Shrub, what exactly do you expect to be in there?

—What else could it be, Liliana? The final page.

Shrub inserted the key and turned. There was a pop, then a drawer spilling out the side. Pages and pages fell about. Much more than a single page.

—I'm hearing something, Miss Shrub! There is definitely rumbling!

—We're hurrying, Wit! Quidnose, Bump—help us sort through this!

The many hands gathered and shuffled, attempting to match pages with the numbers before and after. Liliana was flustered.

—I don't understand. So many pages. Is it another book?

Bump was first to make sense of something.—Hey! I know this place! Mobrigger Bridge! I've read about it before.

Shrub identified the pages for what they were.—Wait a moment. "*Mobrigger Bridge.*" This is another story.

Quidnose rustled through.—This—this is a collection of short stories. With such unusual names: "*Skullduggery,*" "*Blah Blah Blah,*" "*The Whippersnapper.*"

—Miss Shrub—

Frances leaned over to Liliana's page. It shook in her hand.

—There's a man—

—What man?

—In this story. "The Most Important Thing Happening."

—What about this man?

Liliana handed her mother the paper.

—It appears that he was—inside our supply closet.

Bump blathered on as reality set in.—But, so many pages are absent. It's like there's a huge chunk missing somewhere near the middle. I haven't done the math, but it feels like it's about—

—99 pages.

Shrub said it. They each stood still. The rumble outside waxed on—but they stood stunned. It was Liliana who truly understood.

—We were never the whole story. Never. We were only one story. 99 pages somewhere near the middle of a greater work: a larger collection. With other worlds and other characters. And by the looks of this, our story reaches in to each and every one of them. Like tentacles. We were so affected with the fact that we were written, we never considered how we might be affecting others. We—we're not even the first story. We're—

Bump interjected.—We're the sixth. The sixth story.

The fatality of it all settled in. The rumble grew louder, stronger. Closer. And then, Liliana had an epiphany.

—Oh! But we've considered it now!

Liliana began climbing to the top of the high precarious shelf that had been storing an entire alphabet of Archive Boxes.

Shrub intervened.—Where are you going?

—One last talk with our writer!

—But—you don't have a camera!

—He wrote us, Frances! WROTE us! Do you really think he can't see us?

—Why would he give us a camera if he could already see us?

Wit answered.—So we would believe that he could.

Liliana arrived at the top shelf. She braced herself as her goose-bumps affirmed this was no sturdy soapbox.

—Liliana! DAUGHTER! Shrub pleaded.—You don't have to do this. After all—it is my fault.

—It's not, Frances. It's not.

Liliana stared up at the dust-rattled ceiling as the room hushed.

—Mr. Hardaway, sir? I mean—Colin? I know we've had our doubts throughout this very long short story. But, we now believe that you wrote us—because you love us. Right?

They each nodded in agreement.

—Your duct tape alone was proof of that. You clearly long for us to make decisions within this story that influence the others. We realize that once we go back to the first paragraph, we will forget everything that has happened. We're sorry. We can't help it. We're forgetful. We're characters. All we ask is that we—that we take some of this with us. The ways that we have molded and shaped one another. A hint of the knowledge of you. It doesn't even have to be a certainty—it can just be a notion. Something knocking around in the foggiest part of our minds that urges us to behave differently. I understand what you were trying to say now about the difference between seeking an answer and finding one. Finding an answer makes me stop hungering, stop hunting. But, chasing an elusive answer, especially one that feels like it might be just around the corner—it pushes me, shapes me. Trusting something that had not been proven to me did more to strengthen the way I was written—much more than knowing for certain ever could have. Trusting you. Please—please—next time, let us—let *me*—see that sooner.

She was done. All was silent.

FOOM! The room began to fall to pieces. Liliana stumbled and caught herself on the edge of the shelving. She screamed.

—LILIANA!

She had broken her arm. Burke, Travis, and Miss Shrub struggled to climb and support her pained body simultaneously. Wit could hear large blocks of cement falling against the outside of the door: their only means of escape.

—If we don't leave RIGHT NOW, we will never get out of this basement!

Miss Shrub responded —Get that door open!

But, as Wit rammed his shoulder against the door, it would not budge. Miss Quidnose recognized an altogether separate crisis.

—Isaac, Bump! Help me!

—Miss Shrub! We're almost to the final page. The page that is missing!

—Not now, Miss Quidnose!

—If not now, then WHEN?!

The roof began to cave in. One large foundational stone at a time. Bump, Isaac, and Wit HEAVED, shoving their bodies against the door to the point of breaking both it and them. The shelving started to tumble, collapse, with Liliana at the precarious top and Shrub about to be buried. Wit commanded,

—SHOVE! SHOVE! SHOVE!

And the men did as the shelving collapsed toward the door itself, Liliana riding it.

The roof gave way. Liliana was thrown from the wreckage just as the shelves beneath her turned to splinter. She tumbled through the air toward the door and inhaled a tumult of dust and residue. Wit managed one last push and—just as the room about them came crushing down, Liliana flew through the door—

The ding of the opening elevator doors startled Liliana. Her mind had wandered, but not too far to fetch. She inhaled deeply as a lesser girl might on her first morning at a new job. She stepped out and into the hallway, knowing that somehow today would be different. Different from what, she could not quite recall, but butterflies filled her stomach. Like nervousness. Or anticipation.

Or love.

It was here that her life would begin anew. The sixth story.

KATHLEEN

Vanessa was pretty sure this was gonna be the day. Yup. Pretty sure. It's been a long wait she thought. Gonna marry Bruce she thought. If the numbskull would hurry up and propose she thought. They had been growing distant lately, sure, but there was something in his voice on the phone. A tad of excitement that hadn't been there since autumn. Not a tad—a smidge. And not excitement—urgency. Either way, wasn't like Bruce to throw a picnic on a workday at lunch. Had to be what Bruce called "a special occasion." Though Bruce has a different definition of a special occasion: certain televised playoffs and war reenactments and when that one band kept coming back into town. But she knew he bought a ring. Left the receipt in his pocket when he threw his jeans in the wash. She knew doing his laundry would come in handy. Bruce always left clues in the pockets. He's thick that way she thought.

She drove into the empty parking lot, her low-air tire light blinking. When was he going to get around to fixing that? His car was there on the far end of the parking lot. He had left the tailgate open. Of course.

She glanced out into the landscaped field. There he was, somewhat of a feast laid out before him on the edge of a pond, seated cross-legged, unscrewing the wine and unwrapping the cheeseburgers. So thoughtful.

She called out in a sing-song that she thought would feel romantic.

—Hey hey!

—What'sa matter?

—Nothing. Why?

—You shouted at me.

—No, I was calling to you. Letting you know I'm here.

—Of course you're here. I told you where we were gonna meet.

—Never mind.

She sat down before the spread he had worked so hard to prepare. Her butt crinkled.

—What am I sitting on?

—It's the tarp that covers the pool.

—The apartment complex's pool?

—I thought it would give us more room to spread out. Have you seen real picnic blankets? They're the size of a nickel. You can't eat anything on a nickel.

—This looks very special.

—I got your favorite. He was holding a bag of potato chips as if it were a handbag she were considering purchasing.

—How are those my favorite?

—You buy them all the time.

—For you. Because they're your favorite.

—I thought we had that in common.

—I don't eat chips.

—Sweet. More for me.

—Look what you did here.

—Yup. We have a bag of potato chips, wine, cheeseburgers, pudding packs, and a head of lettuce.

—You're thoughtful, Vanessa said with a straight face.

—Well, Bruce obliged —it's a special occasion and I wanted to surprise you.

—It was more of a surprise before you had me cook the cheeseburgers.

—I wanted you to have at least one thing homemade. Only the best for my Vanessa.

—So you've told me.

He bit into the cheeseburger, consuming over half the entrée in a single snarf.

—Well?

—Well, what?

Vanessa persisted. —Why are we here?

He wiped his mouth on his sleeve and stood, extending his hand.—Let's take a walk around the pond.

Vanessa had never been to this particular park before. She didn't prefer public property with bodies of water. It was beautiful to behold, but there was always a mild stench from the standing water that made her nostrils restless. Bruce, on the other hand, frequented this location. He loved it so much, he called it "our spot" in a romantic way. He had done the same thing with a song she had yet to hear. The least she could do she thought was to visit "our spot" at least once. Who knows. If he proposed to her here, she may just agree with him.

—Our spot is lovely.

—Oh, you like it too?

—It's growing on me.

—Okay. Here. Bruce stopped at a very specific location and held Vanessa firmly by the shoulders. He stooped down to stare deeply into her eyes.—Vanessa. How long have we been dating?

—A very long time.

—Yes. That's what I think. It's been like five years.

—It's been six years.

—Uh huh. Six. That's like five. You don't have to disagree with me about everything.

—I'm not disagreeing with you. I'm correcting you.

—I think we both understand that we've reached a place where it's time to make an important decision.

—Oh, Bruce!

—So, you're good then.

—Why wouldn't I be?

—Well, I was kinda hesitant at the thought of it, but then she was like, it's for the best.

—Wait, what?

—I've been thinking that our relationship has gotten a bit, you know, dry. What with my shirts not being ironed on Mondays like they used to be and me having to put the seat down and all those things that make you doubt a relationship.

—What are you talking about?

—I didn't notice those things for a long time. I only noticed the good stuff aboutcha: your sour-cream mashed potatoes and the fact that you smell like the candle store. It was like there was a cloud over my eyes, or more like a fog or maybe a fog over just one eye while the other eye had something in it and was watering fierce. But she really helped me see where we need to make some changes.

A mushroom cloud was billowing within Vanessa, threatening to reveal itself out her ears. Vanessa was glad she didn't have the ability to shoot daggers from her eyes she thought lest Bruce already be shred to ribbons.

—*She.* She who?
—Oh. Kathleen.

Vanessa had never heard the name before. Well, of course she had heard the name, it was the third most popular in her book of names for girl babies, but it was going to get crossed off that list this afternoon for sure. She had never, however, heard Bruce speak of Kathleen and she was unaware of a Kathleen in her—or his—life.

—Kathleen? Kathleen who?!
—I met her here. Right here. And you're gonna meet her in just a minute.
—*What?!*
—Now, don't be that way. I was perfectly willing to meet Dorna.
—She's my *sister!* This is your—your—what is she? *What is she?!*
—She's my confidant.
—*Confidant?!*
—Well, that's not quite right. She's more like a guide or a coach. Or a sensei. She's like an alarm clock for the love inside me.

—You—you love her?

—Oh no, not like I love you, Vanessa. You and me, we're special. We're like that pair of pants that you don't throw away because they used to be comfortable even though you can't snap the button anymore. Kathleen's more like the person who buys me some new pants. Like a ninja.

—I—I don't understand. How have I never met her?

—I only see her here.

—Here? At this park?

—Right here. Right dang here. On this very spot.

—You *only* see her on this very spot?

—It's where she first came to me. I think she was attracted to the ring in my hand at the time. You ladies love your bling.

—The engagement ring?

—Dagnab it. Did Kathleen tell you?

—*I don't know Kathleen!* You left the receipt in your jeans pocket. You know, your favorite jeans, the ones you safety-pin shut?

—Thank God. Tell me you saved the receipt. I can't get a refund without it.

—REFUND?!

—That's what I'm trying to tell you. Kathleen showed me the light and that's why we're not getting married.

There was a rumbling, a significant rumbling in the sunlit sky. Something distant and yet unsettling. It made both Vanessa and Bruce stop and gaze into the blue, but there were no clouds, save the stream of a jet plane that connected a straight line across the sky.

Vanessa looked hard at Bruce and told him to explain exactly how they met. Exactly.

He had been in a Brucefunk. They were rare but not unusual, normally arriving at the end of winter. He would consider his last-minute career choice of the gutter-cleaning industry a failure. He would contemplate dying alone of old age in fifty-some-odd years. He would shuffle off and debate how earth had failed him and how all of his friends were happier in better jobs with ladies on their arms who don't ask them to put their underwear in the basket. He thought maybe this spring would bring change. It was a yearly ritual that Vanessa abided, understanding that even shallow demons are real. Bruce had wallowed in his annual sadness a few more days than usual this time and one day, decided that if he wanted happiness, he would have to shove it in the pocket of his cheek like a gobstopper. So, he bought her the engagement ring. It cost a lot, but what's one more credit card? He was on his way home with a gallon of Neapolitan to spring the question on her when he saw the park. He normally stopped to think by locking himself in gas station bathrooms, but there it was easier to get distracted playing online poker on his phone. He saw the pond, and he decided to rend himself of the last iota of sadness on its shore. He had almost finished off the chocolate third of the ice cream when she came to him.

Kathleen.

It was as if someone finally knew what was banging against the inside of his skull. She made him realize that life had indeed been unfair to him. All people had indeed been unfair. He had not chosen lamely in life but rather had lameness thrust upon him. He deserved more. And, the first of these changes would have to begin with the lady who was about to own this sparkly thing, this ring. Kathleen made it clear that Vanessa had not earned it. She had not earned Bruce's love because she did many things wrong. She made moments difficult. It was she who was attempting to turn the ME of Bruce into an US. She must be reprimanded.

It had taken seven visits with Kathleen for Bruce to drum up the courage to bring Vanessa to her. But, he felt he owed it to Vanessa. He knew she loved him as much as he loved her and she deserved at least a fighting chance to change. She deserved an audience with Kathleen, the only way to gain her approval.

—Approval? *Approval?!*

—You're not taking this well. It sounded a lot better when Kathleen was telling me how to say it.

—Bruce, sit.

—I won't sit. I sat whenever my mother wanted to give me a foot massage and I sat when my girlfriends used to pull up a beanbag and I sit whenever you demand that I be still so you can give me a backrub. I'm tired of getting pushed around into chairs. I am taking control of my own life—my own situation.

—You are not. You're just giving the control to a new woman.

—You obviously haven't met Kathleen.

—No. No, I haven't. I haven't met this woman who you believe knows you forward and backward, even though your entire relationship has existed in five square feet of space by this here pond. I, who have nursed you through your surgery, loved you in ups, downs, and the times you so eloquently call "bloated," I have not met the woman who has been manipulating you to betray me.

A distant murmur. Almost that of a crowd, but not down the road or across town. The murmur sounded as if it were beyond the sky—filled with alarm and consternation. And, if Bruce and Vanessa's ears weren't tricking them, was preceded by the faint sound of something ripping.

—She said you would be clouded. She's so funny with her big words. She also said you would be jealous of the truth.

—Oh, I cannot wait to meet this tramp.

—She is *not* homeless and you don't even *know* her.

Vanessa took his head by the ears, palms squeezing him. She brought his eyes to hers. She steadied him, gazed in deep and long. —You're not yourself. You don't realize what you're saying.

—Let me go! She's almost here!

—You're talking polluted! You're a lot of things, Bruce, but none of them would say these words coming from your mouth. Remember when you wanted me to make you that coconut cake and it looked wonderful—it looked more perfect than wonderful—and something tasted off about it and it turned out the coconut manufacturing plant had accidentally filled half the box with laundry detergent and we had to get our stomachs pumped. That's you—and I cannot help but think that Kathleen is where your detergent is coming from.

—You don't know.

—I *do* know, Bruce. And I am the only one in the world who knows Bruce. Whether we were made for each other—designed for each other—or not, we belong to one another now, because we have com-mitted. Remember that? Commitment? I get it. I get your nervousness. Your hesitation. I'm not perfect. I see every detail of you, Bruce, and you see every detail of me and that is a wondrous and explicit thing, but it also has a mother of a downside. Some days all I can see is the seat you left up or the tailgate you left open or how many weeks it's been since we really talked. I see the distance and the awkward minutes and I only hear the many many things you don't say. I can only expect the same from you. But, I am ready to rummage through every flake. I'm willing to separate the coconut into one pile and the detergent into another and learn to tell the difference. What I am *not* willing to do is resign myself to never having coconut cake again.

She broke through. She could see it in his eyes, the more personal she made her diatribe, the more she risked ridicule and having these words used against her, the more his eyes cleared. The more he saw her for who she had always been. When she finished, she released her hand. He pulled his head back, his eyes still transfixed. His head sweating, red imprints of her fingernails on his cheeks and ears. He had the look of an addict who had just been startled alive by a Taser. The frown, the furrowed brow, it all lifted. His eyes became at peace. He looked into her face and said—*Vanessa.*

She knew it had been necessary. She had not realized the depth, but amid loving him, she had built up an immunity to liking him. Her speech was revelatory even to herself. That chasm must be bridged if she were to deserve the ring that moments ago, she indignantly saw as her own.

—I love you, Bruce. And I want to be your wife.

—I don't know what happened to me, Vanessa. It's all true. All true. And I am madly, desperately in *lurkvh*—

His body jerked backwards spastically as if an invisible force sacked him. He flipped sideways high high in the air and came spiraling down like a yard dart on the opposite side of the pond.

Okay she thought.

She ran to him, yelling his name, at first assuming his body had an adverse reaction to his profession of affection. Until, of course, she saw the thing wrapped around his neck.

She hated snakes, but thought it would be rather prudish to proclaim a love-laced diatribe and then wuss out when it came time to rescue her man. She grabbed at the slithering thing as it attempted to wrap around his windpipe—but she could find no end to it. This was not a snake at all she thought. Not at all.

—No worries, Vanessa. He eked it out in a constricted whisper. —It's just a hug, just a friendly embrace. Like a sister.

—What are you talking about?

—Kathleen.

Not a snake but a tentacle and Kathleen arose out of the pond's darkness and scum. No, she *was* the pond's darkness and scum. A half ton of her, slithering amphibious mass with tentacles and spikes and a fiery tongue, smelling like the paper factory when the wind shifts east. A head with a hundred eyes rising out of the murk and bleakness. She was not a *she*. She was a *thing*. A monstrosity that appeared rather unpleased with Vanessa, hurtling out of the water in her direction, waving Bruce above her like an ornament on a car antenna.

Vanessa instinctively ran like fire, bolting away, but Kathleen was a torment, fast and sleek. She shot the edge of one of her feelers downward toward Vanessa like a scorpion might sting and slashed the back of her left thigh. Vanessa writhed, diving into the recesses of the playground climbing structure where Kathleen's beefy appendages began bashing away at the treated wood, unable to get through to her. Kathleen howled as the wood splintered and stuck like toothpicks into her calloused flesh. She shook Bruce violently in retribution, as a crocodile might an antelope.

—WHAT IS GOING ON, BRUCE?!

—I don't think she thought your speech was very sincere.

—ARE YOU CRAZY NUTS?! She's a MONSTER! She's a DEMON!

—You've barely gotten to know her, Bruce said as Kathleen squeezed so hard she cracked one of his ribs. —Ow. Insincerity kinda riles her up.

—I think anything that might take you away from her kinda riles her up!

—This is completely platonic.

—I DON'T think she's looking for a DATE, Bruce. I think she's looking for a MEAL.

—She's not my type. But, that doesn't mean she didn't have some reasonable suggestions.

Kathleen changed tactics and began shooting spikes out of a haunch on her back. It made it difficult for her to aim, and the javelin-sized weapons shish-kabobed the rockety horses on the preschool lawn.

—She wants to kill me, Bruce!

—Well, what are you looking at me for?! You're the one who ticked her off with your manipulation.

—Manipulation?! I was sincere!

—Sure you were. You're always sincere when you can't get me to do what you want, and I believe you because I know you love me. I do. And I believe that you think what you're saying is a new beginning. I do. But, I also know it's not gonna last. Because having me love you back is not always the thing you're trying to get me to do. Soon enough, I'll forget to say I love you the moment you need me to, or I'll move in to kiss you when you're not in the mood, or I'll forget to fix the one thing you deem most important while fixing three other things that don't matter to you. And it will be all that you see. And this moment, this moment that changed us temporarily will be erased from our memory.

—I DON'T THINK THIS MOMENT WILL BE ERASED FROM MY MEMORY.

—You won't be able to see how my love is growing. Every single dang day, I see more clearly who you are and I love it, but it also frustrates the fool out of me and just when I think I've got the words to say it, the distance grows.

—So, this is all me?! ALL ME?!

—Of course not! You're not listening. It's mostly—

But, Kathleen did not like this at all. She decided to utilize a new weapon to obtain her prey. She decided to use Bruce himself. Still grasping him like a sledgehammer, she thrust Bruce's body down into the climbing structure, it finally splintering into a hundred pieces. Bruce landed in the grass like a wet rag doll, and Vanessa was exposed.

Vanessa ran to Bruce, who mumbled incoherently about excusing his emotional tirade today because he's pretty sure his blood sugar is low.

Kathleen saw Vanessa touching Bruce's chest, caring for him, and let out a hideous banshee shriek, shooting her tongue toward Vanessa like a flaming missile. Vanessa reacted fast, dodging only slightly but grabbing onto the tongue itself as it retracted.

Vanessa found herself hurtling through the air, the stench of Kathleen's acrid breath increasing rapidly. As the mouth became a cave, Vanessa let go and landed rather harshly onto Kathleen. She hung from two of the spikes, one fist wrapped around each. She was just beneath Kathleen's chin. Kathleen was bucking wildly, Vanessa's feet knocking against her throat. This was causing Kathleen to retch and Vanessa was able to feel the tender spot in her trachea. She considered kicking harder, but Kathleen bucked one last time and flung Vanessa into the water playzone. A large slab of concrete, completely exposed.

It took Kathleen a moment to reorient herself. Vanessa stood absolutely still, considering a sprint to where Bruce's unconscious body lay—but Kathleen was already on alert. She snorted and shook violently, scampering in a serpentine pattern looking for her lunch. Vanessa did not move.

In the brief respite, Vanessa noticed again the distant rumbles like thunder, the faint ripping sound, the ethereal voices speaking as if from the skies. But before she had a moment to consider these sounds, Kathleen saw her.

Another roar as she reared up on her hind end and charged toward the water playzone. Vanessa was stunned. Her left leg was ablaze inside from the gash; Kathleen was between her and Bruce, and there was nothing—nothing to shield her from the oncoming wrath. This is it she thought and closed her eyes, clenching her fists, imagining all the ways she had feared her relationship with Bruce might end, and yet never quite anticipating this option.

Kathleen was within yards now. Vanessa could hear it, feel it as the ground vibrated and swelled around her—and then.

Phhhhhssssssst!

Kathleen screeched, stopping thunderously in her tracks.

Vanessa opened her eyes, soaked to the bone. The sprinklers had come on. The waterfalls and mists and attractions of the waterzone crafted rainbows out of the sunlit sky. Kathleen reared back, eyes the size of china dishes. She retreated a half-dozen feet and began pacing in wait.

It dawned on Vanessa that, pond creature though she was, Kathleen could not bear *fresh water*. She thrived on the scum and stagnation of water that never flows, never moves along the rushing streams, never purifies.

This is us she thought as Kathleen paced around the circumference of the waterzone, waiting out the timers on the attraction. Our love requires the painful rush of the water over the stones and twigs though we might resist it she thought. I saw my dissatisfaction as an indication that I was superior to Bruce, that he needed my affection in order to fix him. Bruce saw the pain as a reason to make it all end. We were both wrong. It takes all of it, all the hesitations, habits, irritations, failures—it takes seeing all of that, ramming into all of that full force, and then loving anyway. That is the thing. The thing she hates. Kathleen wants the stagnant, the gross, the relationship with scum and scabs where each retreats to their corner, never growing or changing—only resenting the pain. Bruce needs me, but more surprisingly, I need Bruce. To keep me raw and fresh and real. No. Not to keep me. To *make me more.* We rub off on one another to keep each other human. To know and be known. To discover a love deeper than the one in all the storybooks where the prince slays the dragon. That's what Kathleen detests. And that's why she's about to tear us both limb from limb.

The sprinklers stopped. The timer ended. The mucous-laden razorous pit that Kathleen used as a mouth emoted a snide smile, and Vanessa knew it was over.

She just now figured out this relationship, and the next time she and Bruce would be together, it would be as a jumble of bones in a lump of leviathan dung. Is that irony or is that apropos? Probably neither.

Oh well she thought. The picnic was a nice thought.

Kathleen arched her back and scrubbed the ground with her chin, snarling and preparing to pounce upon Vanessa.

Vanessa stood her ground, closed her eyes, clenched her fists, and thought—just thought—for one more chance to make this right with Bruce, just one more chance, I'll take anything, any option you've got, no qualifiers. I knew we were special once. Special. Just like anybody who chooses to love. In this absolute scenario where there is no reasonable way out, I'll accept any old act of God.

And darkness began to fall.

A terror from the heavens.

It shushed like a fire mixed with a torrential rain, startling Vanessa out of her moment and causing both she and Kathleen to look upward into the afternoon sky.

RIIIIIIIIIIIIIIIIIIIIIIIP!

The sky was torn open vertically from top to bottom, literally ripped like a sheet of paper. Vanessa grew wide-eyed and fell backward to the ground as Kathleen skittered, fearful, rushing to Bruce and hovering over him, her easiest kill. The sky ripped outward top to bottom like a V and then, in the crease of the destruction: a face. An angry, tightly wound face of a woman, seemingly at the end of herself, staring down with fervor, muttering something about "special" having consequences.

The world began folding in on them, the pond rising to their west side, the playground being crushed into heaps of scrap metal. Kathleen squealed and gripped Bruce in her jaw. Vanessa held on tightly to the sprinkler bar as the ground turned ninety degrees and became a wall of dirt from which she hung. And then, ridges and hillsides formed, up becoming down, the world crushing in on itself. This place—them—it was all being crumpled up like a discarded piece of paper.

As the pond water rained down upon them from above, covering them with slime and overgrowth, Kathleen lost her footing. She was slick, scum-laden, and unable to maneuver the crevices and land shifts. Vanessa realized she finally had the upper hand and leaped from apex to apex, crushed corner to crumpled mesh. She dove underneath as the jungle gym folded above her, mashed into a hundred separate things. A single metallic rod snapped off, sharp at both edges. Vanessa grabbed it and sprinted hell-bent toward Kathleen.

Out of her element, Kathleen scraped away from Vanessa, gripping at whatever could give her balance, her tail squeezed between folds, tugging to free herself. She hissed and seethed, Bruce hanging unconscious from her drooling maw.

Vanessa caught up and leaped atop her tail, scaling her to the neck and attempting to beat her over the head with the metal pole, but it was like trying to break open a stone piñata with a drinking straw. Kathleen wriggled her head, flailing her tail, attempting to swat Vanessa off of her. Vanessa turned the metal rod on its end and attempted to stab the monster in the head, but Kathleen's tail caught her, throwing her off-balance, and the sharp edge instead sunk deeply into Kathleen's shoulder.

Kathleen yelped angrily and hurled Bruce from her mouth, his body catching onto a folded precipice. Vanessa's body, too, was thrown and Kathleen whirled around, fumes snorting out her nostrils. Kathleen's eyes were death notices, her legs ready to pounce. Vanessa stood her ground and met the creature's gaze.

—I'm not afraid of you—because I know now where you come from.

Kathleen hissed from deep in her throat. She paced an arc around Vanessa, searching for sure footing from which to pounce.

—I thought you were a demon, but now I get it. You're not from hell. You're just from us. Bruce and I did this. Our relationship built you. I'm not afraid of you, Kathleen, because you are mine.

Raging, Kathleen closed her eyes in concentration and grunted hard. There was a creak and then a pop as what appeared to be decrepit and disintegrating wings separated themselves from her back, unfurling as scales and scabs fell to the ground. She howled in fury. These wings hadn't been used in a while. She must want to get to me pretty dang badly Vanessa thought.

Vanessa stood solid, no weapon in her hand, and awaited the inevitable. Kathleen sprung in flight, and was midair between her launching point and Vanessa when suddenly—suddenly—gravity ceased to work. The two of them hung midair for a fleeting moment. Then, reality reversed and Kathleen began flitting and falling the other way, the way from which she had leaped. Vanessa, too, lost her footing and was falling forward atop Kathleen. Their world had been lifted, weightless, hurtling toward something. All began to grow stifling hot as the sky above them shifted from blue to black and the heavens alit with fire.

Actual fire. The sky was becoming a black mesh, the sort of texture you would find in, say, an office trash can, and all around them was ablaze. They stopped moving with a jarring thud. The sky became the ground beneath them as Vanessa hung from the crumpled heap she had just been standing upon. Her world was upside down and she was about to be sucked into the blaze.

Vanessa glanced about in a panic. Where was Bruce?! He must have fallen—but no, he couldn't … she refused to acknowledge the awful truth, knowing full well that everything between her and the horizon had fallen into the blaze.

Everything except for Kathleen.

The creature moved sleekly along the ceiling ground, talons, spikes, and claws holding her aloft. She moved slowly and steadily toward Vanessa, her eyes daunting but without motion. Her prey was finished, no options remaining.

Vanessa met her stare, considering all the tiny changes she could have made in their six-year journey, all the choices that could have averted this disaster.

Of course, the sky ripping open, the crumpling, the fire—those were probably unavoidable either way.

Kathleen reached her face-to-face, the aroma unbearable. She did not attack immediately, but rather met Vanessa's gaze as if to say *look who gets the man this time*. And Vanessa was satisfied. She would meet her end, yes, but she would meet it along with Bruce. She would meet it with clarity, the first time she had that in almost a decade. Let Kathleen have her day. Vanessa would still be with Bruce in the end, charred reunion though it might be.

Kathleen reared every weapon on her natural armor: the talons, the tongue, the spikes, the tail—all ready to strike, her eyes locked on Vanessa's face.

Vanessa closed her eyes softly.

Shink.

A gargled wail broke the silence as if all the universe's ghosts from dead relationships past emoted a yowl all at once. Vanessa opened her eyes just in time to see Kathleen roll back upon herself, blood spouting from her throat, a gaping hole in the soft spot.

She released her talons and tumbled headlong, grasping for the pain on her neck, swatting at it like a mosquito. She folded upon herself frontward and backward, headfirst into the inferno, bursting into a blaze that reeked of sewage and then, in a spectacular expulsion of carnage, separated into a dozen pieces, finally devolving into ash.

Kathleen was gone.

Vanessa turned to her vanquisher. It was Bruce, hanging by one arm, a long, bloody red spear in the other.

—Where did you come from?
—I climbed the wall of the can. At least it felt like a can. That's where I got this thing. It's really heavy.
—I don't think we'll need it any more.

Bruce dropped the weapon, an enormous red ink pen, back into the blaze from which he had pulled it.

And just as neither Bruce nor Vanessa could hold on for one moment more, their world righted itself, pulled up, out, and away from the fire. The sky turned blue again, the ground stable and smoothed as if by an unseen hand. They were back where they started, only without the cheeseburgers.

—I'm so sorry, Vanessa.
—No, Bruce. I'm sorry.
—No, Vanessa. I'm—
Vanessa stopped him there.—Maybe we should just back up and start again. Differently.

He looked at her with love. There wasn't really room to begin again. The park still stood, but the pond and playground were gone. It was all raw and barren. Not because of a clean slate, but because of all they had just been through.

273

—I'm Bruce.

—I'm Vanessa.

Though crumpled and singed at the edges, they stood upon a blank page.

THE VERY LAST SANDWICH IN THE ENTIRE WORLD

Downtown was dead.

And the whole wide world was just about to join it.

Not a soul to be seen nor heard, save two.

Two men were dressed for success, if smackdowns could be considered successful.

Identical tailored suits all the way to the buttoned-up vests and suspenders.

Why suspenders? Why not? This was war.

War over what? Thank you for asking.

There, at the abandoned intersection of 12th and Valencia, sat an object:

Five inches square in the crossing of two one-way streets.

'Twas the sandwich.

Both men knew of its existence, each yearning to stake the claim.

All hell was about to break loose.

The sun glinted off the face of the aluminum foil wrapping,

A signal fire for the battle at hand.

A war cry emanated from the man in the Taupe suit at 11th and Richmond.

Another yawp from the gentleman in the Auburn suit

Rolling off the awning of the Ginsberg Building.

Each a quarter mile

From the object they had sought so hard so long so far so good.

They ran at one another like kamikazes, hell bent on a collision

—the sandwich at its crux.

They ran.

Ran. Ran. Ran. Haha.

To lock horns had they had horns.

Like bullets from a gun attached to another gun aimed back at that first gun.

Set upon one another like a fury that would leave the other but dust.

Like sneezes.

And so forth.

—My sandwich, said Taupe.

—My sandwich, claimed Auburn.

—MY sandwich, countered Taupe.

—I DO NOT CONCUR! It is MY sandwich!

Taupe was first to approach the sandwich, faster,

Having cross-trained with a focus on cardio.

His arm outstretched, hand taut, fingers nunchakus.

The entrée almost his.

But of course Auburn pulsed.

Handsmack upon fist, then palms outstretched.

Invisible energy shot out of his fingers like they taught us in third grade.

Before we didn't believe them.

VWONG. Like microphone feedback. Seriously.

Taupe was shot backward feet-over-face into a billboard,

The sandwich unmoving.

He was back on his feet in a nanosecond, fist to hand,

Returning an energy blow to fend the insult.

He arched his back and thrust his left palm forward,

Auburn dodging the pulse as it took a chunk out of a nearby building.

Auburn had a tender grace about the physicality of his fighting.

Taupe just looked stupid.

I hate to say it because he's already got the lazy eye but there it is.

Awkward.

Nerd.

Given the option, one would choose Auburn first

In kickball.

Four more pulses.

Taupe, Auburn, Auburn, Taupe. Then they ran out of carrots.

Just when it gets good they always run out of carrots.

They eye each other in a panic and glance around their surroundings frantically.

Ah, THERE!

An abandoned roadside vegetable stand.

Why?

I dunno. Again: war.

They each sprint to the carrots and begin munching them like rabid animals,

All the while staring each other down with battlelust

Which is a word I just now coined.

With each new downed carrot,

Auburn and Taupe snap their fingers to check for sparks.

Taupe is reenergized first. He claps and pulses again. Haha.

I'm sorry. The way Taupe moves just makes me snicker.

Auburn dives for cover, a carrot stub still protruding from his lips.

Rubble flies.

Auburn gets one more good shot in. He misses Taupe and hits an automobile.

It is destroyed in a ball of white-hot flame

And another car's security alarm begins to beep.

Annoying. Hate that.

Both Taupe and Auburn are exhausted now,

Out of energy pulses again.

Suckers.

They breathe heavily, bracing themselves.

They eye the vegetable cart. No more carrots.

Auburn pulls out his car keys and turns off the car alarm.

Oh. It was his. My bad.

He stares.

The other he stares.

They both make an all-out sprint for the sandwich.

They reach the sandwich simultaneously, each hurtling toward it at the same time. Their collision causes both to miss. Fisticuffs ensue.

It is not very impressive. Slaps, bites, and sloppy punches.

I wish they had more carrots.

You really should see the way the energy shoots out of their palms

When they have enough carrots.

Very cool.

But, hand-to-hand—not really their milieu.

Just sad.

Finally, depleted, they cease,

Lying next to each other and breathing heavily.

The sandwich between them.

Auburn reaches slowly for it.

But Taupe grabs his wrist.

—Touch my sandwich and I'll kill you, Taupe states convincingly.

—You know, I don't believe we've met.

—Hello. I am Man.

—What a coincidence, observes Auburn —I am also Man.

—What a coincidence. So am I.

—What a coincidence.

—Yes, what a coincidence. I mean that we are both Man.

—What a coincidence.

—Now that I look, you do seem familiar. Are you certain we haven't met?

—Yes. Yes. Quite certain.

—Because you look amazingly like my brother.

—That so? You know, now that I think of it, you would look exactly like my brother, had I ever seen him before.

—But, think no more of it. That couldn't be, for my brother's name was Man.

—What a coincidence. My brother's name was also Man, had I had one.

—What a coincidence. My name is Man.

—What a coincidence. So is my brother's.

—Amazing. One world, and we're all Man.

—Except for my sister. She is called Woman.

—Amazing! My sister is also called Woman! But, she has passed.

—As well as mine. She was killed while fighting over the very last corncob in the entire world.

—You don't say!

—Yes, I did.

—Well, don't say it again.

—Now I have all the corn, but no Woman to show for it.

—Too much sadness.

—Too much corn. So I suppose we are brothers.

—Not at all. My Woman was killed fighting over the very last corncob holder in the entire world.

—Ah, then the similarities have stopped.

—But the fight has not!

—Give me my sandwich!

—You mean my sandwich.

—Of course I mean my sandwich!

—But I have a bill of purchase.

Taupe unfurls what is indeed a bill of purchase for something. Very long. Very impressive.

—And so have I.

Auburn's bill of purchase is longer.

But less impressive.

Larger font.

—How could we have both bought the same very last sandwich?

—We couldn't have.

They exchange and review.

—Ah ha! Taupe exclaimed. —You did not dot your *i*'s!

—There are no *i*'s in Man.

—What a coincidence! There are no *i*'s in my Man either!

—Proven, Auburn observes. —Man hath no *i*'s.

—And you hath no sandwich.

Another sprint to the sandwich.

Why? War. I'm a little tired of explaining that.

Auburn reaches. Taupe steps on his hand. Snapping knuckles.

Auburn howls in pain as they both drop to the ground,

Face-to-face directly over the sandwich.

—Try that again, Auburn threatens —and I will take off my clothes and roll on the sandwich.

—No!

—I will lose a hair in it.

—No!

—Then—I will say foul words!

The world stands still.

Taupe holds his breath, pregnant with concern

Over what would come out of Auburn's mouth next.

—Foul words! Foul words! Auburn wails. —FOUL! FOUL! FILTH! Extremely foul word!

—ARRRRRRNGH! Stop it! Stop it! Stop it! Taupe relents. —Have you no decency? Have you no humanity? Have you no heart?

—That depends, Auburn offers. —Have you no sandwich?

—You do not understand. I have traveled the world searching for this: the very last sandwich in the entire world. I have climbed mountains. I have swum oceans. I have braved deserts.

—Why?

—I forgot where it was.

—I am not interested in what you did for this sandwich.

—Are you interested in what I can give for it?

—No. What?

—My entire life.

—Your entire life?

—For starters.

—For a sandwich?

—For the very last sandwich.

—Well, I can give more than my life.

—And that is?

—The lives of my family.

—Ha! That's nothing! That's less than nothing. That's not a thing. That's no thing.

—No thing?

—I would give all that I am for this sandwich.

—All that you am?

—You see, with this sandwich, all the world is at my mercy. All the world needs me. I would have the POWER OF THE SANDWICH!

—There would be other food.

—Yes, but no sandwiches.

—Ah, I see.

—So, alas, we both have need of the exact same very last sandwich.

—Ah, if there were only a way we both could have the exact same very last sandwich.

—We cannot. It is why we are at war.

—My my. That sounds manly.

—My my?

—What what?

—You say my my as if this battle is yours yours.

—No no. Well, maybe. Which reminds me. Perhaps we should know exactly what sandwich we are dealing with.

—You mean?

—Yes, the manner of sandwich.

—I never considered that. Remarkable.

—Well, thank you.

—Yes. I wonder what kind of sandwich it is.

—And, how do we find out?

—Why, we could open it.

—No, no! There has to be a more clever way.

—A more clever way to identify a sandwich?

—Man! You've hit it right on the head!

—What? What have I hit?

—You said there is a more clever way to identify a sandwich!

—My my.

—Yes. Your your.

—You said it first.

—Yes, but you reassured me! You are remarkable!

—Well, thank you.

—We will smell the sandwich!

—It could be thousands of years old!

—That is why you must smell your sandwich.

—You just said it was yours.

—Only after you said my my.

—But it isn't mine mine!

—You claimed it!

—I didn't claim the smell!

—You claim the power, you claim the smell!

—If I smell it, will it belong to me?

—That depends.

—On what?

—On what it smells like.

—All right.

Taupe leans down tentatively.

He seizes his Tuesday tweezers out of his vest pocket

And peels back the teeniest corner of the aluminum.

He brings his nose within a centimeter.

He sniffs.

—Soooo. What does it smell like?

—It smells like al …

He collapses.

War.

—Man?

Auburn had seen many well-dressed men die.

This was his first war, of course. His first battle.

But he watched a lot of television.

He had never seen someone fade to nothingness so fast

As if death was an urgent matter,

An appointment.

Taupe lay there, a victim of toxicity.

Auburn took his Wednesday tweezers out of his vest pocket

And checked under Taupe's eyelid.

It was a day early for Wednesday tweezers,

But this was an emergency.

Taupe sat bolt upright.

—… batross!

—What? replies Auburn.

—It smells like albatross, states Taupe.

—I assumed you were dead.

—What a coincidence. So did I.

—Oh Man.

—What what?

—Did you say albatross?

—What a coincidence. I did say albatross, Man.

—I am allergic to albatross.

—How would you know?

—I was stranded on a desert island with a blind man. Long story.

—I see.

—So I am allergic.

—What a coincidence. I am not.

—Oh Man.

—Then, I suppose you shall discontinue your manly-sounding war.

—Absolutely not.

—But you cannot eat this sandwich.

—I do not want to eat it. I want to have it.

—What good is having when eating is out of the question?

—Having the sandwich is not about me eating it. It is about you not eating it.

—Seems irrational and unfair.

—A life lesson.

—Ahh, ahhed Auburn.

—So I MUST have the sandwich.

—Ah ah ah. You gave me the sandwich.

—I most certainly did not.

—You said depending on the sandwich, the sandwich would be mine, Taupe heralded.—The sandwich inevitably was albatross, which you were inevitably allergic to. Albeit that was a coincidence, thus making this sandwich very dependent.

—Ah ha! But you said that the sandwich was given to you by me?

—Certainly.

—Which means that you accept the fact that the sandwich was mine to give.

—Probably.

—In which case, I take the sandwich back.

—You cannot do that.

—I can do whatever I please. I make the rules.

—Why do you make the rules?

—Because I own the sandwich.

—Foul word.

—So, logically, legally, and even coincidentally, the very last sandwich belongs to me.

—Not altogether, debates Taupe.

—And why not altogether? questions Auburn.

—I touched it last.

—You what?

—I touched it last.

—That is childish!

—I am childish. I touched it last.

—Yes, but I touched the actual sandwich last.

—What do you mean the actual sandwich?

—You only touched the wrapping. I touched the actual sandwich 'neath the wrapping.

—When did you do this?

—When you were unconscious.

—I don't believe you.

—You don't have to believe me. I make the rules.

—Well, it doesn't matter.

—What?

—It doesn't matter that you were the last to touch the actual sandwich because I was the last to touch the almost actual sandwich while we were both conscious, which is a new rule!

—New rule?

—Very new.

—So, you were the last to touch it?

—The very last.

Auburn taps it with his foot.

—Were not.

Taupe taps it with his foot.

—Was too.

—Mine!

—Mine!

They tap and claim, claim and tap.

The nonbrutality of it all quite tedious and cumbersome.
A bit of a yawner of a war.
Not that anyone else downtown was paying attention
Except the one fellow in the window of the sixth story.
But still.
And then, She arrives.
Her clothing is neither Auburn nor Taupe and yet both plus.
She speeds into the intersection as if out of nowhere,
Though in reality it was more than likely out of somewhere.
She speeds in.
She speeds out.
From some faraway place.
But in between in and out, she stomps on the sandwich.
It means much to her.
And yet nothing.
She wants it destroyed
And only hers.
It means everything.
The albatross sandwich.
But she cannot quite recall why.
Taupe and Auburn stare in collective awe—awfully.
—Look! Look what you've done! accused Auburn or it may have
been Taupe
(does it matter? the answer is no.)
—What? What have I done?
—You've provoked that woman to stomp on my sandwich.
—You mean my sandwich.
—Of course I mean my sandwich!

—Oh agony! Will it never end, this sandwich-themed bickering?

—But it must end. Eventually, eventually … maybe sooner.

—How?

—There is one way!

—That one way being?

—A game of chance.

—You are mad.

—Yes! Yes! A last resort! A contest, a gamble, if you will.

—You would dare gamble on something as important as a sandwich?

—Man, my man, you cannot expect to win except through losing.

—Then how should I expect to lose?

—You should never expect to lose.

—Then, I shall expect to win!

—Oh, I don't expect that.

—What game of chance?

—Have you a deck of cards?

—No.

—A roulette wheel?

—Not on me.

—A gun and one bullet?

—I certainly have not.

—A coin?

—What a coincidence! I have a coin.

—No matter. I have one as well.

—Then, we shall have a coin toss!

—Are you ready?

—Wait! How will we decide which coin to toss?

—We will draw straws.

—Who will draw first?

—We will toss a coin.

—Ah.

—Call it.

—Yes? What?

—Heads or tails?

—Excuse me?

—Choose a side of the coin!

—Am I choosing which side faces up or which side faces down?

—You are choosing which side faces up.

—And who made that decision?

—Choose!

—Heads! Facing up!

But the coin does not make it to the ground.

It could not. It lingers midtoss, frozen within the spin.

Taupe and Auburn also find themselves incapable of movement,

Save their eyeballs, of course.

When will someone figure out how to freeze the eyeballs as well?

Oh science.

You can harness the destructive power of carrots,

But cannot freeze one simple eyeball.

Irony.

The culprit is the She.

As they linger in tableau

Like the end credits of a television program

She saunters between them

as if out of nowhere (again: somewhere).
She wears a bowler hat
Which (let's face it) is a fashion mistake.
She pockets the coin,
Scoops up the albatross sandwich
Which is barely held together by its foil.
Taupe and Auburn gape at her or at least their eyeballs do.
Hard to tell otherwise.
She stands behind the vegetable cart
Which has somehow transformed into an auction table.
She bangs a gavel.
The men are unfrozen.

—Look! Look what you've done!

—What? What have I done?

—You have provoked someone to do something with my sandwich!

—You mean my sandwich.

—Of course I mean my sandwich!

—Auction! She declares.

—Did she just say auction?

—Auction! She repeats.

—Oh, I just love a good auction!

—Just what are you auctioning off this morning, auctioneer?

—One dependent and slightly trampled hypoallergenic albatross sandwich in unmicrowavable wrapping.

—We'll take it!

—Hold on! She interrupts.—This is an auction. What would you give for this sandwich?

—We would give anything!

—What would you do for this sandwich?

—We would do anything!

—Would you give anything?

—Anything!

—Would you do anything?

—Anything!

—Because, I don't know if I should let a handy and valuable item like this go.

—Let it go! Let it go!

—You don't understand! We had this very "very last" sandwich once and lost it! Our need for this sandwich is unsurpassed!

—What if I asked you to kill your friend? She asked.

—Anything.

—What if I asked you to kill yourself?

—The moment I had the sandwich.

—What if I asked you to betray your family?

—Done.

—What if I asked you for two left shoes?

—But—

—I don't have two left shoes.

—That is my price! she declared. —Two left shoes! I must have two left shoes!

—Why two left shoes?

—Because I must must must have them!

—But nobody has two left shoes.

—I've got a lot of left shoes, She said.

—Then why do you need two more?

—I've got more than a lot of right ones.

—Oh agony! The sandwich, mere inches from my hand, and me with only one left shoe.

—HOLD ON! Providence! I have a left shoe!

—What good does one left shoe do you?

—Nothing at all!

—You see!

—But, with my left and your left, two wrongs make a right! See?

—I do see! Auctioneer, here are your shoes!

—Here is your sandwich. Be careful.

She is gone.

Half-barefoot, they hold the sandwich between them.

—Why did he say be careful?

—He?

—Yes, he.

—He was a she.

—He was not a she.

—She was not a he. She was the sandwich-stomper.

—He was the sandwich-stomper?

—*She* was the sandwich-stomper.

—Implausible. She had a hat.

—What a coincidence. She looked remarkably like my dead sister, had she looked like a man.

—What a coincidence. My dead sister was a man.

—No matter. Give me the sandwich. It is mine.

They grapple.

The sandwich smushed betwixt the two of them and leveled by the earth.

Is smushed a word?

I suppose anything can be a word when you're at war

Except smushed probably.

They roll. They roil.

Sweat pours. Grunting and whatnot.

Finally, they stand, the sandwich belonging to both of them and neither.

—It! Is! Mine! declared Taupe, rather emphatically.

—Under what authority?

—The authority of owning the bigger half!

—How do you figure that you own the bigger half?

—I have a bigger foot, hence, a bigger shoe, hence, the bigger half.

—Yes, well I gave the second shoe, thus obtaining the second half, which is logically always the larger half.

—Under whose logic?

—Under yours.

—How do you figure that?

—I don't.

—Foul word.

—Then we have established nothing! We know no more whose sandwich the very last is than before!

—On the contrary, we now know that the sandwich is definitely either mine or yours. Before, it simply should have been.

—Then, how are we to finalize the matter?

—A game of chance.

—She took my coin.

—No. The ultimate chance.

—Being?

—A shootout.

—I don't follow you.

—You're following me now.

—I meant figuratively.

—But I'm walking in a circle and you're right behind me.

—I mean I'm not following what you *mean*.

—I don't understand.

—Precisely.

—The last alive obtains the sandwich. No more argument.

—That is the first sensible idea you've had today.

—Why, thank you.

—However, due to an expected lack of thinking, we have forgotten a useful tool.

—Being?

—Weapons.

She appears.

—Weapons for sale! She declares.

—What a coincidence!

—Are you gentlemen in need of firearms?

—As a matter of fact, we are in desperate need of these two very pieces of weaponry that you have before you.

—Well, it just so happens that I am willing to let them go at a very reasonable price.

—And what price is that?

—Two left shoes.

—But—we already gave you our left shoes.

—I'm sorry. Two left shoes. I must must must have them. That is my price.

—Kind madam and fine madam, is there *nothing* else of worth to you?

—Well—if I must settle …

—Yes? Yes!

—I suppose I could take all of your—

—Yes?! Yes?! *Anything!*

—carrots.

Taupe and Auburn stare one another in the eye.

Hmm.

—A sidebar.

They skitter.

They consider surrendering their life force.

—What would he want in the carrots?

—What would *she* want in the carrots? And I'm stumped. Other than the source of all of our virility and power, they hold virtually no value.

—True. Except for essential vitamins and minerals.

—Agreed. And you could stab someone with the pointy end.

—Yet we have no more.

—Not entirely true for I am just now recalling a significant stash hidden away in my vest lining.

—That you did not feel as we scuffled heartily?

—Adrenaline and whatnot.

—Which prompts me to remember the baker's dozen of carrots nestled in the knife strap attached to my thigh.

—Those could have come in handy.

—Yes.

—And the knife as well.

—Goes without saying.

—So—we surrender the carrots, we receive the sandwich. She holds all the power in the world, but we have our albatross to continue to war over.

—That word war is so overused. I prefer to consider this a healthy disagreement.

—With violence.

—Yes. Right. That's why I said healthy.

—I see no downside.

They return to the Barter swiftly,

Eager to solidify the transaction

Before she changes her mind.

—Here are our carrots.

—Here are your guns.

—It is appreciated.

—And what are the guns to be used for?

—To snuff out one another's lives.

—Albatross has that effect. Well—I must go. Be careful.

She did.

They didn't.

—Why did she say "be careful"?

—Superstitious fool. What harm ever came from guns?

—Or albatross?

—Except that one time on the island.

—Goes without saying.

—How must we conduct the shootout?

—We will walk paces, turn, and fire.

—Who decides the paces?

—I do.

—And who decided that?

—We will count TEN PACES!

—What a coincidence! I was just going to say TEN PACES!

—Now we must turn and count them.

—Count what?

—The paces!

—Oh yes, the paces. Say, if I lose, it was a lovely battle.

—Yes, same to you.

—Oh, and if I win, it was a lovely battle.

—Yes, same to you. Turn.

—One, two, three, TEN!

Neither counts to ten.

Taupe and Auburn turn and fire simultaneously.

Auburn hits Taupe in the leg, opening a major artery.

Aren't they all major?

Only if you don't want to hurt the artery's feelings.

Taupe hits Auburn in the spleen.

Funny word spleen.

Except right now, of course.

They both hit the pavement.

They begin to bleed out.

Both suits ruined.

They crawl wearily, soiling the pavement red, scraping at the concrete, pulling themselves toward the albatross sandwich.

Each reach arm outstretched, hand taut, fingers nunchakus.

—I—said—ten.

—What—a coincidence. So—did I.

Inches from the sandwich

So handsome

They die.

She arrives as if out of somewhere

And tends to the sandwich,

Sweeping it into a dustpan and shuffling its remains into the refuse pile.

She then sits on the hood of Taupe's car,

Rubs her fist to her palm

And sends out an enormous blast of energy.

VWONG. Like microphone feedback.

A pulsating force directed at the Hardaway Building.

And she watches as it begins to tumble to the ground.

MOBRIGGER BRIDGE

Oliver ruminated on the askew screw. A useless and delightful thing. He twirled it between his left thumb and forefinger. He liked the way the inconsistency of its bent caused it to roll farther down his thumb as it pivoted.

—Throw that'n away, Todd said. —It's worthless.

Oliver rolled his eyes at another ignorant missive from Todd Hobbs. That's right. Todd Hobbs of Todd Hobbs' Odd Jobs. You've seen the commercial. Oliver is the one smiling in the background behind the wheel of the van. Todd made him give a thumbs-up in the commercial. Oliver didn't like that.

Oliver thought the screw a sad sort of thing. He had just removed it from where it had once served a purpose: securing the top of a screen door. Over time, it had rusted, bent under the strain of all the slammings—become more of an annoyance than a benefit. It was no longer capable of being a screw. Oliver knew Todd was right: he should toss it aside—or rather, into a garbage receptacle. A screw in the grass was a lawn mower accident waiting to happen, and Oliver was quite determined to avoid being the conduit for an accident. Oliver was, by nature, quite careful.

Todd was saying that Oliver was not listening to him. But Oliver was. Always. Unless, of course, the Other Voice was trying to tell Oliver something at the time. Right now, Todd was going on and on about the screw being defective, knowing full well that that's why Oliver wanted to hang on to it. Oliver tucked the crooked item into the chest pocket of his coveralls—another souvenir to a job well done.

Oliver was finished with the screen door, and so he bent it this way and that to illustrate that it no longer caught at the top. Miss Ottanot (the customer) clapped her tiny hands like a prayer and whisper-squealed her delight. The door had aggravated her for as long as she could remember. The sound of it scraping the top of the metal jamb had been horrendous, and when she threw the force of her shoulder against it to pry it open as she so often did, it would rattle like a bedspring. She leaned into Oliver to kiss him on the cheek in gratitude.

—For fixing it so well, Miss Ottanot offered.

But Oliver jerked backward before contact. Todd corrected her.

—Sorry. He don't like to be touched. And he never says anything.

—Oh. Would you care to see my gun collection? I'm just about to clean my Colt M1911. It's a dandy. Just precious.

—No thank you, miss'm—but we do accept personal checks.

Women were always leaning into Oliver. He was told he was quite handsome, and considered it a great nuisance. That sort of business seemed a bit of a waste of time. Todd assumed Oliver had no need for love. But Oliver was bursting with love. He just didn't see the purpose of affection. Todd liked to call Oliver simple. Simple is the go-to word for an individual who resists vocabulary. Oliver did not speak. He was concerned that if he spoke, he would not be able to listen. And if he could not listen, he might miss the Other Voice when it gave him an important instruction, which seemed to be quite often these days.

Oliver lived by the Other Voice. Somehow it brought him peace, even though he regularly did not understand it or the consequences of its commands. Todd knew nothing about the Other Voice, but this was the way Oliver preferred things. No one could know about the Other Voice. It would make them think he was plumb crazy. Full bore crazy. But, Oliver knew he wasn't. He was just quieter than most. As of yet, there had been no need to tell Todd about it. Todd always took Oliver to the right place at the right time whether Todd knew it or not. Oliver often found himself faced with a choice. To the right or the left, up or down, one way or the other way—and if he would listen closely, the Other Voice would steer him well. It was the reason that Oliver considered every decision important—and every defective thing necessary. Todd, on the other hand, had different priorities.

—Thinking of getting a new hairstyle, Oliver. A swoop to the left this time, down over the eye. Not too differ'nt from what I got going now, jes' the other side—the left side. My neck hurts on the right side from flipping it out of my face alla time, so it's basic'lly for health reasons.

As they zoomed down the freeway, Oliver observed a housefly inside the car. He must have flown in at Miss Ottanot's house. How surreal for him. He will work his way across the dashboard and fly out the other side once they are parked downtown. He'll be thinking to himself how did I get here and where did my family go. Then, he'll die later today like all flies do, still fairly confused.

—You really took your time fixing that screen door. We gots two more jobs today and we hafta be finished by sundown. Important day. Important day. So, I'm with you—excellence and whatnot—but when we gotta get it done, gotta get it done. And I need botha these payments today if'n I'm gonna take Barbara away tomorrow for a weekend special. Sheez. I still gotta fit in that haircut. All I'm saying is you kinda took your time.

Oliver turned to Todd quizzically. Todd had not mentioned that they had an extra job today. Oliver knew they still had to tend to their maintenance contract with their largest client downtown. It was a hefty day's worth of work that should finish out their Tuesday. But, an additional job? Important? Today? Todd rarely kept the details of a new job from Oliver—and Oliver did not like it when Todd did.

—Why you look'n at me like I didn't mention the other job? I did. Didn't I? I did. Course I did. I always fill you in—but maybe I didn't cuz it was last minute and the details are need-to-know and you don't always seem to want-to-know, so need is sorta another step above that.

Oliver pursed his lips and stared.

—I hate it when you do that with your lips. I don't need your approval. It's why it's called Todd Hobbs' Odd Jobs, not Oliver Hobbs' Odd Jobs. Cuz I'm the boss—even though we're equal part-ners. And because nothing rhymes with Oliver. Todd grabbed his newspaper and smacked the dashboard. Dead housefly.—B'sides, we're still gonna get to the reg'lar Tuesday job first. We hafta do the other job at a set time later this afternoon down at Mobrigger Bridge.

The two words set Oliver's eyelids on fire. He could not explain why—he listened for clarity from the Other Voice, but none came. He gazed at Todd suspiciously. Oliver didn't know how he was going to do it, but he was quite certain he was not going to allow his brother to drag him anywhere near Mobrigger Bridge.

—Been working on my abs like in that infomercial they play during J. Aaron Epsom ev'ry night. Bought wunna them Abatronics—bends you automatically like with batteries so you can do crunches while you sleep. Here. Punch me as hard as you can.

Oliver did not.

Todd pulled into the parking lot of a large impressive building with a large impressive word emboldened over its large impressive door. Oliver had been here many times, enough not to be impressed. There was, as usual, a line formed out the door and down the block— but Todd and Oliver bypassed it. A checklist was waiting for them in the management offices. A week's buildup of fixes that all fell under the Hobbs brothers' areas of expertise. Enough to fill a Tuesday.

—So give it some elbow grease. Double-time. None of that lol- lygagging you did over Miss Ottanot's screen door.

After several hours of changing fluorescent bulbs, tending to plumbing leaks, and mending a rather large hole in a rather small break room wall, Oliver was escorted outside by Phillip, the one slightly amicable security guard. They walked toward the back of the building exterior. Oliver liked this specific contract. It was higher security than the other jobs, which meant the assignments specified great detail. Oliver liked detail. He liked it a lot. It kept him at peace. He was very good at taking instructions and following them to the letter. He also liked that when the job was especially sensitive, security would escort him. Oliver liked to be observed by experts. He liked being double-checked.

Oliver did not like it when choices were unclear. He did not enjoy the weight of the world rising or falling on his assessment of the options laid before him.

—Don't see why management felt the need for me to join you on this one, Oliver. I mean to say: we trust you. Phillip plunged into his nostril with his forefinger because Oliver's back was to him, but Oliver could hear the digging. —Then again, I don't see why I can't be trusted to do something as small as this all by myself. I mean—it's what? An air vent cover?

Oliver nodded, quite content. He followed the instructions he had been given to the letter, removing the old vent with a special tool provided him by the building management.

—Course, I can be a bit scattered with the honey-do's, bringing the wrong wrench and so forth. The company insists upon precision with their little details and you have certainly proven to be precise. And you don't give excuses. You definitely know how to make the higher-ups happy.

Oliver knew this task wasn't nearly as simple as Phillip assumed. No task was simple for this client. Oliver meticulously cleaned each vent divot, tiny though they were. He soldered the malfunctioning chip in the security beacon tucked just inside. He replaced the soiled polymer with a new filter management had provided him and began securing the bolts tightly. He had made his way around the periphery of the vent and was working his way to the top left corner—the only portion of the vent unsecured and slightly jutting out.

That is precisely when he heard the Other Voice.

—*Wait.*

Definitively. And louder than he had ever heard before—as if the Other Voice were nearby. Oliver turned briskly toward Phillip to make certain the word had not come from his mouth.

—What's a matter, Oliver?

The Other Voice had never told Oliver to wait. Never. It had always told him what to do. It had never told him to stop doing. Oliver stood, the tightening tool in one hand, the screw held carefully in place with his thumb and forefinger. Oliver held his breath, perplexed at this missive. And the Other Voice spoke again.

—*Not yet.*

Oliver was so startled by the directive that he dropped the screw. He quickly dropped to his hands and knees, searching the grass, as his thoughts became scattered.

This didn't make any sense to Oliver. Why did the Voice tell him to pause his efforts? He sat up into a kneeled position and listened carefully for clarification.

Silence. Absolute silence.

It was a new sensation for Oliver. Others might describe it with a word like emptiness or panic. All Oliver knew was that for the first time, the Other Voice was suddenly gone.

He sat unmoving, the tool still in his hand.

—Now, what on earth is this all about?

Phillip's words brought Oliver back to reality enough to see Todd walking toward him down the alleyway between this building and the next. Todd was not alone. He was being escorted by two police officers.

In the holding room, Todd rocked back and forth in the chair, then suddenly out of the chair—then suddenly back in the chair again. The room was windowless, but Oliver noticed a handful of dust bunnies gathered or swept into one corner. They danced playfully as if manipulated by a gust of air conditioning nearby that was too slight to cool down much of anything. Todd prattled.

—Man oh man. I'm just gonna have a field day. Didja see that one cop grabbing my elbow like I was arrested? And today of all days. What time is it? I ain't arrested. They cain't arrest you if they don't know nothing.

The last sentence gained Oliver's attention. Todd noticed.

—And also if you didn't do nothing. You don't think they got listening devices in here, do you? I did like that cop's watch, though. I saw that watch in a catalog in the department store bathroom. You think I'd look good in that watch? I would. Course, I'd have to get a suit coat.

Two detectives interrupted Todd and sat at the other end of the table. Most would call their outfits similar, but Oliver knew one wore a white shirt under his gray blazer while the second gentleman's shirt was bisque.

—I am Officer Johnson and this is Officer Jameson.

—I know my rights.

—Yes, Mr. Hobbs—and you are welcome to call an attorney, but you are not under arrest. We just need to ask you and your brother a few questions.

—I ain't calling no attorney. That'll just make me look guilty.

—We haven't accused you of anything.

—I'm still not taking that bait.

—And—you are his brother—Oliver Hobbs?

Oliver nodded tentatively. Where was the Other Voice? Where was the peace that came from its company? Oliver had never needed its companionship more than right this moment—and it had abandoned him.

—And you are mute? I understand you are mute but not deaf.

—Todd was quick to reply —It's called *selective mutism.*

—What does that mean?

—He has the ability to speak but he don't. Not since the accident.

—What accident is that, Mr. Hobbs?

Oliver shook his head no.

—He's asking me, Oliver. You cain't talk anyway. So, we was jus' kids. Little ones. I mean Oliver was always little even for being younger. He still dragged his blanket around—called it his mush. Even at four. Can ya believe that? Oliver's screaming something awful 'bout his mush, jus' screaming along like a cat underwater and not none of us can find it anywhere. Daddy didn't do too well with

the baby screaming. Momma left a few months before and Daddy
didn't take that too good. And I was running all around trying to
find the kid's mush and Daddy jus' gave up and drove away to go buy
a new one and then he crashed and then he died.

—Was he high? Was he drinking?

—Oh, I don't think that mattered much. Daddy got real good at
driving drunk. Craziest thing. It was cold and we'd been leaning against
the hood of the car. You know—it's warm for a coupla minutes when
Daddy turns the engine off. And Oliver's mush got caught on the grill,
just dangling there. It's why he was screaming in the firs' place. It wasn't
lost. He jus' couldn't get his mush unstuck—but insteada saying that,
he just screamed a buncha nothing. Once Daddy got to the main road,
that mush musta been flapping around like a wounded bird when it
untangled itself and blew up onto the windshield. Daddy couldn't see
nothing and drove right inta a whole messa trees.

Oliver pursed his lips and stared.

—I really hate it when he does that with his lips. You see what
he's doing with his lips? I hate that. Can we go?

—Why? You in a hurry?

There was silence for a few moments before Officer Johnson
placed a photograph on the table and asked if they knew the man.

Knew. Past tense.

They did not know him and Todd said so.

Officer Johnson asked if they were absolutely certain they had
never seen the man before.

—I dunno. How'm I supposed to remember every guy I ever
met? I mighta seen *you* before, but I wouldn't remember. I mean, I'll

remember *this time* cause it stands out, right? But, have I run into this guy at Whales or the Casa del Pancake? How should I remember? Would you?

Officer Jameson clarified that they were likely to know the man in the photograph's sister, a Miss Esme Ottanot, who had just killed the man today right around lunchtime.

Wait, what?

—That's a mistake.

—No, assured Officer Jameson —It isn't.

—But, we was just at Miss Ottanot's this morning and she was happy, even tried to kiss Oliver.

Oliver found himself very confused indeed.

—We didn't do NOTHING.

—Miss Ottanot wasn't expecting her brother, continued Officer Johnson. —She wasn't expecting anyone. He snuck right into the house to surprise her and she shot him.

—*After* we was there, right?! What's that gotta do with us?

Oliver began to feel a bead of sweat forming at his hairline. He knew exactly what it had to do with him.

—Miss Ottanot claims the reason she was surprised was because she didn't hear the screen door stick to the jamb.

Todd was at a loss for words. So, that's what it takes, Oliver thought.

—Evidently, the doorbell was broken and her brother didn't see the harm in sneaking on in. He caught her by surprise.

—But—but, we just fixed that door this mornin'.

—Maybe you should have fixed the doorbell.

Oliver absorbed what was being said. How was this possible? The Other Voice. The Other Voice had led him to Miss Ottanot and her squeaky door. How could his compliance have ended so tragically?

Todd was regaining his limited vocabulary.

—What we done ain't no crime! It was jes' an odd job! A Todd Hobbs' Odd Job!

—Odd, indeed.

—That's not a crime. That's a coincidence.

—We thought the same thing—at first.

—At first?

Officer Johnson pulled a large manila folder onto the table and began pulling one photo out at a time. A lady in a kitchenette. A man in a foyer. Two gentlemen in an automobile. More.

All dead.

—This first one was taken a few weeks ago. She used a metal knife to clean out an old toaster oven she didn't realize had just been fixed. Electrocuted. This one: slipped on a newly installed and waxed floor. Broke his neck. These two: swerved to miss some traffic cones that had been set out while an office exterior was being painted.

Oliver began to turn green. Todd just stared, his mouth hangdog.

—It's a fluke. It's all jes' happenstance.

—Of course we thought the same thing, Johnson interjected —Until lunchtime today. It was something Miss Ottanot said that gave us pause.

—Whadid—whadid she say?

—She said the same thing somebody said at every one of these crime scenes.

Oliver knew what she had said.

—She wished the silent man had never done that odd job.

The room remained still for some time while Todd turned, wide-eyed, and gaped at his brother. Oliver knew all eyes were upon him, but all he could connect with was the hair stuck to Officer Jameson's blazer. It flitted as if half of it wanted to stay put and half of it yearned to fly away. Oliver stared and tried his best to find the Other Voice. It was distant the first time he heard it. Maybe again. But, nothing. There was nothing.

Officer Johnson continued.

—These all do seem like random coincidences. Certainly not the sort of premeditated killings someone could pull off with an intricate plan. They leave too much to chance. Far too much. So then, please tell me, as the Hobbs brother who WILL speak, why each one of the deaths in this file is a chain reaction that began when your brother Oliver put his hand to fixing them.

Oliver stared at the hair.

—What do you *know*, Mr. Hobbs?

Jameson interjected —Don't make it personal, Johnson.

—What is your secret? Why are you really so afraid to speak and how does it shed light on these deaths? What is it? You can read minds? Tell the future?

Oliver's eyes locked.

—Are you one of those idiot savants who sees numbers dancing in your head and somehow knows when fixing a door will kill someone?

Oliver felt his palms ache. His fingernails digging into them, fists clenched.

—Or are you just very bad luck?

Oliver vomited all over the table, causing both detectives to lift their coffees and shove their chairs backward. It was the screeching of the metal chair legs against the concrete floor that yanked Todd out of his stupor.

—Have we done anything illegal?!

Neither detective answered as both were trying to wipe the previous contents of Oliver's stomach off of their photographs.

—Have we?! Have we done anything besides be in the wrong place at the wrong time?!

—Not that we can prove.

—Then, I'm pretty sure you gotta let us go.

—I will tell *you* when it's time to—Officer Johnson didn't get to finish his sentence. Another officer, a woman, shoved her way brusquely through the door.

—Johnson! Jameson!

—Debra, can we get a mop in here? There's…

—Forget that. Come quick!

Officers Johnson and Jameson scrambled after her, leaving the door open.

Oliver sat, spent, uncertain if what was dripping down his face was a tear or the remains of his breakfast. He glanced up to meet Todd's anxious gaze.

—Oliver—what have you done?

The melee in the next room hit a fever pitch. It sounded like gasps of shock and despair. With no Other Voice to guide him, Oliver was uncertain what to do next. Todd stood up hesitantly and worked his way to the open door. After peering out, he spoke.

—Come on, brother. We're leaving.

Oliver thought this an unwise decision, but without counsel or another ride home, followed Todd's lead. As they exited, they passed the break room. It was filled to capacity with police officers, all staring at the television. On the television, a building had collapsed somewhere downtown.

Todd was driving very fast, arguing out loud to no one in particular that they weren't exactly escaping. After all, the police had left the door open and moved on to more important things. Oliver found it difficult to focus. His head was spinning—and silent. The absence of the Other Voice should be bringing him clarity now—but the silence was noise. Troubling thoughts inserted themselves. Thoughts of who he might have been listening to, and what it seems had come from his obedience.

—Didja see that building come down? That huge one down-town? That wasn't the one where we worked last night, was it? Where you installed that camera and monitor on the sixth story? Naw. Dang it. Cain't be late! We've got eleven minutes. Hafta be there at 3:17. Hafta. Important day.

They were not slowing down, speeding past the off-ramp that led toward downtown. Oliver glared at Todd suspiciously.

—Are you crazy?! There's no way I'm head'n back downtown.

Oliver scrambled to clarify and pulled the tool out of his chest pocket—the tool he had been given by the management of the last job. He waved it in front of Todd's face.

—You can finish that job tomorrow. They'll be closed up and empty the rest of the day. Just like ever'body else downtown. Look.

Oliver followed Todd's finger toward the black cloud on the horizon emerging from the middle of a cluster of high-rises. Rising from the place where the tallest building stood just this morning. The building Todd and Oliver had worked inside just last night.

This was not reassuring. So much information. So much devastation. So quickly. And the Other Voice absent.

Oliver closed his eyes and concentrated.

There was no way around it.

He didn't mean to. He didn't. He had meant well. Always meant well. He wracked his brain and attempted to determine if the Other Voice forced him to do those seemingly insignificant things. No. Not really forced. It just eased him into those moments. Coaxed him. Never really giving an explicit direction. Instead—an urge to do something. Something seemingly helpful. Always seemingly helpful.

But then—something new this afternoon. For the first time, the Other Voice had asked him to wait. To not do something. Why hadn't the Other Voice done that the other times—when Oliver's actions were about to cause irreparable damage? The Other Voice must have known. Did the Other Voice want those awful things to happen?

Or was there no Other Voice at all? Was it possible that it was all just him?

Just Oliver.

But how could it just be him? He didn't know the future—didn't wish ill on others. Maybe Officer Johnson was correct. Maybe Oliver was bad luck. But then how to stop the pattern? Disobey the Other Voice? The Other Voice was gone now. You can't disregard orders you don't know. The only thing that made any sense was for Oliver to stop doing odd jobs completely. To stop helping anyone. Period. To stop doing anything at all.

But wasn't the absence of doing anything a choice as well? Wasn't waiting an action? Stalling could do as much damage as moving forward. Standing could wound as much as running. It was all happenstance. Coincidence. So, why was Oliver in the middle of it? No. At the start of it. Always at the onset. He was the spark that lit all of these bombs. Why? Why? *Why?*

Oliver couldn't remember the last time he had so many thoughts of his own.

—When we get there, I'm gonna need jus' a bit of help. I'm gonna have to step out of the van real quicksies and get something from a fella. So, you'll hafta switch with me and drive from then on out.

Todd took Oliver's silent stare into the distance as disapproval.

—Just some guy. A business associate. You don't know him.

More silence.

—Jes' this one time! I never make you drive. Won't even be far. It's only seven miles to our apartment from Mobrigger Bridge.

And Oliver realized where they were driving. For a moment, he forgot his existential crisis enough to take a stand against his brother's extra errand.

—Do this one thing. This one errand, Oliver. I cain't explain it yet—but we won't have to do these odd jobs no more. And you won't cause no more accidents. It's an important day.

Oliver hesitated.

Why did he feel so demonstratively against this errand? Why did it set his head on fire?

He knew why.

Because of the Other Voice. This morning, when Oliver first heard about Mobrigger Bridge, the Other Voice had set off an alarm in Oliver's head. The Other Voice wanted Oliver to stop this from happening. He was certain of it. Perhaps the Other Voice was wrong—or rather misleading him. If Todd was correct and this errand to Mobrigger Bridge could end their need to perform odd jobs, it would be the exact sort of thing the Other Voice would dissuade.

But, that doesn't necessarily make the errand wrong.

Oliver hesitated.

Now is as good a moment as ever to disregard the Other Voice. Perhaps this time, no one will die.

Todd pulled the van down a neighborhood street and doubled back, parking under the shade of a tree in front of a small empty residential lot. He stared into the distance and said nothing. A police siren wailed in the echoed faraway. Oliver could see Todd's neck hairs standing on end. They relaxed back down to his nape as Todd realized the authorities were all headed toward the incident downtown.

—Some timing, huh? Crazy. And we *should* do this. We should. 3:17. Hafta be on time. Hafta.

Oliver connected the dots, though he was certain Todd was only talking to himself.

Todd held his hand motionless over his dangling keys and after a ten count for certainty, turned the ignition. The van crept slowly toward the shallow slope leading down to the flood drainage canal that Oliver knew would eventually lead underneath Mobrigger Bridge. Todd looked this way and that until he was convinced the van was out of the sightline of passersby. Oliver saw Todd's shoulders relax as he stepped on the gas and headed northeast.

The bridge was a dot in the distance—the yawn of an insect—as Oliver fixated upon it. He glanced at Todd, seeing hesitation in the eyes and determination in the foot pressing the gas pedal. Something inside Oliver wanted to grab that steering wheel now and turn it around—as if the mouth of the bridge was a precipice—but Oliver stood firm. No. If he was going to resist the Other Voice, it would require conviction.

But Oliver's gut churned.

He had never gone so against his own instinct. Every follicle, every nerve ending fretted. This was not good. Simply not good. And yet—

The Other Voice had agreed with Oliver's instinct. The Other Voice. The one that had led Oliver down so many regrettable paths. How could it have been wrong so many times and yet right now? Oliver must deny what he felt. He *must*. He must stay the course of this foolish errand.

Trees whished past at the top ledge of the drainage canal, blurring into a dark mesh of nothing very pretty.

Mobrigger Bridge was becoming clearer. Not long now. Oliver could see the faint outline of something there. Something mustard. A taxicab. Someone stood outside of it. A man with a cardboard box.

No.

This is not good.

Oliver gripped the dashboard and closed his eyes.

The motor revved, struggling to live up to the weight of Todd's foot.

Oliver thought. He focused, uncomplicated by the Other Voice.

He thought his own thoughts. He came to his own realization.

He never felt like this when he obeyed the Other Voice.

Never.

His instinct had always agreed with it. Every single time. Because regardless of the destined outcome of each good and generous act, the choice Oliver made was still the right choice for Oliver. It was still the best option to help. To look for ways of making someone's world better. It wasn't merely the urging of the Other Voice.

It had always been Oliver's instinct as well.

He and the Other Voice had agreed. Always agreed.

Oliver reasoned through this truth.

Regardless of how tragic the outcome, had there never been the Other Voice at all—had Oliver decided and acted upon his own nature—he would have made the same decision every time.

It seemed foolhardy now to deny acting upon what he knew to be right simply because he didn't know where that action would fully lead.

The engine screamed in pain, the van barreling forward.

Oliver's bottom lip quivered. He knew what must be done. The only thing that would actually stop Todd now. Oliver opened his mouth, not quite a yawn, not quite a gasp for air.

Todd glanced, then turned toward him in disbelief, for he could see what Oliver was attempting.

And as they hurtled at breakneck speed toward Mobrigger Bridge, Oliver forced out a single word.

—*Wait.*

Completely flummoxed, Todd slammed on the brakes—the screech echoing throughout the surrounding trees. The rear tires drifting and leaving the stench of burnt rubber behind. Todd stared.

—What? What did you just say?

The man outside the taxi was a hundred feet away from them now. He appeared displeased, uncertain how to respond to this turn of events. Oliver spoke one more time.

—*Not yet.*

Todd gasped, not realizing how long he had been holding his breath. Todd stared.

—Did you—did you *say* something? Did you say *wait?*

A shadow passed over the windshield, blotting out the sun.

—Wait for what?

The windshield burst.
Shards of glass flew about the inside of the van.
Chaos and confusion.
As Oliver came to his senses, the rearview mirror dangled a few inches from his face. There were broken things and radiator steam everywhere. All was quiet, save the hissing of the brutalized vehicle. He could not see out, because the windshield was blocked by something—something protruding through the broken glass.
Hands. Two hands.
Oliver shoved his door open with his foot and wriggled his way free from the passenger seat of the van.

A man.

A man had fallen out of the sky.

A man had fallen out of the sky and smashed directly into the windshield of Todd Hobbs's van.

Evidently hands first like a swan dive.

It took Oliver a moment to gather his wits. He glanced at Todd, who had also made his way out of the vehicle, completely bewildered. Todd's face was bloodied. Oliver attempted to help him, but Todd suddenly remembered why he was here and spun on his heels to gaze down by Mobrigger Bridge. The man with the cardboard box was snapping photos with a high-speed camera.

—NO!!

Todd began charging toward the man, but the man darted the other way, discarding the cardboard box (clearly empty) as he sprinted. Todd ran as far and as long as he could, but would have struggled to keep up with a toddler. He stopped, palms on his knees, stooped over and spitting blood. The taxicab hurried away.

Oliver stared at his brother and then back at the van.

A body.

Where could it have come from? Not Mobrigger Bridge. It was too far away. Of course, any place this body could have come from was too far away. Was he a jumper? His landing gave the appearance of someone who had time to realize he was falling. But, falling from what? Where?

Oliver turned back. He could barely see the taxicab now. A dot on the shimmering hot landscape.

Todd was puking on the pavement.

Oliver stepped closer to the human on the hood. If the fall didn't kill him, whatever was sticking out of his eye probably did. Because he had to be dead, right? Oliver attempted to mop the sweat from his own face with his hand and found his fingers sticky and wet.

Were his hands bleeding? He didn't feel an injury there. Or was it the blood of the stranger?

Oliver looked down to see that it was neither. His hands were not red.

They were blue.

His hands were covered in *ink*.

Oliver made his way back into the van. It seems the stranger had been holding a blue pen. It had broken open and the ink was dripping from Oliver's hands.

Oliver turned around at the sound of an oncoming motor.

It was Officer Jameson.

They had been followed.

Oliver had never minded waiting rooms. The woman seated a few yards away from him had her back turned enough so that Oliver could see several independent gray hairs comingling with the brunettes. He counted seventeen and wondered how many of them were caused by whoever she was waiting for.

The swinging doors—the one to the right labeled ENCY and the other labeled EMERG—made a sound much like the grocery entrance. Out came Officer Jameson. He held two coffees.

—Seems your brother needs some stitches on his face. Probably going to be several hours. The building collapse victims are the priority. The man who fell on your car is evidently alive—but barely.

Officer Jameson handed Oliver one of the coffees. The one that appeared the least bitter, the most dulled by dairy. The sun was setting outside. They both sat in silence as the EMTs wheeled in a woman who appeared lifeless—her mouth wide open in a frozen scream. She wore a wedding dress. Oliver stirred his coffee, the cloud of cream forming an ouroboros. Jameson interrupted his thoughts.

—You're going to be separated from Todd for quite a while. Blackmail is serious business, especially against someone as well-connected as Mr. Eeley—but we think your brother was just the courier, not the instigator. If Todd lets us know who he was working with …

Oliver kept staring into the coffee. Unmoved. The ink on his hands now making a mess of the Styrofoam cup.

—Too much bad news to handle today, I suppose.

The officer sighed deeply and removed his hat, scrubbing his short haircut with his bitten fingernails. Eight gray hairs.

—You're going to be on your own now.

As hard as he tried to keep still, Oliver knew that Officer Jameson detected the quaver in his hands, the tiny ripples in his drink.

—Oliver, look at me.

He didn't. He just stared into his coffee. The officer studied Oliver for a moment, considering his next words. He looked about the waiting room and then, after assessing Oliver one more second, spoke just above a whisper.

—Have you ever been in a life-or-death situation, Oliver? I have. I've been in many. Shootings and heart attacks and a near-drowning one time. But once, it was my eight-year-old. My Nissi. She was lying on the floor turning blue and it didn't matter what training I had. That all went flying outta my head. I just knew my baby wasn't breathing and I froze. I absolutely froze. I honestly did not know what to do. And then—then I heard this Voice.

Oliver blinked.

—And it brought me peace and confidence and it helped me. Now, it didn't tell me anything I didn't know. I knew what to do—but the Voice gave muscle to it. Gave me the strength to actually go to those places a person knows about but struggles to land all by hisself. You hear that Other Voice, too. Don't you, Oliver.

Oliver frowned to keep his lip from shaking. He wiped the corner of his eye.

—Today was unfortunate. Officer Johnson's take on the matter was unfortunate. You heard some awful things. Terrible results of your actions—and of course the photos—the proof. But, your odd jobs—they weren't the only thing those cases had in common. In every one of those cases, you played a part, yes. But you did a wise thing. You know who didn't? You know who did not do a wise thing? The person who died. Nobody should stick a knife in a toaster oven, Oliver. A man's gotta be careful on a slippery floor and everyone has to pay attention while they drive. Miss Ottanot was careless with her gun—and your daddy …

Oliver's gaze fell.

—Well, your Daddy shouldn't have been drinking. I think you heard right, Oliver. I think you heard the Other Voice correctly. And more importantly, you obeyed. Even today. I think you did good things there. But that doesn't make it simple. It doesn't undo everyone else's actions. It can't change what the people who don't listen to the Other Voice do. I'll bet there are plenty of times in your life where your actions started a chain reaction of something—wonderful. Unfortunately, there's no stack of photos to prove what bad things *didn't* happen. No. I'm afraid no one gets *living* proof.

Officer Jameson stood to go.

—Like I said, I've been in a lot of life-and-death situations, Oliver. *Everything* is a life-and-death situation. Sometimes they live, sometimes they die. Don't punish yourself just because the dying is the only end anybody wants to talk about.

Oliver sat for a long time in the newfound silence of his thoughts. He sat and thought as Officer Jameson was urgently called back to help locate the man who had fallen through the van window as he seemed to have disappeared. He sat and thought as a stitched-up Todd was escorted in handcuffs out the waiting room doors. He sat and thought as night became darker and darker. And then, he wandered.

Oliver wandered for a very long time. Everything had changed today. Todd would be gone, locked away for years. Oliver's decisions would no longer be simple and clear.

And the Other Voice—it remained absent.

His head was stuffed with the same heavy silence that occupied these abandoned and dusty downtown streets.

In the distance.

In the dark.

He could swear a voice cried out for help.

Uncertainty filled the farthest reaches of his thinking.

It was time to act without clarity.

He gazed down at his open palms.

They were stained.

Stained blue.

Blue as the nighttime with echoes that lingered of Mobrigger Bridge.

ORI G AMI
PAJ AMA

It was thankful for the transition. First handled by the menace, his fingers filthy with the blackness of toner, it was then transformed into something far more beautiful by mere folds of the paper, by the small intentional movement of fingers. Its creator had called him *origami* when he spoke of it to the pretty girl. Oh, she was pretty. She had red hair and it had a thing for redheads. He had called it origami but she had called it a monkey. It didn't understand how it could transition from paper to monkey with mere folding, but was excited for the prospects nonetheless. It didn't have much of a brain, but found that the creator's words filled him with expectancy as he dangled it between the two of them.

I made the wind in such a way as to always shift. To move in ways that even I choose not to predict. And the wind that I made moves the monkey I made in ways that I designed to surprise me. He cannot move on his own. He cannot speak or walk—or even think. And yet the wind will take him on a journey. A journey not entirely of his own making, but a journey he will take part in nonetheless.

The creator then attached a paper clip to the monkey and placed him where he could see the room quite well.

There were worse ways to spend a day and yet not many, it thought (though the creator had told the pretty girl it could not think). A long Tuesday filled with yelling and gunfire and raining indoors and then the creator was silent. He remained on the floor for a very long time indeed, bleeding and staring unblinking at it, the origami monkey.

Odd though.

While the others were fighting among themselves, turned away, the menace leaned down to the creator and opened a small bottle. The others were caught up in their confusion and grief. *We remember nothing*, one said. *We learn nothing. That's not a next time. That's a first time.* None of them noticed the menace as he took the lone tear on the creator's face and moved it delicately into the bottle. As he did, it expanded and turned blue. The menace smiled and sealed the bottle tightly, slipping it into his pocket.

What a sad little moment, it thought. Menaces ought to leave dead creators alone.

Of course, a dead creator would stay put, wouldn't he?

As hard as the monkey tried to locate him, after some time, the creator's body was no longer there—no longer on the floor. Simply gone.

Shortly thereafter, a powerful and rushing wind poured through the room, catching the monkey up in its wake. It twisted and twirled, flittering this way and that, lingering briefly past the stunned stare of the menace whose fingerprints were stained upon the monkey itself—and then it was out the window.

Falling, falling—but not with a kamikaze sort of trajectory. He wafted back and forth instead as if he was the dust bunny between gusts. It was one of the very few benefits of being paper—and yet the paper clip attached to him was giving him enough substance to surrender to gravity. Cascading downward and adrift.

A bird snatched the monkey up in its mouth, and it dangled from its beak. A carnival ride. Oh well. This would be the end, wouldn't it? The bird would feed the paper to its young and the young would not like the taste of him at all with the ink stains and paper clip. He would be spit out into a ball that would make up the nest. The thought was not seemly. But he was after all only paper and had already celebrated more adventure than most.

And then the bird fell from the sky.

Hit by a flying mound of debris. Where did that come from?

Oh. The building was collapsing under the weight of what the menace had accomplished. Large portions of the building were plummeting to earth like an asteroid on fire and the origami monkey in the mouth of the bird found himself tumbling along with them. But, as the bird fell, life leaving her, her beak inched open. Moments before she thudded to the pavement, the monkey slipped out of the small crevice and was once again a slave to the breeze.

Chunks of concrete came crashing down, metal beams jutting out of each. Shards of glass and a snowstorm of green Post-it notes fell in torrents. Each created its own squall, guiding the monkey up and around through the maze of debris. The monkey considered how there were moments he had thought it unfair to be less real than the people around him. Lighter and without deep thought. Thin as paper. He now understood his creator's cleverness. The force of this epic roiling around him left him unscathed, creating a new rescue of a breeze upon each violent act.

And then, in one tumult, what was left of the Hardaway Building came crashing down. Sad, the monkey thought, such nice and complicated people seated at those desks all day. The wake of it blasted the monkey up above the high-rises where it could observe the dust cloud settling throughout downtown.

All was quiet. His movement was the lull of the smallest autumn leaf over a passage of time.

Its arm bent outward now by the incident with the bird, the monkey caught a crosswind and found itself twirling feverishly. The movement began to make him ill. And then, a breeze just in time. He was now drifting facedown. He didn't know how long he had lingered near the building tops, but could now see movement through the dust. One man. An older gentleman. A figure the monkey had not seen before. He wore a blue jean jacket and scribbled in a journal. He stepped with great intent through the carnage, the pollution of dust. He covered his mouth as his eyes grew red.

The monkey settled softly upon the man's shoulder. Another ride.

The man sighed as he took in the vista around him.

He stepped precariously over boulders that were once wall. Desk chairs and copier machines. He reached a spot and paused, unwilling to trek further. Monkey looked to see what had given the man pause, but all he could see on the ground was a napkin with lipstick stains. From the man's lips came whispered words.

I can't do this any more. It's the boy's turn.

Monkey watched as the man picked a red pen up off the ground and stared at it. Monkey felt the man in the blue jean jacket's shoulders lift as if this item gave him an idea, and then held on as the man turned with a jerk and began to trot down the barren city street. His abrupt movement almost threw monkey off of his shoulder and back into the random unknown, but monkey's bent arm caught onto his collar. He found himself riding bareback through the town, past alleys and parked cars and two dead men in business suits, the dark brown cloud growing thinner the further the man ran. As he ran, he muttered strange things like "Leap—come on, *leap!*" He was so lost in his own thoughts and mission that he gasped when he heard the woman's voice.

I was supposed to be in there.

The blue jean jacket man ran into a lamppost. He was startled, not expecting to find an individual in the middle of the street, much less to be addressed by her.

Oh my goodness, I didn't mean to startle you.

I'm—I'm fine.

The man was thrown to the ground, as if by an electrical charge. He gripped his head as if it was pounding.

Are you okay? Is—is there something wrong with your head?

I can't—I'm sorry—I don't have time to get involved …

He shooed her hand off of him, but she refused to redact her politeness.

Were you in that building? I need to get you to a hospital.

No—no, I was not. But, it's terrible—terrible. I must, I need to—

You've got a thing on your shoulder.

A—a what?

A monkey. A little paper monkey.

She motioned to it. It was the first time his existence had been recognized since the creator. It felt good despite the circumstances.

That is, it felt good until the blue jean jacket gentleman flicked him off of his shoulder with his thumb and forefinger, the monkey dashing to the pavement. The gentleman stared at it momentarily, the collar it had ridden upon so far away like the tip of a skyscraper. The gentleman seemed cross. The monkey didn't hold a grudge, though.

What building was that? What building just fell?

I don't know. I'm not from around here. Please—

It was the Hardaway Building, wasn't it? The home of Shrub & Sons Publishing?

I'm sorry, I—

Then the man grabbed his temples in pain. And disappeared.

The woman didn't see it. She was staring at the empty space where the building had just been. When she turned back, she assumed the man with the blue jean jacket had simply run away.

The monkey wondered why he was the only one to notice these things.

The woman, quite heavy, struggled to lower herself cross-legged onto the pavement in the middle of the one-way street. The monkey appreciated the effort to bridge the distance between them. She stared at the crisis ahead of her, the rubble of what had been.

And she wept.

Such a curious thing, thought the monkey, these tears. She did not know the people in the building or she would have certainly been inside the building herself.

She wept for what must have been an hour. As she sat in her despair, the fallen papers from the building collapse reached her, drifting across the lane like tumbleweeds, filling the street with little green squares. She picked up her phone and dialed a number.

She began to speak, though it didn't seem to the monkey that anyone was on the other end listening.

Um, this is Saphsa. I just thought I owed you this. You were right. The world came crashing down around me. Another fresh start away from you amounts to nothing. Just thought after what I did last night, I would give you the opportunity to gloat. But, of course, you're not there. Of course you're not there.

She paused for a moment without hanging up the phone.

You won't have to worry about me any more. If you ever see me again, I won't remember you any better than you remembered me.

She pushed a button on her phone—and threw it abruptly in the direction of the rubble. Odd, the monkey thought. People seem so in love with those things. Oh well. Fickle.

Saphsa sat in the middle of the abandoned street, head in hands.

She saw the monkey again.

She reached down, her fingers missiles aimed at it. She picked it up with her thumb and forefinger and rolled it around in her fingers. She seemed to admire its handiwork. She spoke through tears.

You're a clever thing.

They were happy words coming out of a sad mouth. It couldn't tell if she considered it a delight or a disappointment. She broke gaze with him and instead stared out toward what was recently the Hardaway Building. Her eyes were moist; she breathed in and out through her nose, and then seemed to shift into a new idea, glancing again at the monkey.

I wonder.

She carried the monkey and retrieved a portfolio that it had noticed on the sidewalk. She must have dropped it when the building came down. Saphsa pulled something small out of an envelope inside of it: a tiny pair of what appeared to be silk pajamas. She eased them on to the little paper creature. A perfect fit. Monkey had no reference point for the act of sighing, but considered the act something it would probably do right now, had it been aware of the first step. It did not know what it looked like in pajamas, but instantly appreciated the concept of wearing clothes. It must have added to its cleverness because amid her despair, the look of the monkey made her smile.

Briefly, yet a smile still.

She tucked Monkey into her shirt pocket, its little head peering above the cuff like a sleeping bag.

She stood up and began to walk the opposite direction, away from the wreckage.

They walked intently for a half hour, others emerging out of their hidden spaces and apartments, wandering aimlessly in lieu of retreat. Only Saphsa appeared to have an intentional destination. Monkey enjoyed the ride.

It had been an education, this day. Observing the change in people, the transition between what he assumed was considered humdrum and ordinary suddenly turning into crisis and chaos. The look on the face of the redhead this morning as the creator folded him—it was so curious, so at peace (though she would not have thought so at the time) compared to the faces around him now. Wandering, not merely in the legs, but in the eyes also. People everywhere, but not really seeing one another—instead staring at the space in the horizon that a building used to occupy. It made them suddenly lost. Or rather, it made them realize they had been lost for quite some time. Monkey considered the realization a good thing because now the people could stop wandering and instead pursue something. But the monkey would not have said the thought aloud, even if it had a mouth.

Saphsa stopped walking.

Monkey could not help but imagine that she must stand out in this crowd as she was the only person staring at a different building than the one fallen. Saphsa was glaring up at a building with a very large word over the door: XtraX. She pushed against the glass door and found it unmoving. She pushed and pushed and eventually banged with her fist. She pressed her face against the glass and peered inside. She began to call out.

But no one was inside.

Saphsa fell to a crumpled heap against the door and wept. She wept so deeply that Monkey reasoned people must be waterproof.

And then, a voice.

We're closed.

A gentleman walked around from the outside corner of the building. He carried a small toolbox and wore a uniform with his name on the chest.

Miss—are you going to be all right? Did you know someone in the Hardaway Building?

Saphsa wiped her nose and eyes.

Not yet. But—I was supposed to.

Well, I'm afraid we've closed early today.

The sign says the lobby will be open until 7:00.

We've evacuated. Everyone's gone home to be with their families.

But, I need something extracted.

I'm terribly sorry. I'm certain we will have additional grief counselors here when we reopen.

When will that be?

Could be a while.

Please, Mister—

He sighed. Monkey was beginning to like the sound of sighs. They always came before the truest parts of the conversation.

Just call me Phillip.

This is urgent.

Everyone's gone home. There's nobody here.

You're here!

I'm not supposed to be. I only came back because I remembered an odd job that had gone unfinished. Now, I'm done. Now, I go home.

Phillip politely walked away from her.

Monkey had never seen the look in Saphsa's eyes on another person before. Of course, Monkey did not have a breadth of experience here, having just been folded into existence around lunchtime. It was not the look of a wanderer, but of someone who knew exactly where they were headed—and did not want to go there.

Please.

He turned.

You'll have to wait and have your grief removed just like everyone else, miss.

This is not about grief. It's about—a broken heart.

Phillip pursed his lips, uncertain.

If you had read our pamphlet you would know that we cannot extract a broken heart because the heart itself is necessary to live.

But you can extract what caused the broken heart.

You believe so?

I need for you to erase my memory. There is too much pain.

And nothing good?

What?

Is there nothing good worth holding on to? Nothing at all?

Certainly, but the bad outweighs it.

Are you sure it doesn't just outweigh it today?

Saphsa's eyes communicated that she did not think she would make it past today.

Please.

Listen—I'm only Security. I'm not really qualified—maybe you should go to a counselor?

What good would that do?

You could—bring your need to someone bigger than you.

Monkey could tell by the look on Phillip's face that he knew he shouldn't have said it, but the words had already been spent. Saphsa was angry.

If there's someone out there bigger than me, why do I need to bring my need up to them? Why can't they just bring the answer down here?

Phillip appeared to have some empathy—but it was all for naught. He uttered eight words with finality.

I'm terribly sorry. I've got to go home.

And with that, Phillip walked away.

Saphsa wandered into the alley next to the XtraX building. She leaned against the brick wall for a long time before fishing in her pocket for change. She then eased into a telephone booth and dialed.

Monkey did not hear a voice at all on the other end of the phone. Instead, he heard a series of beeps.

Uncle Howard. I figured you wouldn't pick up since I'm not calling from my cell phone. I—I just need you to know that I love you and that you should not take what I'm going to do personally. I don't have time to write a note. I'm certain the police will find my body somewhere underneath Mobrigger Bridge. Again—I'm so …

Her voice trailed off, breaking down.

She left the phone dangling off of the hook and crumpled into a corner of the booth. Monkey wished desperately that he could give Saphsa a pair of silk pajamas of her own. She sat there, wiping tears from the corners of her eyes with the back of her hand, wiping her nose on the collar of her shirt when she felt it.

A small square of green paper.

In the flurry of the collapse aftermath, it must have floated down, getting stuck between her neck and her lapel.

Saphsa reached over her left shoulder and dislodged the thing. She was about to use it to wipe her nose when she realized.

Words. Handwritten words. Monkey recognized the handwriting from earlier today.

It hurts to know.
But hurting and knowing is better
than a life in silent oblivion.

Saphsa gasped out loud, her mouth hangdog, her eyes the size of coins.

Her tears became bewilderment. She burst out of the phone booth, looking around for someone, anyone who could have heard her and written such a thing.

But, there was no one to be found. They had all walked away toward what had once been the Hardaway Building.

Of course, Monkey knew where the little note had come from as he had seen it earlier today on the Pretty Girl's desk. He wondered how the Pretty Girl had known her scribblings would matter so much to someone else. Even though he didn't understand, he was grateful she had taken the time to write these words down. They may have been nonsense to the Pretty Girl, but they seemed to be quite valuable to Saphsa.

Saphsa slowly lifted her eyes to the sky—not the empty space of the tragedy—but higher. She whispered.

Thank you.

She folded the small green square delicately and placed it in her shirt pocket, not realizing she was dislodging the origami monkey. Another gust of wind picked it up and forced it rapidly down the alleyway beside the XtraX building, where it pressed against an air vent attempting to draw it inside. Monkey could not keep itself from surrendering to the vacuum for very long.

But Monkey did not mind. Because Saphsa now had very different eyes. Very much like the Pretty Girl when she had been in conversation with the creator. Monkey considered that what it was feeling must be like sighing, for it was even better than the feeling of the silk pajamas.

The vacuum was relentless. It pulled Monkey toward the top left corner where a slight gap had been created between the vent and the wall. A gap created by a defective and askew screw that had mistakenly been placed there to hold the entire thing together.

It was a small slit—but perfectly sized for the Monkey to disappear inside.

Monkey knew he must relent.

And as the powerful force drew its origami body fully inside the ventilation system, monkey noted that the last thing he saw was Saphsa walking away in the exact opposite direction of Mobrigger Bridge.

THE LAST DROP

Sebastian was haunted. Not by the drop of God, but rather by the details within the recesses of his soul that it persisted in shining a light upon. He could feel the drop roving about inside him like a helicopter searching for a criminal, drudging up buried pain and scraping scabs. It was pain unlike Sebastian had ever known, not because it was worse than deception or murder, but because it released all of the bottled remorse from every single one of Sebastian du Guere's evil acts combined.

He felt on the verge of madness. The things Sebastian had done in the last twenty-four hours, the man he had become—the creature he was becoming. He did not believe he could actually go through with this final con—knowingly leading another broken human to her demise. He did not know if he was capable of giving in to the treachery—and then remembered the details of this evil day. The crimes against human decency he had already committed. The murder of his precious Robin. The selling of her soul to the man who had one eye and bandaged hands. Well, *now* he had two eyes, thanks to Sebastian. The guilt poured upon him, smothering. He no longer recognized himself. Paranoid. Filled with remorse yet hardly any other genuine emotion. Why had he allowed the drop of God to touch his tongue? He both wished he had never seen the bottle and craved what remained inside of it. But the man had taken that bottle far from him, withholding its contents until Sebastian contacted him with the exact details of when and where this new deceived soul would be made available.

—But, how do I remove someone else's soul intentionally? Sebastian had asked —the removal of Robin's was an accident—a tragedy.

—You'll figure it out, the scarred man had replied.

He had given Sebastian a number to text when the victim was ready. The scarred man demanded he be present at the transaction— a piping-fresh soul seemingly better suited for his purposes than a previously buried one.

Sebastian mindlessly folded and unfolded the paper with the scarred man's number as he stirred his bourbon with his finger in the shadowed corner booth. He found it ironic that whiskey cooled his throat compared to the drop of God he had tasted just an hour ago. He knew he was putting himself at great risk by loitering in this public place, but he did not know where else to look for a lost soul to trade for his own. This backstreet dive seemed as good as any.

But, of course—finding a lost soul was one thing. Removing it—that remained a puzzle.

He was also able to keep an eye on the news here. He was stunned how little had been reported about his dealings in the afternoon. The fall of the Hardaway Building had overshadowed all other stories. The only update had been rapid. A report that the Chivenchy daughter and father had been murdered at her wedding and that the estate had flown the bodies to Silver City, intending to cremate both come morning in order to put the tragedy behind them as quickly as possible. There was a photo broadcast of Sebastian as a person of interest in the investigation, but it paled in the public's recollection next to the images of the downtown carnage. Sebastian found himself outraged at the neglect of Robin's remembrance, devastated that her body would be decimated by flame a hundred miles from here as soon as the sun rose.

He took another drink in protest. His Robin. The one he loved and destroyed.

He looked about for a victim.

—Youwanna bourbon? I ken getchanother bourbon. The voice at the next booth startled Sebastian. It was hushed and mumbled as someone drugged by a dentist.—Did'n meanta startle ya. I'm laying low myself.

—Who says I'm laying low?

—This joint is nowhere. Ya don't have to hide in the corner to get lost. You hide in the corner of dis place, yer really trying.

—You're in the corner.

—Just like I said. Don't worry. I'm not gonna call the tender over. Got a bottle myself. The man poured Sebastian another glass, then shoved it in front of him, the contents sloshing against its sides.

—Could you please not draw attention?

—Youthink I wanna tension? If I did, I could jes snap my fingers (which I do not know how to do acshully). Sheesh. You're like Howard with the accusations. It was *his* niece and *his* show and *his* contract and if I knew going to dinner with her could make my teeth fall out and ruin his network, then he shoulda thoughta that. Right? Rightright.

—Your teeth—fell out?

—Dees are fakes. Not that it matters.

—Who are you?

—Orvin. Orvin pointed a pickled finger at Sebastian while the other three and the thumb tilted the glass precariously over Orvin's own trousers.—Yer in big huge trouble, aren'tcha?

—Wait. You're that Epsom fellow. You're on television.

—Nope. Not after tonight. Butchoo are.

—I'm what?

—On telebision.

He pointed his pickled finger at the monitor. The report was back on. Another old mug shot of Sebastian filled the screen. Sebastian pushed himself further into the shadow.

—What are you going to do?

—Whatdyou mean what am I gonna do? Yer bizness is yers.

—You heard what they think I did.

—They're nod right.

—They are.

—They are wrong.

—And how can you say that?

—Because you, my friend, are heavy of heart. Very burdened. Cold-blooded people—people like me, their heart never weighs much. Never. Neverheavy. Those words go good togedder. He pointed at the screen again.—I've been watching you writhe around and drown your conscience in this stuff here for an hour and I'll promise you one thing. There is no way that you killed that woman like they say you did. Because you—you miss her.

Sebastian listened intently. Here was someone who had made his fortune off of brutalizing others for laughs—how was that different than a long con? Perhaps Epsom could be his next victim—but he was too famous to be missed—and Sebastian couldn't imagine that his soul would be all that desirable to consume. For a moment, Sebastian thought Epsom was asleep, but Epsom shook his head as if his eyes had been frozen.

—But, that isn't why I called you ober here.

—I didn't realize you had a reason.

—I'm gonna tell you a story. A story I'm reading. Or I did read it. I'm finished. But, I didn't finish it.

—I don't have time for—

—Shh. Truss me. You wanna make time. Dere's a surprise at the end. Epsom took his wallet out of his sportcoat pocket and began rustling through it as he spoke.

—There's this girl named Valencia. Or no. Victoria. NO! Vanessa. I remember now because it was the same as that one intern with the tiny dog. She kept that puppy in her purse like it was attached to her car keys.

—Vanessa.

—Right. A girl named Vanessa and she loves dis fella named Bruce and they've loved each other a longlong time. Really long. Like too long. Like they've hit that place where you start to notice all the lousy stuff'n get tired of one another and kinda forget what love even is, you know. Like on the third date.

—I need to be going, Orvin.

Epsom fanned out his credit cards like a magician and began working through them. His eyes never connected with Sebastian's.—Shush. Lisven. I mean listen. And learn to me.

—You're very intoxicated.

—Learn. They forget what they loved. They kinda forget who they loved. It's a very touching story and then this monster comes in between them and it makes them remember what and who they loved.

—A monster?

—A monster between them. You get it?

—Of course I get it. What happens to them?

—I dunno. I didn't finish the story. Who finishes stories?! The point is what happened to them is what happens to any of us, man! The monsters get in between us and love or truth or whatever and screw it all up. The monsters—the monsters win. Das whad I'm trying to tell you. Love is not worth the pain.

—That's not a surprise.

—I haven't gotten to the surprise yet. Didja hear about Earl Eeley?

—I don't know who that is.

—Everbodies knows who that is. He's Earl Eeley. He owns XtraX. Personal friend of mine. Tried to kill himself today. Pilled himself to death.

—I saw that on the news. He died?

—He tried to die. Didn't work. But, he tried, man. Richest guy in this town and the monsters got between him and his whatever, too. AH! Here it is. *Now, the surprise.*

Orvin plopped one black credit card onto the table. A reflective, jet black card with no writing on it at all. He propped it upright against the bottle of whiskey.

—What is this?

—Iss—magic.

—Nothing is magic.

—Iss the next best thing.

—I don't understand. There's nothing on this card—how am I supposed to know what it's for?

—Only people like me know what it's for. It is one of the many perks of a luxurious and privileged life. Did I jes say luxurious correctly? I need anudder drink.

—I need to leave.

—You need to LISTEN! He grabbed Sebastian's wrist.

—Dere are only four people in the world wid one of these and I wasted—wasted mine. Used it to keep erasing my memory. Starting over. Over and over. I kept wiping it clean until I couldn't remember any of the good parts—and now that's all bit me where the sun don't shine.

Sebastian realized what the card was.—You mean to tell me that this is a pass—a pass into the XtraXion machine?

Epsom pulled him close and whispered.—A *lifetime* pass.

—Lifetime? But you can only use it once.

—Dat is the biggest lie of 'em all. Epsom picked the card back up and teetered its corners on his thumb and finger, spinning it like a well-hewn diamond.—I have connections, you know. All the famous people. They wanna be on my show. Or they wanted to be on my show. I could introduce 'em, you know, to all sorts of other famous people. Earl Eeley *loved* famous people. Absolutely *loved* them. Treated me like a rockstar if I would juss let'em sit backstage and introduce'em as my friend, my buddy. Man. We used to have some fun times with his money. Did some crazy stuff up there in Silver City. Anyway, my comedy was getting rough. I was only getting real laughs from the mean stuff, and then I was regretting saying anything. Too much thinking. It was really becoming a problem. Had to hire a whole messa writers. Then, Earl tells me he can have that removed. I said *what?* He said yeah. The whole regret thing. The memories. All the people I mistreated with my mouth and stuff. I won't remember any of it anymore. The guilt'd be gone.

—You can't just remove guilt.

—He takes me after hours down below the building and puts me in this tank, see. And the next thing I know, the memories, they're just gone. GONE! Whoosh. You like that word? It's kinda a sound effect.

—Sure.

—So, everything's good, right?

—Right.

—*Wrong.* Because the memories and the guilt being absent—it's not enough. Because I got the same old mouth—and I keep hurting people over and over. I don't think not to do it cuz I don't remember regretting it the last time. New stuff. New words. It didn't fix nothing. It just erased stuff. So, I tell Earl that I'm not letting him backstage no more and he says all I need's a tune-up.

—A—tune-up?

—*Right.* I say, I thought each person could only do this once. He says that's just something they tell customers like turning your phone off on the airplane. It keeps people hungry and urgent for the procedure. Then, when they run outta customers they'll have a "breakthrough discovery" that everybody can do it a second time. Genius marketing stuff. Anywho, he gives me an after-hours lifetime pass.

Sebastian plucked the card out of Epsom's hand.—That's what this is?

—Dat is what dis is. And I wantchoo to have it.

Sebastian just stared at the man.

—Why would you want me to have this?

Epsom rubbed his fake teeth with his tongue. He seemed to no longer be thinking completely clearly.—Because your pain seems pretty deep. Pretty deep indeed.

—And what about your pain?

—Das the problem. Doesn't work for me anymore. Being wiped clean feels worse than regretting now.

—Why?

—Cuz at least I feel something. Epsom pushed himself out of the booth, staggering for balance.—Giving you this—it's the only thing that might help me. Epsom threw several bills down to cover his tab and began to walk away. Sebastian whispered loudly, risking detection for the sake of an answer.

—How do you know that?

Epsom turned back for a moment before departing.—My blah told me to do it.

And with that, he was out the door, sloshing his way toward a new sort of existence without his shiny black card.

Sebastian stared at the shiny black rectangle in front of him. Halfway through the man's diatribe he had considered using the black card to obliterate his own guilt, his own memory. But, what good could that do if the man who could forget anything still couldn't live with himself? He pocketed it, having a much better idea regarding what it might remove. He slipped out the fire escape into the alleyway.

Sebastian had wandered the streets for an hour, the drop burning within him more fervently by the minute. He had avoided the site of the Hardaway collapse due to the large crowds, finding it easier to wander aimlessly without detection in the far abandoned recesses of downtown. If he were going to find his pawn, it would have to be someone alone, perhaps homeless. Time was running out and Sebastian was running through the scenarios in his mind. Why hadn't he conned Epsom? Epsom was as broken as they come. This was not a good time for Sebastian to lose his taste for deception, especially now that his own vitality was on the line.

Deep down, Sebastian knew why he had not seized the opportunity with Epsom. The man's soul was spoiled—already missing too much. The scarred man would have spit his soul right back out. However, Epsom had given Sebastian a precious gift: the black card. The after-hours key to XtraX. Certainly, this—*this* was the way to remove a soul. This was what the scarred man must have had in mind.

Sebastian was now on the outskirts of town, the very darkest parts of the shadows. He glanced up and could see the top of XtraX Tower in the distance in front of him. He realized he was standing atop Mobrigger Bridge. He studied those letters: XtraX, and his heart began to sink. He had lost so much. What really was left to gain? Say his plan thrived. Say he deceived someone out of his or her soul and bartered it back to the scarred man. What then? Life as it was before tasting the drop of God? What sort of existence was that? Did he truly believe that the scarred man would surrender the entire ounce of God—if that was, in fact, what was inside that bottle. And what would an ounce of God actually do to Sebastian? After hearing the fate of Earl Eeley, he did not want his guilt buried or extricated, but he certainly did not want it exposed either. It seemed—no it felt—as if that is what an ounce of God was meant to do.

There didn't appear to be much of a choice remaining.

Sebastian stepped up onto the concrete sidewall of Mobrigger Bridge, the one facing downtown. He glanced down to the concrete below. It seemed very far down indeed. He closed his eyes and stated aloud what he expected to be his last words.

—I'm sorry, Robin, so sorry.

His knees buckled, ready to pounce to his demise—but hesitant still. When:

—Is someone there?

Sebastian stopped cold, still crouched. A woman's voice. Beneath him. Under Mobrigger Bridge.

—Is someone up there? On the bridge? I can't see very well in this, um—in this low light.

He hesitated to answer.—Yes. Yes, someone is here.

—Please. What story are we in?

Sebastian was silent. He stepped down quietly and made his way below the bridge. He found a woman there. Early thirties, wearing a skirt with no curves or pleats. She smelled of hand sanitizer and room-temperature corn tortillas. She merged all her words into one lengthy whisper as if speaking secrets to a companion living deep in the pocket of her tartan blazer. She was huddled into herself, cold and covered with dust.

—What are you doing down here? You're filthy.

—I don't want those things with the sirens to take me. They looked for me among the wreckage of the building, but I broke away.

—You—you were in the Hardaway Building?

—Hardaway. Her eyes lit up.—That is a word I remember. Yes.

—We need to get you to a hospital.

—NO! No sirens. There is something I should be doing.

—But, you're hurt.

—I'm only shaken. But, I—um, I must be here on purpose. If I learned anything last time it is that I am here for a reason.

—Here?

—I—I don't remember. The only thing I remember is Mobrigger Bridge like it was words on a page. Some of the last words I remember reading, so I—um, hurried here and waited. And then you come and you say Hardaway and that, too, does something inside of me. Yet, I do not know what. This means something, right? Doesn't it?

—What is your name?

—Name?

—You don't know your name.

—I know it. It's somewhere—on the tip of my tongue.

—Why did you ask what story we are in?

—Yes. A story. That is what I am here for. It's as if I was caught in one story and then suddenly I was thrust into another while all my friends remained behind. Thrust into this story. Your story.

—Another story? You mean another floor of the Hardaway Building?

—For a reason. There must be a reason that my friends continued on and I ended up here. Your story is outside. Mine was inside. I wanted terribly to be outside, but I can't say that I'm certain I like outside all that much. Forgive me. My thoughts are muddled and memories confused. It must be from the collision of stories.

—Miss, breathe slowly. You were in the Hardaway Building when it collapsed. All of the stories of that building did collide. They collided and fell atop one another and were crushed into rubble. That was the disaster.

—This collision is not the disaster. This collision is the solution. She was crazy. Disturbingly so. A gift.

—I think you and I meeting here at this bridge. I think it might have been meant to be. What is your name, young man?

He considered an alias but then decided he really had nothing to lose.—Sebastian. Sebastian du Guere. And yours?

—As I said, it's on the tip of my tongue. Just over the hill, but I haven't quite climbed it yet. And I do feel very much that this, mm, meeting was intended by Mr. Hardaway.

—Who I would assume is dead now.

She had the look of trauma now—as if she was remembering, regretting.

—I believe maybe you've had a severe blow to the head.

—I'm, I'm jumbled. Confused. As if my mind were a jigsaw and I, um, can't seem to locate all the pieces.

He felt evil simply considering it.—I can remove that confusion.

—I don't understand what you mean.

—I know a way of removing whatever it is that you don't want. If I removed your confusion, all else would become clear: your name, the reason you are here.

—That doesn't sound quite right. How would you even go about that sort of a removal?

—Do you see that sign in the distance?

—XtraX. Now, that—

—Sounds right?

—It does. It sounds like it was meant to be a part of our story.

Sebastian stood beside the woman, staring at the neon sign in the distance, suspicious of how neatly she fit into this plan. It felt like—well, to be honest, it felt too perfect. Like a long con. But, again—he had no real alternative.

—So, you would be willing to go there with me.

—What do I have to lose? Except for, mm, the thing I will lose.

He texted the number as they walked. The digits the scarred man had given him.

```
I have found someone.
    Of course you have. Where do
    we meet?


The XtraX Building.
    You figured it out.


Of course I did.
    I will meet you in the north
    alley. Use your keycard.
```

Sebastian turned off his phone and slid it stealthily into his pocket, walking more aggressively now in order to keep up with this woman. As he broke into a trot, he could not help but wonder how the scarred man knew about his keycard.

They were less than a block from their destination when Sebastian began to doubt himself again. For this woman's assurance that they were headed down the right path, he had a deep unsettling that she was not the only one being set up here. She began to slow down her gait as the entrance came into view round the corner. Sebastian seized the opportunity to take her by the shoulder. She instinctively turned around.

—You feel it, don't you?

—You're creeping me out, lady. Feel what?

—The foreboding.

—Look. Are you certain that this building feels right to you?

—Why? Do you have something to tell me, Sebastian?

—I don't even know you.

—You could go a lifetime in relationship with someone and not have as actual a moment as we just shared. I am still discombobulated, yes—but, mm, I know enough. I know I am not the only one in crisis here. You were too quick with a solution, too quick with your offer for it to be happenstance. And as much as I think I've always loved the word happenstance in stories, I'm beginning to have a distate for it in my own.

He didn't know what to say, his plans unfolding before him, his own fate a multitude of possibilities, none attractive. He choked back an actual tear, not understanding where it came from.—I don't have a choice.

—What are you really trying to take from me, Sebastian?

—It's not me.

—Sebastian, how can you say it isn't you as you stand here?

Sebastian swallowed hard and told her of the deceptions that colored his entire life. Where he had come from and where it had taken him. He told her of Robin and the many changes of his heart that led him from loving her to ending her. He told her of the scarred man, the ounce, the fire, the agreement—all the way up to this very moment. It poured out of him like infection from a purge. When he finished, he was lighter but breathless.

—My soul is corrupt. I intend to trade yours for mine.

—I don't believe that is how it works.

—I can't risk that chance.

—Sebastian—I believe I knew a man like the one you speak of—I thought I even loved him.

—Your memory is coming back.

—Some, but only as I say it. Only as you need it. That's the nature of the story. I have to act without full knowledge or the action just isn't the same. The man I knew —his words always rang of truth because that is where they began. But, they never ended in truth. They always ended distorted, tainted. It was the truth that roped me in—that was his trick. He knew the truth always beckons the hungry. The lie was to associate the truth with him. It was the most grievous con of all. Much much worse than your own. You cannot trust what this man is saying.

—But I tasted the drop of God. I know that, if nothing else, it is real.

—Well, that is the truth he would begin with. The detail you must question is where craving an ounce of God should take you as opposed to where he wants it to lead you.

—It isn't like me to not be able to think straight.

—But you know you're being used.

—I don't have any other option. Please tell me—if you know this much—if you know that a con is afoot, why did you hurry here with me?

—I told you. It feels right. Like mittens with all five fingers.

—But the plan is to ruin you.

—The plan doesn't feel right. Just the place.

—We must leave right now. We must run away.

—We shouldn't.

But, a third voice emerged from deep down the alley.

—It's a little too late for that.

And a pulse of light, like a weapon from a storybook or dream, shot in their direction, freeing a chunk of brick from the adjacent wall.—Got to love a little bit of creative power placed in the wrong hands.

She was silent, stunned, as the scarred man emerged from the shadows, wide-eyed at the sight of the woman from under the bridge.—You, the woman stated in awe—it's you.

—What is *she* doing here?!

—She's the one, Sebastian insisted. —She's the last soul.

—She—she can't be. The scarred man's eyes darted.

—Froman, she spoke as if she knew him well. Sebastian was perplexed. They clearly knew one another. Froman gave pause, then replied.

—Miss Quidnose. What a surprise. You weren't supposed to be in this story at all.

—Only according to you, Froman.

—Didja miss me much?

Sebastian was bewildered. —You—you *know* him?

She turned to Sebastian, whispering.—Open the door.

The passkey applied to a series of doors on the north side of the building. Security unlike any Sebastian had experienced in his years of swindling. And yet, the keycard seemed impervious to them all. It was the literal skeleton key that granted passage all along these unhallowed halls. The three of them finally found themselves in a bright white round room.

—Empty your pockets.

—Why would we do that?

—Trust me. You'll be very sorry if you don't.

Froman began emptying out his own pockets: coins, a small knife. He set them in a small receptacle, the only item in the room. The hum of a massive fan began to resound above them. The metal objects began to rattle. Sebastian and Miss Quidnose were quick to catch on and rapidly rid themselves of anything metal. For her, this included a necklace that she was just now remembering held a special place in her heart. She unclasped it none too soon, for the objects began flitting, batting around the room on their way toward the rumbling device in the ceiling. In a moment, the metal was all gone, sucked into the fan and ground to bits. The engine dulled down to a stop.

—What was that?

—The XtraXion device is on the other side of this wall.

—So?

—So—it extracts. At its core is the most powerful magnet on the planet. You cannot have metal of any kind in that room.

—Or we'll lose it?

—Or worse. Catastrophe. Not that I don't love a little catastrophe. But, no need to worry. If you had any more metal on you, it would have just been ground to dust. He pointed to the final door, his leer a mixture of pleasure and veiled threat. He aimed his newly weaponized stubby palms at them both and smiled.—Ladies first.

The door released and Sebastian felt his ears pop as they were exposed to the low hum within. He could hear voices coming from the center of the room, but could not see the source of the hushed chatter, a half-wall separating them. The three entered the vestibule as the door shushed to a close behind them.

Sebastian's mind reeled. Froman knew this woman, this Miss Quidnose. Her life was in deep jeopardy. She had to understand this—and yet she smiled like the lamb intrigued by her own slaughter. Sebastian's gut instinct was to cower and hide from the voices within, but Froman marched ahead as if he had just been announced. Sebastian followed and was soon shoved against the wall.

—What the—DON'T ANYBODY MOVE!

It was a guerrilla group of five, faces camouflaged, irate at the sight of other human beings in this high-security locale. The one pressing against Sebastian had his arm heavy upon Sebastian's throat, practically crushing his Adam's apple. One man, clearly the ringleader, emerged.

—How did you people get in here?! WHO ARE YOU?!

Froman held his hands high, palms out like surrender.—If you'll give me a moment, I'll show you …

The room held its breath, gazing Froman's way. Froman clasped his hands together, shooting pulses out this way and that, ricocheting across the room, turning each man to ash—leaving only the leader behind. He quickly dropped to his knees as Froman walked directly towards him with Quidnose in tow.

—Conrad Reed? Froman said.

—Wha—who—who are you?

—The only reason you remain alive is because you have not completed that which I need for you to complete. I must say that it took decades to lure you to this point, but I cannot help but admire your handiwork.

And for the first time, Sebastian truly observed what was before him: an enormous tubular and transparent cauldron filled with a red gelatinous mass. Within the mass floated thousands—no, more than thousands—of charcoal black tumors. Sebastian thought he could be mistaken, but there appeared to be distant noises emanating from the device. Not sounds of heat or substance, but of far away moans and agony. When he studied the scenario closely, Sebastian could see that Conrad Reed and his team had sabotaged the device, rigging every potential weak spot with a small explosive device.

—Are these—the extractions?

Froman spoke, motioning to the charcoal floating objects.—
Yes. The infirmities, actually. Of an entire generation. And they
don't stop here. This vat feeds into a literal lake beneath the city.
Can you believe that? The people thought the worst parts of
their lives were being sucked away, disappearing forever without
much of a fight—but instead they have lingered, buried beneath
their feet, seeping their despair upward for an entire community
to soak in. The company never did figure out how to destroy
them. It's a perfect scenario for me, really. I've imagined for
centuries how beautiful it would be to return each bane to its
original owner. Imagine the surprise when the gaping and painful hole these extractions left behind are suddenly filled with a
pain that has grown more hideous over time. Nasty business.
I finally found someone to accommodate the job. Thank you
again, Mr. Reed.

—I'm sorry, Conrad asked —who exactly are you again?

—Who am I? Is that going to continue to be the question from
you three? Isn't it obvious by now? I am the King of Pollution.

—Of our lives?

—Of your *story*.

Sebastian stared at the foul gelatinous mass.—You didn't bring
us here to extract this woman's soul, did you?

—Well, yes. I do need a little pick-me-up, but you've assisted me
in something far more diabolical. Froman hugged the large cylinder.
—This.

—This? This—this vat of cancer?

—It may be cancer to you, countered Froman —but to me—it's
power.

Sebastian and Quidnose found themselves on their knees, Froman's palms outstretched toward their hearts as Conrad rigged each explosive device one by one. Froman waxed on.

—It really is too unfortunate for your kind. You each start out so simple, so difficult to manipulate. Your stories are set in motion with so much possibility, so many random tangents, so much potential involvement on your part to create the ins and outs of where your adventure is headed. If you truly seized the opportunity to play a role in the creative process, I would never be able to predict your actions. Unfortunately for you, you're all predictable. You always assume your own story is the least valuable, so you resort to very petty things to try to make it better than everyone else's. And then hardship and offense come and the next thing you know, you're wounded—angry that someone else got better pages. Ironic. Your stories were written for the purpose of finding one another—helping one another—and instead, you just war one another's stories into the ground. Into little bits of dust and rubble. You characters never learn. You keep making the same mistakes. You just won't listen to your author.

—Do what you're going to do to us and get it over with.

—Brave, Mr. du Guere—or at least it would be brave if you had anything left to live for. When are you going to realize that I don't actually *do* anything?

—You're crazy! Look at all the destruction and pain and death you've caused.

—Destruction and pain and death *you've* caused, Sebastian. Don't you understand? I don't do anything. *Can't* do anything except bounce back onto you what *you* do. I can only reflect your choices and actions. Believe me, I try my darndest to manipulate those choices and actions, but it is *you* who either give in to my coercion or —don't. You create the chaos. You deliver the pain. I simply bounce it right back.

—Then what do you need Quidnose for? She hasn't caused anyone pain. Let her go.

—Oh, I can't do that. Because you brought her to me. You forget our deal, Mr. du Guere. Where you and Mr. Reed are here tonight to make the city grow weaker, Miss Quidnose is here to make me grow stronger. Speaking of which: come now, Miss Quidnose. Inside the device.

Froman picked Miss Quidnose up by her armpits and walked her toward a glass door, a chamber made for stepping inside. He forced her in and began to lock the traps on the door one by one while she banged from inside, protesting—screaming. Sebastian was having trouble keeping his wits about him.

—Don't do this. Please … Take me. *Me!*

—I didn't do this, Sebastian. You did. You had the power all along to simply stop. To no longer be swayed by my words—but you didn't have the strength. None of you do. You're such weak characters, so easily manipulated. Epsom gives you the key and Conrad brings the explosives and you—you bring me the soul of Eleanore Quidnose.

Conrad Reed looked up for the first time in a while, his eyes betraying a sincere bout of thinking. His words sounded like epiphany.

—Her—her name is Eleanore?

—Yes. It certainly is. She never knew that. Not that it matters.

—It matters to me.

Froman pushed a series of warning buttons as the lights in the room dimmed. He then grabbed hold of a lever that he pumped three times before thrusting it upward.

The room pulsed as if every ounce of electricity in the neighborhood grid was being channeled directly into Miss Quidnose. She shook and grit her teeth as the tubular fluid glowed. Spasms of thin lightning climbed the walls of her chamber, shooting across its epicenter and licking against her skin. The tremor of it all finally forced a burning scream from her as the others witnessed her struggling—literally wrestling to keep her soul inside.

Tears poured down Sebastian's face. He had never felt remorse like this, never ached for a tragedy he had caused to this degree. He finally couldn't take it anymore and lunged toward the power apparatus. Froman's reflexes were quicker than Sebastian had anticipated and he shot an energy blast a few feet ahead of him. It would have fried Sebastian to a crisp had Conrad not grabbed Sebastian and doubled backward, hiding behind the device itself. Froman threw up his arms in protest.

—DON'T MAKE ME FRY THE EXTRACTION DEVICE!

Conrad agreed. —He's right. That thing blows and we're all toast. We'll find another way.

Froman pressed his face against the glass and stared Quidnose in the eyes, obsessing over her pain.—You were never loved, Miss

Quidnose. You knew it in your story and you find it again here in his. No man ever cared for you.

—YOU CAN'T HAVE IT! I'M KEEPING IT! she screamed.

—I know it burns, but think of what you will lose. All the pain and regret. All the lonely years that await you here in this world where your friends do not even exist. What did Albert Colin Hardaway ever do for you? He gave you one story and just when you figured it out, he strands you in another. The moment you get rid of the villain there, I find you again here. He made you a defective character—with a defective soul. Why bother holding on to it?

—BECAUSE IT'S MINE!

—Nothing is yours, Miss Quidnose. Nothing except your loneliness. Give it up. This man, this Sebastian—the one friend you have made here is no friend at all. He brought you here to your demise for his own benefit.

—HE TOLD ME! HE TOLD ME THE TRUTH!

—And yet you came. Because you knew, didn't you?

—I KNEW NOTHING!

—You knew you were supposed to come here and suffer.

—I—I DIDN'T!

—You knew it was the one thing for which you were created. For which you were written. I'll give you this, Miss Quidnose. You wasted your story filled with insecurity, thinking that as a character you served no purpose while, all along, you existed for one very pivotal reason.

Her eyes met his. She had run out of words.

—You are the crossroad at the collision of stories. You are where we all meet and crash to our end. Right here is where I needed you all along—and you fell for it.

Sebastian saw it. He saw the same look in her eyes that he had seen in Robin's and he realized just how duped he had been. He was not sent out this evening to find any random victim. He had been sent out to find one specific soul. Hers. Eleanore Quidnose. He knew now and he couldn't believe he had not thought of it before because he had seen someone surrender a soul—and it had not been accomplished by a machine. It had only happened because she had been loved—loved and betrayed. Quidnose was not here by accident. Froman drew Quidnose here—to break her heart.

Quidnose stared cold into Froman's eyes. Sebastian watched as her mouth slowly opened. Dark smoke started to emanate from it. Sebastian could not help but cry out.

—NO! Eleanore!

A billowing dark cloud. It screamed upward within the chamber, ramming itself against the plexiglass. Ramming so hard that, as Froman unlatched the door, it flew like a spasm into the ramparts, whirling like a tornado of spiders, winding itself tightly to the pain and falling, wafting like cotton candy into a small pulsing organ that Froman caught in the palm of his hand.

Eleanore Quidnose lay lifeless on the floor.

Sebastian crumpled, head in his hands, as Conrad Reed stared in horror. Froman consumed the soul into his rotting mouth and unraveled the bandages on his arms as his hands sprouted fingers and grew into full fists.

Conrad wretched at the sight, horrified.

Froman wriggled his fingers, each filthy black with toner.

Sebastian was in searing pain now from his abdomen, having sprinted across the room. He was through. Conrad instinctively ran to Quidnose's side, holding her head in his hands and whispering— *Eleanore, Eleanore* as if they were lovers. Sebastian pierced Froman with his stare.

—She was innocent.

—Well, if you liked her all that much, you shouldn't have brought her to me. Nobody forced you.

—I kept my end of the bargain. Now, give me the ounce of God.

—It's not for you.

Rage overtook Sebastian as Froman brought the small blue vial of liquid out and palmed it.—What do you mean! We had a deal!

—Oh, Sebastian. Grow up. It was never for you. It was a con. See? The very thing you did all your life? I just bounced it back onto you. Surely, you've figured that out by now. Quidnose's weakness was insecurity so I threw insecurity back at her. I threw resentment and disappointment back at Colin. Looking at your life in detail, Sebastian, doesn't it make sense that you were going to eventually be undone by a greater con?

—But—but why go ...

—To all the trouble? Do you even understand what is at stake here? This took immense planning. Unbelievable strategy. This deception was years in the making. Decades. Volumes and volumes of variations on your stories. Do you know how many times I've almost gotten this far just to be thrown some unexpected curve? Once, you didn't even break Robin's heart. You *changed your ways on the beach and ran away with her*. That one was a nonstarter for sure. But, I've course-corrected. I've thought of everything. To gain access to this room, the explosives to open the device, to have Quidnose here, the ounce of God, to finally do away with Albert Colin Hardaway—so many things had to line up. I can freely release these infirmities and create a fearful, desperate, weak people. The easiest of all to rule. And then, the final step. Now that I am finally at full strength, I will drink the ounce of God. ME! I will be filled with his blue ink—making me the new author of this world. I will be able to shoot it out of the palms of my hands and create whatever awful things I can conjure. It's all been a quite tedious journey and I'm mere moments away from my long-desired resolution. So, you—Conrad. Stand.

Conrad had lost himself cradling Miss Quidnose. He had never intended to hurt anyone. Especially not someone named Eleanore. Froman was lifting him by the shirt lapel. He had indeed grown in strength by consuming that last soul.

—What do you need from me?
—I need for you to do what you came here to do. Blow this mother wide open.

They hid behind the partition as they heard six echoed POPS, each blowing a thick protective latch securing some portion of the apparatus. By the exponential growth of the deafening hum, Sebastian knew that Conrad had been successful. Froman then placed the two men around the circumference of the unlatched lid.

—Now, lift.

Sebastian could feel his vertebrae separating as he inched the mammoth lid, untombing the infirmities inside. He knew from the way it made his teeth vibrate that the magnet at its core was like nothing he had ever encountered.

—And now—if you don't mind, stand against that far wall.

—Why?

—Because I'm finished with you. And I don't think it's just for this draft, either. I do believe we are finally—FINALLY—*done* done.

—*Done* done?! What—you mean you're going to kill us?

—Of course. Where did you think this was going?

—You've barely finished your plan. I mean, sure—you've unsealed the extractions, but how are you going to put them back in the people?

Froman laughed with a brief snort.—You didn't actually expect each infirmity to crawl out of the building and find its former owner one-at-a-time like lost puppies, did you? That was Conrad's plan, not mine. I mean, talk about anticlimactic.

—I don't understand.

—I'm going to do much better than that. I'm going to consume their infirmities myself.

—What?!

—I'm going to feed on their cancer. It's sort of what makes me tick. And then, while wallowing in all of that sadness and insecurity, I will have the most delicious insight into each and every sad, sad person. I will be able to see the gaping wounds. And I will know—I will *know* what infirmities created those holes. I will know because I will be intimately acquainted with each person's weakness. And really, what better way is there to rule than that? Yes, each infirmity will return to its owner, but with my face on it.

—You're *sick*.

—Everyone else is, Sebastian. I'm just going to benefit from it. But first—stand over there. You've already served your purpose. Neither of you ever had this machine extract anything out of you, so all-in-all, you're done. I'm going to blow you to kingdom come—and I'd rather not waste a second blast, so scooch in a little.

This was it, then. Sebastian and Conrad took one last look at each other. A pair of people—strangers before tonight—who had wounded so many in their lives and now truly felt as if they deserved nothing more than to be blown to smithereens. What was really the point of fighting back? Living a life of anguish and regret? Of knowing they had been Froman's pawns? Having the memory of Robin's lifeless body—of Quidnose's limp form stuck in their mind's eye every last day? Sebastian especially thought back through all of his days and he could think of none that were not marred by falsehoods against others and against himself. Days of ruing his lot and throwing curses upon God and fortune. He suddenly saw so many options—so many moments that he could have turned or chosen—or simply walked away from the path that ended in this collision. But he never did. Not once. Just yesterday, he was close to happiness. Almost married. Ready to disappear hand-in-hand with the one he adored. And he discarded it. For what? For fear. Yes, that is simplifying, but when it came down to it, fear is all that it was. Fear of man. Fear of lack. Fear of being found out for his vast and sundry transgressions. And the fear, weighed against the love he felt for Robin, was heavier indeed. How could he not have seen it?

There was truly no hope for him. He deserved to be obliterated. And how apropos that it would happen here, amid the town's darkest and most secret wrongdoings—amid all the buried taboos and pain. This was where Sebastian would meet his fitting demise.

Froman stood across the room and began rubbing his hands together, creating an energy pulse of his own, one that Sebastian was certain would be far more powerful than any that had come before. Sebastian glanced at Conrad. He was closing his eyes. Sebastian understood why but did not feel that he deserved any consolation at this moment himself. So, he stared his attacker down, ready for his final breath. More ready than he had ever been.

—Sebastian du Guere, Conrad Reed. Good-bye.

In the flash of light emanating from Froman's palms, Sebastian expected to be overtaken in flame—but instead—and quite suddenly—the room itself was ablaze. Discombobulated, it took Sebastian a moment to realize what had happened.

Froman's pulse—his death shot—had been returned upon him. Bounced back.

For standing between the two men and Froman—was a third gentleman who Sebastian had never seen before.

He had appeared out of nowhere.

He wore the strangest blue jean jacket.

And he was holding a small mirror.

He had suddenly appeared between them and Froman at the exact moment of the blast, mirror at the ready, reflecting Froman's destructive power back upon himself.

—Where on earth did you come from?

—That's a long story, Gary understated.

The pulse generated more destruction than simply reverberating back onto Froman. It ricocheted about and caused the walls to creak and moan. The room felt as if it could implode. The rooftop ached and strained and Sebastian fumbled instinctively for the passkey.

As for Froman himself, he writhed in pain—not on fire, but rather absorbing it internally. The vial of the ounce bounced out of his hand and skittered across the floor, cork barely remaining in place. Froman tried to grasp for it, but he was shaking seizure, writhing—weaker and weaker, wrestling with himself, attempting to keep something inside—and then.

He opened his mouth.

Sebastian and Conrad watched in awe as the dark smoke billowed out of both his mouth and eye socket, his hands shriveling back into stumps—his eye dissolving away. Froman screamed under the pain of his own electricity. The smoke twisted and turned and shaped itself into the two separate souls that Sebastian had seen him consume in the last twenty-four hours. It was as if they thrust themselves outside of Froman, kicking him physically backward, leaning on the apparatus in a heap. The two living things fell wet upon the floor, still beating. Froman limped and groaned, pulling himself toward the controls of the extraction device as the room began to fall apart from the damage of the ricocheted flame.

The third man—the man with the mirror—took Sebastian and Conrad by the shoulders.

—We have to get out! We have to get out of here now!

But it was Conrad who pushed back.—Not without Eleanore!

Conrad and the man in the blue jean jacket took her body and threw it over their shoulders, dodging debris as they made their way toward the exit. Sebastian knew escape would be impossible without his passkey, but he was also unwilling to leave those two souls rolling on the floor.

Froman, bleeding and pulling a gimp leg behind him, was pumping the current lever of the device for all it was worth, his breathing garbled in weakness, ready to throw the switch.

Sebastian knew what Froman was about to do. He was going to climb in to the device—absorbing the infirmities, strengthening himself with evil. It was a horrid thought, but Sebastian felt there was no time to stop him.

Sebastian scooped up the two souls, wrapping them carefully in his shirt as Froman threw the switch to the extraction device. With the lid removed, the bass-like hum was deafening. Sebastian clutched his ears and lost his equilibrium, falling against the wall. When he got his wits about him, Froman was inches from pulling his damaged body into the tank.

—I will find you, Sebastian du Guere! This cancer will restore me and I will make it my mission to hunt you down! I WILL MAKE IT MY MISSION! Our stories are NOT FINISHED COLLIDING!

Froman eased his mangled body into the sludge. He floated there, arms outstretched, hands nothing but bloody nubs, and allowed the charcoal infirmities to love on him, surrounding him like his offspring. It was clear he instantly began to strengthen, to thrive. From outside the cylinder, Sebastian's eyes met Froman's. They lingered and he could see the hatred inside of Froman. The hatred that fueled him.

Froman knew that he had won.

Until Sebastian uncorked the ounce of God and slowly poured it into the sludge.

Wide-eyed, Froman began to kick and scramble to drag himself out of the machine. But it was too late. The sludge was turning an inky blue. The cancer began panicking, revolting against Froman, wrapping him, enslaving him, dragging him down under the weight of all that torment. Conrad screamed Sebastian's name. They were by the door with Miss Quidnose's body draped over their shoulders. Sebastian turned the extraction magnet to high and ran for the door as the room began to quiver. The keycard opened each door just as the sheer force of what was going on in that room began to cause matter to crumble, walls to surrender and bend. The three of them could not get out fast enough.

Inside, Froman thrashed about and fought against the infirmities that were rabid now, panicking from the power of the blue in which they were immersed. Froman eked his head just above the surface—one last push of strength to free himself from the polluted murk—when the shift in the walls broke open the cover to the air circulation vent. Something had been stuck inside. A small item made of paper—with a tiny metal paper clip attached.

And then, in the center of the chaos, everything slowed for the briefest of moments. Froman choked on his own silence, perplexed as he watched the origami monkey taken adrift by the suction of the magnet, sailing past his face—mocking him—and wedging itself directly into the core of the most powerful magnet in the world.

A hush.

A heartbeat.

And the city shook underneath the weight of what happened next.

As Sebastian, Conrad, and the man in the blue jean jacket passed the threshold of the building into the alleyway with Quidnose in their arms, a supersonic blue ripple floored them. The blast shot across town, felling them in its awesome wake, resounding like a nuclear bomb throughout. The wave passed from person to person across the city limits, its effects at times dramatic, at times subtle; some found clarity. Some found healing. Some noticed very little at all.

In the hospital, Earl Eeley felt despair leave his room like a shadow burned out by the sun. In the closet of her office upstairs, Dr. Ariel Rathbone considered a career change. And J. Aaron Epsom climbed down off of the ledge of Mobrigger Bridge. Some—at least those who had been longing for it—found radical transformation the moment the wave hit them. Others, like Barry Gooz, found it easy to deny the blast ever happened and turned the future fervor into a series of jokes (every third one being the funniest). Some felt a drop—others an ounce—others overwhelmed by it all. And then for some, even a little was too much to consider. For some, it was simply another hopeless night of obsessing about the betterness of someone else's story.

Sebastian heard a faint discussion between Conrad and Miss Quidnose about what a lovely name Eleanore was and would she be interested in having a cup of coffee to discuss the evening's events. Miss Quidnose seemed very much obliged to the idea, ready to begin another chapter. But Sebastian could not fully appreciate their conversation—instead, he had dropped to his knees, incapable of catching a breath. He felt as if his back had been sliced opened wide. A large piece of shrapnel from the XtraXion device had stabbed Sebastian du Guere in the back as he ran out of the building. His breath was thin, garbled, shallow.

Conrad and Quidnose ran to his aid. Quidnose—alive and well. Sebastian attempted to proclaim his shock.

—You—you—alive …

She cradled his head, sobbing. She began to cry for help.

—She was never dead, Sebastian. Only separated from her soul. I fed it back to her. He showed me how.

Conrad motioned to Gary, the man in the blue jean jacket. Sebastian's words battled.—How—how did you—know …

The light was being lost in Sebastian's eyes. Gary squatted, leaning into him, feeling his forehead.—I've always known exactly what to do. I just never actually did it.

Miss Quidnose wept freely.—Oh, Sebastian. You saved me. You saved everyone.

Sebastian eyed the pulsing soul of his beloved Robin in the palm of his hand. So alive and yet miles and miles away from her dying body.—Not—not—*everyone.*

And so that was that.

After a lifetime of repressed regret, Sebastian du Guere felt it all in spades at the very end. After a lifetime of missing the point, he finally made his existence matter in a few frail minutes. Sebastian du Guere felt the breath of life leave his lungs and closed his eyes, grateful that the long con was finally over.

Quidnose and Conrad huddled over him, tears in their persistent but hushed pleadings. The man in the blue jean jacket simply hung his head.

When suddenly a voice came from the darkness behind them.

—*Wait. Not yet.*

And then—fire.

Sebastian's body filled with heat and light, every pore of his existence exploding with strength. His tendons champions, his infirmities dissipating. All pain was resolving: the guilt, remorse, anger and bitterness—it was all burning away like so much fog on a cool coastal morning. But, not erased. No. The memory of it was all there,